★

HE WAS SIXTY FEET UP AT THE END OF A THIN PIECE OF STRING!

Suppose he bumped into something? He looked round nervously for gulls and accidentally let go with one hand—but he didn't fall! Very cautiously, he let go the other. He could fly! The parachute was keeping him aloft.

The platform slid past underneath, then the beach restaurant. They were nearing the harbour. He had a moment's panic about the promised dip in the water but he remembered that would come on the second circuit. He would worry about that later. On the flotilla, one or two tiny figures looked up. He wanted to shout but already they were at the place where he'd snorkelled yesterday and there, her dress billowing round her, was another female person who didn't wave because she was lying face down in the water.

★

"Livingston has a lively wit that can be deliciously wicked at times."

—*Washington Post Book World*

A Forthcoming Worldwide Mystery by
NANCY LIVINGSTON

DEATH IN A DISTANT LAND

NANCY LIVINGSTON

A G.D.H. PRINGLE MYSTERY

INCIDENT AT PARGA

WORLDWIDE®

TORONTO • NEW YORK • LONDON
AMSTERDAM • PARIS • SYDNEY • HAMBURG
STOCKHOLM • ATHENS • TOKYO • MILAN
MADRID • WARSAW • BUDAPEST • AUCKLAND

INCIDENT AT PARGA

A Worldwide Mystery/February 1993

Published by arrangement with St. Martin's Press
Incorporated.

ISBN 0-373-28001-7

This book is dedicated to those
who go down to the sea in ships,
particularly Andrew & Peter, the competent crew.

(It has nothing to do with *anyone* who ever sailed in a flotilla)

PROLOGUE

THE MINISTER WAS very young. The unexpected size of the congregation had unnerved him so much, his challenge rang out, reverberating down the nave, bouncing off stone columns and walls.

"Therefore if any man can shew any just cause why they may not lawfully be joined together, let him now speak or else hereafter for ever hold his peace."

He paused long enough to make them all anxious. Perhaps it was deliberate. He was, after all, unlikely to see any of them again. He bent over his book. A small sigh rippled through the church as the witnesses relaxed. In the minister's hand, the carefully marked stresses he'd been taught at training college gleamed blood red on the flimsy paper.

"Excuse me..."

Oh, God!

It wasn't a nutter. At least, not the sort they'd discussed so amusingly at college over cocoa. The minister's thoughts were racing now. Was it a religious maniac? No such luck. The mild-eyed man in his early sixties looked completely sane as he waited patiently between bride and groom. He cleared his throat and spoke again, "I fear this marriage cannot take place."

There was a collective intake of three hundred and fifty breaths. The entire congregation waited expectantly for the minister to act. And do what, for Christ's sake? He glanced frantically Heavenwards but it was Saturday, the Sabbath, and God being Jewish was on a day of rest.

"Why not!" He hadn't intended to shout. As the echo of his cry died away there was absolute silence. People stood on tiptoe. The bridegroom was motionless but the bride half-turned and the stranger addressed her directly.

"Because it was murder," he said.

ONE

IT HAD BEGUN on a day so raw it took every ounce of energy to stay warm. A day when white collar workers struggled to reach the haven of cosy offices. Those like G. D. H. Pringle, who had taken early retirement, stayed at home, listening as the central heating switched itself off, a sound more terrifying than the Last Trump, but he couldn't afford to leave it on all day.

He already wore thermal underwear. Now he buttoned up his cardigan. Was this why they had won the last war? Yesterday the gas people had sent a demand for higher contributions. He wanted to ignore it but now the temperature had fallen yet again. Mr Pringle sighed.

To add to his misery, the icicle that appeared with the first snowdrops had begun to peep out from the end of the wastepipe. Like the one that sank the Titanic, seven eighths of it were invisible, expanding inexorably. He pleaded humbly with the plumber's answering service.

He thought longingly of the public library, that warm retreat for those liberated from employment, where his was the chair nearest the radiator. But today his friend Mrs Bignell had arrived unexpectedly. The crash of furniture below reminded him. Mavis Bignell had solved the problem of keeping warm by doing his Spring-cleaning. She was a widow with whom Mr Pringle had an understanding concerning Tuesday nights, weekends and holidays. Their relationship was circumspect because they belonged to a generation for whom decorum was a way of life. Today, however, was different.

His Help was due, but Mavis declared a good going-over was too much for one woman on her own so she'd come to give a hand. She shook out her apron. Mr Pringle asked wildly if any of it was really necessary. Why, only the other day he distinctly remembered hanging curtains out to dry. Too much washing could weaken them.

"That was this time last year, dear." Mavis pulled the apron tight over her magnificent bosom. "Why don't you go up to your study. We'll bring you a coffee when we have ours." She smiled, all golden warmth in the morning, but he was too chilly to respond. He retreated.

Up here, in the room which housed his art collection, the Help was forbidden to set foot. Unfortunately Mr Pringle seldom remembered this. Occasionally he flicked a cloth about, but he wasn't really surprised when there wasn't any improvement. Today, his pictures failed to comfort him: a February sun low in the sky showed streaky walls, a grubby tinge in the curtains.

Renée had chosen the colours in the early days of their marriage. He picked up her photograph. He had to nowadays, to remind himself what she'd looked like. Sometimes when he tried to conjure up her image, parts would be missing. Once it had been her face. He'd felt hugely guilty as though he'd consciously obliterated her. The photograph had faded. Colours were still discernible—Renée in her flowered dress on a summer afternoon—but the richness had gone. Fingerprints on the dusty frame reproached him, too. Perhaps he had better let the Help come in here—if only he wasn't so blessed cold!

The previous evening there'd been one of those worthy television documentaries. Senior citizens must keep themselves fit, it warned sternly, dwindling national resources were better deployed among the young. Keep fit, exercise and stay warm. Either that or die quickly because there was also a chronic shortage of hospice accommodation.

Mr Pringle began walking briskly round the study. He turned smartly and caught his knee against the desk. The pain was exquisite. He felt dizzy. The doorbell rang. Let the women answer it, he felt too sick to move.

"Post!" Mrs Bignell called up the stairs, "There's a package for you. Feels like a brochure."

Back in the study he opened it. She was right, it was a holiday brochure. Who on earth had sent it?

On a glorious sea a yacht floated, shimmering white and silver against the blue. The water was so clear, Mr Pringle could make out the entire shape of the keel and darker patches of seaweed beneath. It was the only boat in a sickle-shaped bay bordered by rocks, cypressus and olive groves.

On deck a girl stretched out in sun worship. As he gazed at her, a childhood memory returned of lying on hot sand, feeling the sun burn through his skin until he could bear it no longer and rushed into the bracing North Sea. It had only been hot on that one afternoon, he reminded himself truthfully, for that had been England. This was Greece. The letter that fluttered out was from his nephew, Matthew.

'My dear uncle,

'I hope the enclosed doesn't come as too much of a shock and that you haven't already booked your holidays because of a scheme I want to put to you . . .' Booked his holidays! Mr Pringle didn't begin to consider such things until July, never in February. He was puzzled as to why Matthew should write, though. He hadn't seen either of his sister's boys since before Renée's funeral.

He rummaged through family photos—Enid and George on their wedding day. His sister should never have worn satin, she looked unnatural. Tweeds would have been more appropriate. Mr Pringle shook his head remembering when nursing had been Enid's vocation and how mankind's suffering had increased as a result. Never mind. She had formed some kind of bond as she'd eased George Shaw on to a commode. Six months later they were married. He

couldn't find a recent picture of Matthew so went back t
his letter.

'Have you ever considered a sailing holiday? If so, now'
your chance. My girlfriend Liz and I are sailing round th
Ionian islands this summer in a flotilla, hence the enclosed
There's a spare berth—would you like it?'

Good Lord, thought Mr Pringle.

'You don't have to worry about the sailing bit, Liz and
will take care of that. What we need quite frankly, is some
one to share the cost. All our chums are up to the ears i
mortgages, babies or both...'

Mortgages? How old was the boy now? A moment'
thought and Mr Pringle realized Alan must be twenty-six
Matthew twenty-four! Mentally, he lowered the length o
their trouser-legs.

'This holiday isn't a cheapie but you won't need a lot o
cash once you're out there.'

Mr Pringle broke off once more. Cautious by nature an
a career in Her Majesty's Tax Inspectorate, he turned to th
price list. It certainly wasn't cheap. Matthew had ticked
fortnight in June.

'Not too crowded but sea warm enough by then,' he'
scribbled. It was also less expensive.

'Before you say "No", try a weekend sailing on the So
lent at Easter. Liz and I have booked a SHE 33 so that I ca
brush up my day-skipper's ticket. If you survive Englis
waters, Greece will seem like paradise—sun, sea and ret
sina! The trip at Easter is free because Liz and I don't thin
anyone should fork out for being cold, wet and miser
able—you have been warned!

'All the best,

'Matthew.'

TWO

"YOU'LL NEED A blazer. And a cap with a badge like Noël Coward wore when he went down on HMS *Kelly*."

"I ought to spend the money having this room redecorated."

"I shouldn't bother, dear." Mavis looked round disparagingly. "Once you start, you'll have to do the rest. Going to Greece will be far cheaper, believe me. Besides, you might even enjoy it."

Cleaning was over and thermostats were springing to life all over the house. He and Mavis sat in front of a gas fire with a tea tray. She was indulging in hot buttered scones, which was how she nourished her splendid thighs. The brochure lay beside the cups.

"You should go, dear. Do you the world of good. You deserve a nice holiday. I only wish I could join you but..." And Mavis gave an expressive sigh, "I will not spoil your tea by describing what happens when I step on to a boat. I'm not built for it, that's the honest truth. How are you when you're on the water?"

Mr Pringle didn't know. Outside, in the sleet, the icicle gleamed malevolently. The plumber hadn't been, but then Mr Pringle never really believed he would.

"Perhaps I could risk the weekend at Easter, to find out whether or not I'm suited to it."

"That's a good idea. Especially as your nephew's standing treat. What's he like?"

"He has charm." Remembering Enid, this still surprised Mr Pringle, "And he used to be quite a handsome young chap."

"Takes after you then." Mr Pringle blushed.

"I'm sorry you don't care for sailing," he said impulsively, "I should like to have suggested you accompany me." Mavis was touched.

"We'll go shopping tomorrow and find you some woolly vests. You'll need those under your blazer."

THREE

HE FELT A COMPLETE IDIOT. He was a briefcase and umbrella man. In a suit, he knew what to do with his hands. Now, in Oxford Circus Underground, he'd nothing but a scarlet sailing-bag.

"Hi, uncle. Hope you haven't been waiting long?"

For a split second Mr Pringle didn't reply. He recognized Matthew, but the sheer good looks and vitality were something new. Enid's straw coloured hair was here translated to dark gold. Matthew's dark eyes had thick lashes. In anyone less exuberant the result might have been effeminate but there was no danger of that. Matthew pumped Mr Pringle's hand enthusiastically.

"It's good to see you again."

"And you. How are you?"

"Fine. Let's get out of here." He swung the red bag on to his shoulder, "I hope this is full of warm gear. According to the forecast, we're in for a bit of a blow. Liz is up top in a taxi." Mr Pringle followed the navy blue guernsey.

Side by side on the back seat, he thought what a contrast the two made. Matthew, all shining vitality, the girl waiting quietly to be introduced.

"Liz, meet my uncle, once the scourge of tax dodgers. Now transformed into a human being."

"Hallo." She was dressed identically to Matthew, jersey and cords emphasizing her stocky figure.

"G. D. H. Pringle. How d'you do."

Straight dark hair and heavy brows gave her a determined look, but as they shook hands he felt a tremor of nervousness. "Elizabeth Hurst." Mr Pringle admired

womanliness and wished the girl wouldn't hunch her shoul
ders so, concealing her femininity. He smiled encourag
ingly. Elizabeth Hurst lowered her gaze, apparently
embarrassed.

Matthew carried on chatting. Mr Pringle found himself
watching the girl covertly. She appeared to be near enough
Matthew's age. It surprised him to meet a modern girl who
lacked self-confidence.

"And when we get back on Sunday night," Matthew was
saying, "we planned to stay overnight at Liz's place. It's a
super house, there's even a landing-stage at the bottom of
the garden. We plan to drive up to town on Monday morn
ing. Will that be okay?" Mr Pringle assured him it would.
He no longer had to rush anywhere.

"Do you live with your parents?" he asked politely. There
was an awkward pause. Elizabeth glanced at Matthew, her
face expressionless.

"I'm afraid I didn't explain." Matthew sounded apolo
getic. The girl thrust both hands between her knees and
stared at the floor.

"They're both dead. Drowned. Sailing is part of the
therapy to help me get over it."

"Good Heavens—I'm most terribly sorry!" He was con
fused. Why on earth hadn't Matthew warned him? The two
day frolic on the Solent took on a new dimension.

"Oh, it's all right, honestly. It was nearly a year ago and
I'm over the worst. Really." The girl was leaning forward
anxious to convince him, "I love messing about in boats—
I've done it all my life. My father used to race, you see. He
went in for ocean sailing in a big way, which is how he and
Mummy died. They were trying to win a Round the World
when it happened. He was Leonard Hurst."

"I—see." He didn't.

"Chairman of Freezer International," Matthew added
helpfully. Mr Pringle was none the wiser. He vaguely re
membered hearing the name.

"They were making the voyage alone," Elizabeth continued, "so no one knows for certain what went wrong. Father always taught me—make the preparation as thorough as possible. The rest is in the lap of the Gods, including bad luck. He said it was stupid to worry about that." All the same, Mr Pringle did.

"And was that what happened? Bad luck?"

"There was a typhoon. Freak weather, everyone said." She shrugged. "The yacht was found eventually but their bodies were never recovered, which wasn't really surprising."

Mr Pringle's small stock of courage ebbed away. In the silence he attempted a joke. "I hope the weather will be clement during our expedition." Elizabeth Hurst looked at him in surprise.

"Didn't Matthew tell you? We're in for a bit of a blow."

They collected Elizabeth's car from Regent's Park and Matthew drove it the rest of the way. In the comfortable back seat, Mr Pringle dozed. Chatter between the other two was of winds and tides, none of which sounded favourable. He'd rather not know about them. He was slightly worried at Matthew's attitude. Was his nephew taking advantage of Elizabeth's obvious wealth? He hoped not. As far as he knew, there'd never been a gigolo in the Pringle family.

They stopped at a Service Station. "Your last chance before we have to use the heads," Matthew warned. Mr Pringle locked himself in a cubicle. Tonight he would sleep on board a boat: it was an exciting thought.

As they drove through Portsmouth he felt hopeful. Perhaps it would be a proper boat, on the same scale as the Mercedes? But elegant houses gave way to suburbia and finally petered out in ugly semi-detacheds. Matthew pulled up.

"Got an anorak?" Mr Pringle shook his head. Too late he remembered Mrs Bignell suggesting he might need one. He watched apprehensively as Matthew and Liz struggled into layer upon layer of clothing. Surely this boat—any boat—had some form of heating?

The Easter gale barely stopped short at his skin. Mr Pringle blinked away the tears. Outside, the noise of the sea was overpowering. He could see the black edge of it sucking away at pebbles. On the opposite side of the road, in the semis, sensible people were watching television but he'd committed himself to three days of pleasure.

"Can you help with the humping?" asked Elizabeth. Fully laden, he followed her blindly, sailing-bag over one shoulder, Matthew's binoculars on the other and a heavy carton of supplies in his arms. They staggered along a narrow jetty, further and further out to sea.

"Mind the steps," she shrieked, the wind tearing away the sound.

"Where?" Her torch shone on the flight which descended to a concrete pontoon, heaving with the force of the waves. He watched as she attached an outboard motor to a rubber dinghy, he was appalled. Where in God's name were they going in that?

"Can you help me launch it? And whatever you do, don't let go!" Good grief! Was he supposed to put both hands in the water and get them wet? Matthew appeared out of the murk and thrust a pair of rubber boots at him. "Put these on. Keep your feet dry."

Mr Pringle sat to unlace his brand-new sailing shoes. If he'd had any idea what it was going to be like . . . ! An icy wave slapped down on to the pontoon and caressed his buttocks. He stopped worrying about his feet.

They indicated that he was to make the first journey out to the boat. "Get yourself on board, we'll cope with the rest," yelled Matthew. "You get settled in."

The wind was fiercer now and the dinghy was awash. His scarlet bag bobbed about in three inches of water and he sprawled on top of it, soaked to the skin. Liz handed him the torch to light their passage, a tiny pimple of light in the blackness.

They headed out to sea, rising with each massive wave and toppling into the troughs. They would drown! Mr Pringle experienced a fear greater than he'd ever known and consigned the contents of his stomach to the deep.

After that, he didn't even try to help. Elizabeth lashed the dinghy to a shape which was the yacht and pushed him up the ladder. He slumped in the cockpit while she unloaded, stowed, lit oven, heater and lamps, and finally dragged him down into the cabin.

"Put dry clothes on. We'll fix you up with oilies tomorrow—and get that inside you." It was a tumbler of brandy. It shone like liquid gold. He registered that, on board a boat, Elizabeth was in her element, all diffidence had vanished. Mr Pringle obeyed orders and began to undress.

She put a casserole in the oven. When the smell of herbs in a meaty sauce reached him, he found himself whimpering with hunger.

"You can have another drink once you've put some clothes on," Elizabeth said curtly. He looked down, puzzled. Good Heavens! He was in his underwear and they'd only been introduced a few hours ago. He reached for a towel.

"Back in about twenty minutes!" she shouted, ramming the washboards home. He was alone.

He pulled on a sweater without difficulty but trousers were another matter. He finally solved the problem by lying on the floor and heaving them up like pyjamas. Overhead, the gimballed cooker swayed menacingly. It was safer to stay where he was, so he unpacked by grabbing things from his sailing-bag each time it slid past. Then the bag overturned, emptying itself. He scrambled after his belongings. The boat canted one way then the other. Mr Pringle hurtled from port to starboard, sitting finally on the box of provisions Elizabeth had stowed on the bunk.

There was a slow but inevitable realization that she packed groceries the same way he did, with fragile items on top, like eggs, butter and yoghurt. He thought about nipping out in the morning to buy some more, and to get his trousers cleaned, then the boat lurched again and he remembered where he was.

As he could no longer sit, he went in search of a mop to swab the floor. The yacht had the measure of him now, curtseying unexpectedly, throwing him off balance.

He seized a bulkhead for support. The door slammed shut, trapping his fingers. Pain drove all other thoughts from his mind apart from the need to soothe the agony and use the heads.

Beside the minuscule lavatory was a panel of instructions. He studied them carefully. Panic built up inside. Four fifths of the world's surface was covered in water, all he wanted to do was add his half-pint, but one false move and he could pollute England. Or, if his aim was bad, it would swill about in the bilges and everyone would know.

Mr Pringle half squatted, clamping his shaky knees round the bowl. As the floor shifted beneath his feet, he grabbed the lavatory lid and it banged shut, catching him first between the eyes, then in a much more sensitive area. This time the pain nearly made him swoon.

Something plopped on the floor. He knew it must be a tear, but it was blood. Where on earth was it coming from? He peered in the mirror. Where the lavatory lid had made contact with his forehead, was a deep gash with blood pouring from it. His new jersey already looked unpleasant. Mr Pringle tried staunching the wound, but his swollen fingers couldn't manage the handky. He remembered a pack of Elastoplast in his sailing-bag and made his way back to the main cabin, holding on to the immaculate teak with bloody hands.

He was surprised to see that those items he'd left on the floor were swimming to and fro in a greasy liquid. It took a moment or two longer before he realized Elizabeth must've had milk tucked in among the groceries. The yacht suddenly tipped perilously. He was going to capsize! If only he'd been able to relieve himself first.

"God Almighty!" Matthew lowered himself through the hatch, taking great care where he put his feet, "You have been making yourself at home, haven't you?"

"There were one or two little mishaps," Mr Pringle admitted.

He was stowed in the quarter berth while they cleaned up. From there he learned that the boat belonged to someone called Frank who would be arriving shortly. Matthew wondered aloud whether he would recognize his property. To make doubly sure Mr Pringle could do no further damage, Elizabeth had zipped his sleeping bag up to his chin. He didn't care. She'd also given him more brandy to deaden the pain. If she'd amputated his hand he'd have been none the wiser although he did wonder about the other area.

He watched sentimentally as she scrubbed the floor. Would she and Matthew make love tonight in the little cabin up front? If Mavis had been here, Mr Pringle would've attempted to. On second thoughts, perhaps not. But the movement of the boat no longer troubled him. It was quite soothing once you got used to it. He slept.

FOUR

HIS FIRST WAKING THOUGHT was that he'd died because he was zipped inside a shroud, then he smelt bacon and egg. He must be in paradise.

"Bloody hell!"

Mr Pringle opened an eye. The Angel Gabriel had a leathery complexion. He was examining one of Mr Pringle's pairs of trousers and looked disgusted. Mr Pringle closed his eye quickly but Matthew had spotted it.

"Morning, uncle. Meet Frank. Would you mind dressing in the cockpit because Liz is in the heads. Breakfast is nearly ready."

It wasn't that simple, transfering a shivering, ageing body from pyjamas to vest and pants. There was the additional hazard of being moored near one of Her Majesty's destroyers, that part of the harbour being shared with the Navy. As he tried to make a discreet examination of some of his injuries, a line of matelots leaned over the rail to offer advice. By the time Mr Pringle sat down to cornflakes, he was pinkly furious. The yacht was up to her tricks again, too. He only let go the marmalade for a second but the jar disappeared. Frank managed to scrape most of it off the bunk.

"It's going to be quite a blow today. Are you lot sure you want to go?" he asked grimly.

"Oh, yes." Matthew was confident, "Lunch in Cowes, right?" Mr Pringle nodded gamely. His fingers had swollen to sausages but this voyage was partly for his benefit. Besides, it wasn't costing him anything.

"When do we leave?"

It wasn't that straightforward. One couldn't simply point a boat and hope for the best, he learned. As the albatross flew, the Isle of Wight might not be that far, but mortals had to weigh up pros and cons.

"Winds, tides, underwater obstacles and sandbanks," Frank explained. "You wouldn't want us to end up aground, would you?" Mr Pringle could think of nothing nicer. He went back up on deck to be out of their way.

Liz appeared lugging a sailbag. She was obviously enjoying herself. The wind stung his cheeks but she drew in great breaths of it. "Isn't this marvellous! I always feel so stifled in London." As she moved deftly to and fro Mr Pringle admitted a sad fact to himself: he was a pavement and petrol-fumes man.

"I fear Matthew made the wrong choice. I lack the necessary aptitude for sailing."

"You mustn't worry. You might get the hang of it." She didn't sound convinced.

"But I do worry," Mr Pringle insisted. "Once we're in Greece without Frank to assist, how will you manage? I shan't be any use."

"You could always rescue me if I fell overboard," Elizabeth said lightly. "You can swim, can't you?"

"Yes. Surely you also?"

"No. Father would never let me learn. He said the best sailors never could. He and Mummy couldn't swim. Father's theory was that it would only prolong the agony if either of them fell overboard. Despite what happened, I think he was right." Her voice quivered but she went on briskly, "I can doggy paddle of course, and I always wear a life-jacket. Apart from that, I take great care not to fall in."

Mr Pringle viewed the choppy water sombrely. He would want to stay afloat as long as possible, he had no death wish. Sooner or later someone was bound to come along. Oceans were full of yachtspeople nowadays. Maybe a lonely lady yachtsperson . . . ?

Frank tugged the straps of his safety harness so tight he could scarcely breathe. He was clipped on to the cockpit rail.

"Whatever happens," Frank ordered, "don't try being clever. If I shout—you jump. Got it? There's no room for democracy on a boat and I'm in charge of this one. *Stand by to let go forrard!*"

Down below Elizabeth started the engine, at the helm Frank eased back on the throttle and up front Matthew unhooked them from the buoy. *Green Timbers II* eased her way past the shelter of the destroyer, out into open water. As she did so, the first of a thousand waves crashed down on to Mr Pringle.

He lost count of the number of times he was sick. The difference between up and down wind soon became clear, but not soon enough. No cleaning firm would accept his trousers now. Water ran down the borrowed oilskins, filling the large borrowed boots. His glasses were covered in salt. When Frank ordered him to take the tiller, he couldn't even see the compass.

The wind increased. They reefed in the mainsail until all that remained was a tight triangle of canvas that thrummed in agony. Despite their explanations, Mr Pringle couldn't understand why they zig-zagged all over the Solent. He wanted an end to the purgatory.

A seagull squawked derisively and Frank yelled that he must keep his eyes on the bloody horizon—what a stupid thing to say. There was no horizon, simply a wall of water whichever way he looked. The Isle of Wight had vanished altogether.

"As it's nearly Force Eight," Frank screamed, "We won't bother with 'Man Overboard' drill this morning."

A squall blotted out the sky. The sea was rougher. He hadn't enough strength left to hold the tiller, his arms were being wrenched from their sockets. Through the cabin hatch, Matthew tried to hand him something.

Lunch! The sandwich fell from Mr Pringle's nerveless fingers. It floated about in the cockpit until it separated into component parts of cheese and mush. He was finished.

Suddenly Elizabeth was sitting opposite, feet braced as she took over the helm. With a shock he saw she was smiling.

"Doesn't she go well in this weather?" she cried. He was dumbfounded. That anyone could actually enjoy all this...? "We're not going to Cowes... Yarmouth instead ... prettier harbour." He didn't believe her. They were protecting him from the knowledge that there was no hope left.

Suddenly Frank and Matthew began tossing equipment out of the cockpit lockers with some urgency. Frank grabbed the tiller now and Liz leapt below. She began turning the key. For the first time, she looked alarmed. Even Mr Pringle realized that the engine was refusing to start.

"You! Tie this on up front at the double!"

He set off with the fender under his arm. There was a special knot for this job; he remembered reading about it. Up front it was much more dangerous. When a wave knocked him over, he stayed on his knees. He got to the pointed end and sat, feet dangling either side of a stanchion. He couldn't manage the knot so he tied a bow instead. The yacht dipped—he was underwater! Nothing of his past life rose up apart from the final remains of his breakfast. Gasping for breath, he resurfaced and saw both boots and socks were missing. Nude feet! He stared at them incredulously. The boots were Frank's but there was no sign of them now.

They were heading directly at a jetty. People on it were waving. Out of politeness Mr Pringle let go a hand to wave back. The fender disappeared. They were so close inshore he could've reached out and shaken one or two hands. Beneath his thighs, the deck vibrated. The engine had finally come to life.

They backed off, headed out to sea and turned in a tight curve to race inshore, parallel to the jetty this time. They shot through the opening in the grey sea-wall and immediately, the whole universe changed: no noise, no waves, nothing but flat calm. They were in harbour.

The others rushed about but he stayed where he was, clinging to the stanchion. As they rafted up alongside another boat, he saw the German flag fluttering at the masthead. The front hatch lifted and a foreigner stared at him.

"What was it like?" the foreigner asked, "out there?" Mr Pringle broke the habit of a lifetime.

"Not too bad," he lied, "Just a little bit of a blow."

HE WENT BACK by ferry because Frank declared he couldn't afford to lose any more equipment.

"Matthew still wants me to go to Greece, though, because of sharing the cost." He was in Mavis's double bed. She had greeted him with rapture in The Bricklayers where she worked part-time behind the bar. Now they were alone.

"Perhaps you'll take to sailing once you're out there?"

"I'm afraid that's most unlikely. No doubt Elizabeth could pay the extra herself but Matthew doesn't want her to."

"I can understand that. Who did you say her father was?"

"Leonard Hurst of Freezer International. He and his wife were drowned—"

"Oh, that Leonard Hurst!" Mavis stared at him. "You didn't tell me she was an heiress."

"She isn't, not yet. According to Matthew she doesn't inherit the trust money until her twenty-fifth birthday later this year."

"All the same..." Mavis sank back on her pillows, "he's done all right for himself, this nephew of yours."

"Yes..." Mr Pringle felt uncomfortable.

"What was her place like, where you stayed last night?" He tried to find words to convey the luxury.

"Very, very splendid. Neither Matthew nor I could afford to return such lavish hospitality. He is still studying to be an accountant having failed his exams last summer."

"I shouldn't worry, dear," Mavis turned over on her side. "He won't be the first young man whose face was his fortune. And you never know... If they do decide to get married, they might be happy." Mrs Bignell never had high hopes of matrimony.

FIVE

THE GLARE FROM the white dust at Preveza half blinded him. He hurried across the tarmac. He'd become separated from Matthew and Elizabeth, but once he reached the shade, he looked back for them.

The baggage trolley arrived. The handlers at Gatwick had been very thorough, he noticed, it would've needed forensic science to determine his sailing-bag had once been scarlet. A tubby young man strolled up and examined its battle scars.

"Bit of a sailing man, I see," he said aggressively.

"Oh, hardly!"

"Been cruising, have you?" He thrust pudgy hands in his pockets, lowering his jeans below the belly plimsoll line.

"I went on a short cruise earlier this year," Mr Pringle admitted, "in coastal waters."

"I've always wanted to do that. Never could afford to. Dinghy on a trailer man, that's me." He gave a short unfunny bark of laughter. "Own your own boat? Or are you in a syndicate?"

"No, really, I…" The conversation had got out of hand.

"Couldn't afford to do that, either." The silly fellow leaned forward, his bottom lip jutting jealously, "What's your line, as they say? Got your own till?" Mr Pringle felt brutal.

"I'm retired. Three years ago I was an Inspector in the Inland Revenue."

The silly chap's feet began walking away, the rest of his body following as best it could. "Got to go," he muttered, "the wife's waiting." Despite himself, Mr Pringle sighed. It was ever thus.

Matthew came hurrying up. "What a crush! They can't all be for the flotilla?"

"I sincerely hope not. Where's Elizabeth?"

"She's following. Oh, great! The Fairchilds have made it after all." He beamed at Mr Pringle. "They weren't sure if they could so I didn't tell you about them. It was too crowded on the aircraft to go and look. Hi...! Over here!" He began waving vigorously, but Mr Pringle had spotted Elizabeth making her way across. Matthew couldn't have seen her otherwise he'd have gone to help with her bags. Mr Pringle frowned. Should he go? He could see she was suffering, patches of sweat darkened her blouse.

The family were waving now. Even at this distance, Mr Pringle could clearly see that two of them, sisters, looked most attractive. The elder was taller with gold hair thick about her shoulders, she moved swiftly towards Matthew. The younger, paler and more sylph-like, kept pace with her parents.

The elder girl drew level and for the first time, Elizabeth noticed. Her expression changed. For Mr Pringle it was a frozen moment. Matthew had obviously not told her about the Fairchilds, either.

Mr Pringle stayed where he was and let his nephew sort out the awkward situation. He watched the introductions with Matthew's arm firmly in position round Elizabeth's waist. The Fairchild sisters made polite gestures, the elder ceasing to sparkle. They began to move in his direction.

"Uncle, I'd like you to meet Mr and Mrs Fairchild, James and Kathleen. And this is Charlotte...and Emma." Mr Pringle didn't like to look at Elizabeth. Close to, the taller girl was even more dazzling. She smiled and he raised his panama.

"G. D. H. Pringle." She was as beautiful as a ripe peach. What on earth was Matthew up to?

BEYOND THE TINY immigration hall, coaches were waiting. A tanned girl separated them into groups. Those staying in villas or hotels filled three coaches, mariners climbed on board the fourth.

Mr Pringle deliberately sat apart. He wanted to be quiet for a while, the heat was tiring. And Mr Fairchild was the kind of businessman he'd always found intimidating. He'd been glad to leave them behind when he'd retired.

Sitting in the back row of the coach, he estimated there were seven boatloads. The tanned girl was introducing herself as their hostess, Kate. With her were the flotilla skipper, Patrick, and John, the engineer. Mr Pringle watched their neutral expressions. Surely one or two fellow passengers looked promising?

Out of habit, he made his own assessments. One foursome, roughly his own age, were loudly nautical. Home Counties, he decided, Schedule D, forty to fifty thousand a year and up to every dodge in the book. Two families, with noisy teenagers, appeared to be travelling together (PAYE). The silly tubby fellow and his wife sat apart. Mr Pringle wondered idly who had the misfortune of sharing their boat. The Fairchilds, with Matthew and Elizabeth, were sitting at the front.

Mr Pringle closed his eyes. He liked a little nap in the afternoon.

"Hi." It was Kate. She sat beside him. "I just wanted to tell you a little bit about the flotilla. I've given Matthew the inventory for your boat but this is something to help you get to know each other."

It was a diagram with eight boats, one slightly larger than the rest, named *Zodiac*. "That's the lead boat with Patrick, John and myself. The rest are like this..." Beside *Virgo* and *Libra* she wrote Hansons and Clarkes, and indicated the families travelling together. "Don't ask me which is which, the mums are sisters I gather. One lot have just had a win on Ernie, the other are spending Dad's redundancy money, so they tell me. And on *Scorpio* we have the Gills."

The silent foursome were nearest to where he sat, but he'd hardly looked at them. There was an air of tension and Kate murmured, "I don't like to ask what's wrong...Mrs Gill looks as if she's forgotten to cancel the milk or something." She went back to her diagram and her voice slipped into neutral, "On *Aquarius* we have Phyllis and company."

Mr Pringle nodded at the group from the Home Counties, "Over there?"

"That's right." Kate consulted her clipboard, "All from Surrey." Mr Pringle felt smug.

"*Pisces* is our singles boat."

"Singles?"

"Those who can't make up a crew among their friends. We fit them together. This trip there are three, not four." From her tone Mr Pringle felt sure there was a problem. He waited. "The skipper of their boat," Kate continued, "is Louise—she's Canadian, by the way. And she's asked me to tell everyone...that she's an alcoholic."

"Dear me!"

"Yes, I know," Kate sighed, "but she did ask. That's her." Mr Pringle glimpsed straggly hair above a headrest.

"Who are the other two?"

"Roger and Maureen Harper. He likes to be known as Roge." It was the tubby fellow and his wife. Mr Pringle tried to look sympathetic.

"If only we'd got another boat," said Kate, "Louise could have had it to herself and one of us could have helped on *Pisces*. But *Leo* got sunk last week."

"Good Lord!" All Mr Pringle's fears came flooding back.

"Three yobbos from Tunbridge Wells," Kate sounded bitter.

"Were their bodies ever discovered?"

"Oh, they were all right. It was the boat that went down. They undid a jubilee clip." He wanted to know more, but Kate was scribbling again.

"The last two boats are *Aries* with your friends the Fair-childs—"

"I've only just met them," he protested.

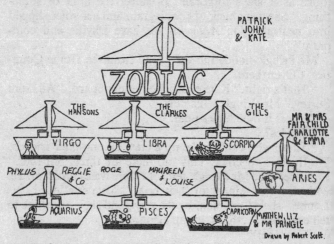

"Ah, yes, they're your nephew's friends, aren't they? Anyway they're on *Aries* and finally on *Capricorn* there's Matthew, Elizabeth and yourself. There we are, that's the lot." She handed the diagram over and asked, "Are you keen on astrology?"

"Definitely not."

"That's good. We've had all kinds of trouble since these boats were named. People wanting to change unfavourable signs, that kind of thing. It's all rubbish, of course." He didn't like to ask if *Capricorn* was a good omen. Kate stood, assuming her bright, hostessy manner. "I think it's going to be a really good trip."

"You mean there are other sorts?" Her smile flinched, just a little.

"You have been sailing before, haven't you?"

"Only for a day. Sufficient to discover I have no aptitude whatsoever. I am here..." he wanted to make a clean breast to someone, "because Matthew was obliged to find a person to share the cost and all his friends had mortgages. Or babies." Such candour was so rare, Kate warmed to him.

"Between you and me, Mr Pringle, I shouldn't worry. I think you'll discover you're as competent as most of them. In fact, you may find you're *more* experienced than one or two." Confident she'd put him at his ease, Kate left him. Mr Pringle clutched his diagram. Less experienced? There was no chance of it being a good trip. The signs had been more propitious for the *Marie Celeste*.

THE ROAD ROSE in gentle curves and the landscape opened out. There were fewer villages or newly built villas. There was the occasional donkey or goat tethered in the terraced olive groves, that was all. At the highest point, the coach stopped. They could smell the wild sage and hear the cicadas.

"Your first view of Sivota Bay," called Kate, "Five minutes for photographs." Mr Pringle stayed where he was, taking it all in. He looked where the land rolled away towards the deep blue sea and at the curve of the bay. He didn't want to waste time, he wanted to get there, to feel the warm salt water on his skin.

"How goes it?" Matthew was beside him.

"Splendidly." There was silence for a moment. "I'm very glad you invited me," Mr Pringle said shyly. "I hope I won't let you down."

"Not a chance. We're going to make a competent crewmember out of you yet." Such faith, thought Mr Pringle, such trust.

The turn to Sivota was as sharp as a bend could be. They pivoted on back wheels and tried to ignore the drop. The descent was rapid until the road petered out in a track. The

rest of the journey was on foot and they wandered through
the village, nodding at women who peeped at them over
balconies. An old man lifted a dignified hand in greeting;
and there, suddenly, were the boats—a silvery white line of
them moored sterns-to along the quay. Young Clarkes,
Hansons and Gills raced to be first on board. Mr Pringle
paused to wipe his face.

Where the quay ended, the trellised verandah of a restaurant stood out over the water, Ianni's place, where Kate had
said they would dine tonight. Greenery and bougainvillaea
shaded the white tablecloths. Even as he watched, a broad-
shouldered man with a laden tray emerged from the kitchen.
Condensation ran in icy rivulets down a dozen bottles of
beer. Mr Pringle found himself sitting in the first plastic
chair.

"'allo," said Ianni. "Welcome to Greece."

THEY DRANK, they unpacked and Mr Pringle offered to
help, but he could see the other two managed better on their
own. He listened as Patrick and John explained the engine
checks without understanding a word. Finally, he undid his
shirt collar, put away his tie and went up on deck to watch
the rest.

On the port side, the four from Surrey were settling in on
Aquarius. Phyllis rallied them with piercing cries, "No, no
Reggie! Not like that. Remember what happened at Poole!"
Two of her crew had already mutinied. Reggie joined them.
Eventually Phyllis did the same and the four sprawled in the
cockpit as duty free gin bottles emptied and the slices of
lemon in their glasses turned dark pinky brown.

To starboard, on *Aries*, the Misses Fairchild divested
themselves of clothes. As first one then the other appeared,
Mr Pringle forgot to close his eyes. Both had on bathing
suits, but not in the full sense of the word—his holiday was
getting better all the time!

It didn't take long for the rest to join in. Soon the harbour was a mass of bodies, splashing and squealing. Mr Pringle went in carefully, using the swimming ladder—it was so warm! A little way out he trod water and looked back at the flotilla, at Ianni's place and the whitewashed houses. It was all so perfect, then he noticed Elizabeth. She was sitting in *Capricorn*'s dinghy, dangling her feet in the water. Out of politeness, he swam back.

"Did you know they were coming?" she asked. Inwardly, he sighed.

"I had no idea. I've never heard of the Fairchilds before today."

"She used to be Matthew's girlfriend."

"Which one?"

"Charlotte, of course." Of course. Who would glance at Emma if Charlotte were there. No doubt the younger girl would blossom once she'd emerged from her sister's shadow. Mr Pringle came back to the present with a stab of annoyance. What right had Matthew to upset things? This little cloud threatened to swell out of all proportion and spoil the holiday.

"It was all Matthew's idea," Elizabeth said quietly, "He told the Fairchilds about the holiday and suggested they might like to come, too." Mr Pringle could see Matthew in the distance, trying his hand at wind-surfing.

"Perhaps that's all there is to it," he suggested lamely. "I mean, he's a sociable chap. He probably thought it would be more fun to have some friends along . . ." She looked at him and he dropped his gaze. "Look, why not forget all about it—I'm sure it means nothing to Matthew—and let me teach you to swim. I once taught Matthew's mother and she was hopeless. She used nearly to drown me, too, pulling us both under, but I managed in the end. Come on."

He flopped backwards out of the dinghy and re-surfaced, blowing a spout like a whale. She laughed, and he felt thankful the cloud was beginning to disperse.

SIX

THAT EVENING AT IANNI'S, Kate sorted them deftly into groups. Mr Pringle watched as Matthew and Liz sat at a table with Charlotte and Emma. Mr Pringle didn't feel like joining them and anyway there wasn't an empty chair. Charlotte was sparkling again. The other two girls were very quiet. In fairness, he couldn't say Matthew paid more attention to Charlotte, even though she made every attempt to flirt with him.

Too late he discovered he'd been put with Mr and Mrs Gill. There was an air of marital gloom about the Gills and Mr Pringle dearly wanted to ask whether she had forgotten to cancel the milk. Instead he stayed silent while she openly criticized those round about and Mr Gill patronized him on the subject of wine.

"I said, you wouldn't think the Hansons were our neighbours, would you?" Mrs Gill repeated sharply.

"I beg your pardon?"

"Over there. The Hansons, sitting with the Clarkes." She pointed at the large noisy table.

"No, I..." He sought desperately for something to say, "Didn't Kate tell me the families are related?"

"Yes, the wives are sisters. Mrs Hanson—she's the one with dyed hair and a weight problem, she's my neighbour. Terribly sweet. We used to live in Kingston on Thames, of course, but we had to move. One does, doesn't one nowadays—all this getting on one's bike?" Mrs Gill smiled vivaciously and Mr Pringle tried not to cringe. She reminded him of all those ladies who'd ever sold him flags. She went on gaily, convinced she was fascinating him with her chatter.

"Anyway, when hubby came home one day and said—it's going to be Hounslow—I thought, Oh, my God! Well, one does, doesn't one? And then when we got there I thought—well... here we are, one must make the best of what there is—and Shirley Hanson is a terribly sweet person. So persuasive." Mr Pringle hadn't the foggiest notion why she was telling him all this.

"Shirley came round one day—out of the blue—I always call her Shirley but she insists on calling me Mrs Gill—so sweet! Anyway, she came round and said what do you think, we've won on the Premium Bonds and I said how marvellous and she said yes, we're going to Greece. Then she said why don't you come too and I thought, well... why not!"

The evening stretched ahead of Mr Pringle endlessly. He was trapped with the couple nobody else wanted to talk to.

"I thought, the children will benefit from foreign travel. And hubby needs a break—admit it, darling, you did, didn't you? Of course I know we hadn't had a win on the Premium Bonds..."

He'd have a word with Kate before tomorrow night, he wasn't going to put up with this a second time.

"And when he'd discovered what I'd done, thinking it was in all our interests, hubby kept his little problem to himself, because he believes in looking after his family, don't you darling..." Mrs Gill simpered across the table and Mr Pringle wondered whether he could pretend to have an epileptic fit. Help appeared in the shape of Ianni, arms full of bottles.

"Red or white?" Mr Gill clapped his hand to his forehead.

"My God, look at the way he's handling those bottles!" Mr Gill's protest was as synthetic as his wife's social chit-chat. He tried to include Mr Pringle in the conspiracy, "You

just can't explain to these people, they don't understand!'
Mr Pringle stared at the tablecloth.

"Tell me, landlord, have you any decent claret?" boomed
Mr Gill. Ianni understood the word. He smiled happily and
flipped the crown cap off one of the red bottles.

"Claret wine," he said and was gone. Mr Gill poured
himself a full glass and pretended he was tasting it. Mr
Pringle waited for him to spit it out, but he swilled each
mouthful round his teeth, swallowed it and went on repeating the process until the glass was empty.

"Damn raw," he announced, and filled his glass to the
brim again. Mrs Gill pushed hers across. Mr Gill filled it
then she said, "Actually, I think I'd prefer white." Her
hubby nodded benevolently.

"I'll tell the fellow to bring us another bottle." He turned
to Mr Pringle. "Would you care for any of this?"

"If I may." Mr Pringle had been conned like this before.
Gill had two glasses in front of him now, both full. His wife
would no doubt consume the bottle of white—and Mr
Pringle was ready to bet folding money they'd suggest
splitting the bill three ways.

Gill poured again but only to the halfway mark. He made
heavy weather of sliding the beaker across. "Don't want to
spill any," he said blandly. Mr Pringle hoped Matthew and
Elizabeth were enjoying themselves at their table because he
certainly wasn't over here.

"Actually," said Mrs Gill archly, "we were hoping to
have dinner with you as soon as we saw who was on your
boat. It was the Clarkes who made the connection—Jack
Clarke over there, he's Shirley Hanson's brother-in-law—
and he recognized her straight away because he knew her
father." She looked at Mr Pringle bright-eyed as if expecting him to sort through all these convolutions, but he no
longer cared.

"Clarke and I work for the same firm," boomed Mr Gill, that is to say he did, because he's just been made redundant—"

"And of course it was in a very humble capacity," Mrs Gill confided. "Didn't you say a warehouseman, darling?"

"Mechanic—"

"Hubby's in management, naturally. And the Clarkes have spent all his redundancy money, coming out here. So foolish!"

Could he pretend he needed the Gents, wondered Mr Pringle, and escape to the kitchen to have his meal there?

"Freezer International," said Mr Gill, producing his rabbit out of the hat. "And that *is* Leonard Hurst's daughter on your boat, isn't it?"

"WHAT A BLOODY awful nuisance!" exclaimed Matthew.

"I have never had such an unpleasant evening in my life," said Mr Pringle with feeling.

"No, I meant coming all this way only to find employees of Freezers on the same holiday. I wanted to get Liz away from all that."

"It's not all that surprising," Mr Pringle was irritated at the naivety, "You're the one who's always telling me what a big organization it is. Anyway, there are only two of them. And technically speaking I don't think Clarke is an employee any more, now he's been made redundant."

"I hope he's not nursing some sort of grievance about that," grumbled Matthew. "I don't want Liz upset."

Privately Mr Pringle thought it was much more likely he'd be upset by the presence of the Fairchild sisters than by any ex-employee of her father's firm. Aloud he said, "I want to make it quite clear, Matthew, I am not prepared to eat with those people again. Wherever we sail, whatever we do, I must emphasize I want nothing more to do with them."

"That's no problem." Matthew's voice in the darkness sounded surprised. They were on deck, two black shapes

against a molten sea. Down below, they could hear Eliza
beth moving about. "In fact, it rather settles the matter o
our free-sailing partners, doesn't it?" Mr Pringle was baf
fled.

"After the first couple of days we all go our separate
ways, exploring the islands. The only rule is, we go in pairs
Which is why I invited the Fairchilds in the first place."

"But..." Mr Pringle tried to find a tactful way to de
scribe Elizabeth's distress.

"Look," said Matthew, misunderstanding, "it's a pretty
obvious decision. The choice is between that little wart who
accosted you at the airport sailing with the drunk, tha
lot..." He dropped his voice and indicated the boatload
from Surrey, "or the Gills."

"On that basis, I agree it has to be the Fairchilds. I jus
wish you'd warned Elizabeth beforehand," said Mr Prin
gle shortly.

"What...?" Matthew sounded astonished. "You don'
mean...Charlotte and I?"

"Of course."

"But that was ages ago...long before I met Liz. It's over
finished."

"Then you'd better try and convince Elizabeth." He
could feel Matthew staring at him.

"She hasn't—said anything, has she?"

"Not in so many words," replied Mr Pringle carefully
"But I'm sure her feelings are hurt. At your lack of consul
tation, for one thing. Why didn't you *discuss* the Fairchilds
before inviting them?" Matthew shrugged.

"It was a last minute thing," he admitted. "We'd talked
about suggesting it to a few people we knew. None of them
could make it. As I said, I wasn't sure the Fairchilds could
till I saw them on the tarmac." He got up to adjust a hal
liard clattering against a stay.

"You know, Fairchild is on our Board. I see him around
but I can't simply walk up to him and start chatting... I have

to wait for him to speak to me. Which is what happened. He remembered me from the days when I dated Charlotte...asked about holidays. I was enthusiastic, told him about this one, remembered the girls liked sailing, suggested *he* might enjoy it. I even thought Charlotte and Em might be company for Liz.'' He shrugged again, impatiently. ''Christ, how often d'you have to tell a woman you love her before she believes it?''

Mr Pringle wasn't going to be drawn. He rose. ''Might I suggest you go more cautiously in future? I don't think it's easy for Elizabeth, watching other girls enjoy your company so much.'' He shirked any mention of Charlotte's charms. ''Now, it's been a long day and I'm for bed. Are you quite sure you wouldn't both prefer the main cabin?''

''Quite sure. Liz and I will be very comfortable in the forepeak.''

It wasn't comfort Mr Pringle was referring to. On the occasions when he and Mrs Bignell had a tiff, they settled matters much more pleasantly in bed. He thought Elizabeth and Matthew would have been better off in the double bunk, the triangular shape of the forepeak was, he considered, inhibiting. He turned to go. Matthew called softly.

''I'm most grateful you've come on this trip, Uncle. I know Liz could've afforded something better, chartered a yacht with its own crew, that sort of thing. But I can't bear to sponge. With you paying a share, I could just about manage.

''There's sod-all I can do about the money. I expect people do see me as a fortune hunter but when she inherits it, Liz is giving the bulk to charity. She's already decided, and I'm with her all the way. It's nothing but a curse, believe me. When she does get rid of it, perhaps people will leave us in peace.''

In the familiar tunnel of the quarterberth, Mr Pringle wondered. Would they really divest themselves when the time came? It was cynical, he knew, but actual possession would be so different from theorizing. And even if Elizabeth wanted to stick to her ideals, he had a shrewd idea his nephew might weaken.

IN THE FOREPEAK on *Aries*, Charlotte Fairchild examined her tan. "It's coming along..." She sounded complacent. Emma looked at her steadily.

"D'you really think it's a good idea?"

"What?"

"Don't play dumb. What you were trying to do with Matthew." Charlotte stretched, catlike.

"It's a free country."

"Oh, come on, Char. Grow up."

"Listen, he's not engaged to her—"

"You'll get hurt, Char, I'm warning you—"

"You sound just like Pa."

"So? Remember what he told you? Matthew's a good-looking bloke but he's got no money—and you've got very expensive tastes. He's not even qualified yet."

"We'll manage..." Charlotte's eyes grew big. "I love him, Em." Her sister shook her head in disbelief. Charlotte whispered vehemently, "I do, I do! And I'll get him back..." She broke off. "What are you doing?" Emma was raising the hatch.

"Seeing what it's like ... Oh, yes, it's a marvellous night. Give me a hand with my sleeping bag."

"You're not going to sleep on deck?"

"Ssh! Keep your voice down. No, in the cockpit. Lots of others are doing it, look." Charlotte peered at the line of boats. Lights were out. Above them was the gauzy trail of the Milky Way. She could see the shapes of bodies, and listened to the even rhythm of them sleeping. As Emma made her way to the back of the yacht, she whispered after her, "I do love him, Em..." but there was no reply. After that there was silence for a time, apart from the lapping of the water, then an agonized cry from another seafarer.

"Oh, shit!" A bottle dropped from the unsteady hand and smashed on the gravel. Louise, the alcoholic, was on her way back to *Pisces*.

SEVEN

MR PRINGLE WOKE with a start and remembered he'd forgotten to ask Matthew where the jubilee clip was. Were they still afloat? He clawed his way out of the quarterberth. The floor looked dry but he needed air. Up on deck, he wasn't alone. Elizabeth was already sitting there.

"Hi, couldn't you sleep either?"

"I fear I'm not yet accustomed to the bunk."

"I couldn't bear to miss the dawn. Look over there."

The sun was beginning to rise above the curve of the bay. On the far shore, a fisherman was washing down his boat. As a breeze rippled the surface of the water, Mr Pringle eased his spine. It was cool out here and he'd got a touch of lumbago.

"Are you—glad—you came?" She didn't reply immediately but still sat, hugging her knees. Eventually she said,

"It's going to be okay. She's a friend from the past, that's all." There was a small shrug. "Silly of me to get worked up about it."

"And thoughtless of Matthew not to have told you," he answered quietly. She turned and gave him a tight smile.

"I forgot my father's golden rule—Never trust anyone completely."

"Dear me!"

"When you're rich. It's the only way. Of course, it'll be different once I've got rid of it. Then I'll really be sure of a person's feelings . . . ?" He managed to meet her gaze.

"Yes, indeed." My word, he thought, was Matthew going to be able to cope?

Up and down the flotilla, people were beginning to stir, emerging to nod shyly to other pyjama-clad figures. Electric razors started vying with cicadas and, on one of the family boats, children were squabbling over cornflakes. Mr Pringle went below.

Any hazy notion he'd come on a restful holiday was quickly dispelled. Each day began with a Briefing Session. This looked casual enough. Skippers from each boat lounged in a semi-circle round Patrick making notes on their charts. Some even affected not to be listening, but Phyllis asked a great many questions. Not understanding any of it, Mr Pringle wandered off to practise Greek phrases on Ianni. Someone followed him: Louise, the alcoholic. She sat at the same table and ordered an ouzo. He felt nervous.

"Hi, Pring."

"Good morning." Close to, her breath was rancid.

"Listen, you can communicate with these people, right? Only I left Toronto in a bit of a hurry so could you ask this guy if there's a pharmacy round here?" Mr Pringle couldn't oblige. By Lesson Five, *Persuade them in Greek* assumed its pupils were still healthy.

"Perhaps Kate has something in her first aid kit?"

"Not what I need, Pring! Kate doesn't have my sort of problem—did she tell you about that?"

"Yes." Louise knocked back the rest of her drink and snapped her fingers for a second. She had an intelligent bony face but the lank hair could do with a wash. Her clothes looked as if she'd slept in them.

"What the hell, Pring. What's an alcoholic now they've discovered Aids? I mean, fancy having to admit that and have people *know* what you've been up to." Mr Pringle made a small noise at the back of his throat. "So I tell everyone because I figure it's stupid to try and keep a thing like that a secret, right?" Her hand still shook, but she'd stopped dragging on her cigarette as though it were her last.

"A little difficult on a boat, perhaps?"

"Cor-rect! That boring guy Roge made one hell of a fuss about it. His wife's nice, Maureen. How does a shit like Roge get to marry a nice girl like that?" Mr Pringle didn't know.

"Tell you something else, Pring. Roge is out here hoping to find someone with money." Louise shook her head like a dog, repeating the word, "Money, money, money, money, money..." then paused, eyes shut as if waiting for her brains to subside.

"He's got some business deal—he's such a boring bore, Pring. He keeps going on about it. I told him I don't have a spare cent so he's started sniffing around... Hey!" Ianni hurried across with the bottle. How long, Mr Pringle wondered, before Roge discovered Elizabeth?

"Perhaps he'll concentrate on sailing from now on?"

"I doubt it." Louise was gloomy. "If you ask me, the nearest Roge has been to a boat before was in his bathtub." The ouzo was beginning to take effect. "I like you, Pring. You know last night, when you told everyone you're only here to share the cost—boy, you're honest!" Mr Pringle blushed.

"You know what makes me nervous about the Roge situation? I can get violent with someone as stupid as that, know what I mean? He brings out the worst. Which is why I need a pharmacy real soon, see." The small plastic bottle was nearly empty. "These stop me going berserk but there's not enough for two whole weeks."

Roge suddenly appeared at their table.

"You've left the Briefing!" Louise blinked.

"So?"

"How will we know which way to go!"

"Oh, for Chrissake, Roge! All we have to do is find tiddly little Port Spiglia. I mean, once we're out of the bay we should be able to see it." Roge took the chart and hurried off to join the others. Louise lifted her arms in the air, "So, where's the problem?'' Mr Pringle didn't know. It didn't sound very far but then neither had the Isle of Wight.

HE'D ENVISAGED an orderly departure as, one by one, yachts would slip their moorings and follow each other like swans across the bay, but then Mr Pringle hadn't been on a flotilla before.

It was only half a day's sailing. Patrick insisted everyone have lunch before leaving, so they sat in the cockpits, chewing, eyeing each other before first one then another slipped away and pretended to be doing nothing with the anchor.

Engines started abruptly, fumes filled the air. On board *Zodiac* Patrick kept up a running commentary. Kate and John, the engineer, stuck to their lunch. They didn't need to look, they'd seen it all before.

"There goes *Libra*,'' Patrick sounded cheerful, "straight over her own mooring line. Caught it neatly round her propshaft. Revving like hell. Should burn the engine out any second now..." John winced.

"Hallo! Cap'n Phyllis off pretty quick— Oh, no! She's in the wrong gear—she's going backwards!''

There was a graunch as the stern rammed the concrete quay. Phyllis could be heard screaming, "Fend off, Reggie!'' John closed his eyes.

"Are they sinking?''

"Not yet. Fend off...'' Patrick was disgusted. "The poor bloke nearly lost his foot. Oh dear, oh dear, what a nasty dent they've got in their transom now. I hope we've got enough Polyfilla. Oh bloody hell—*Virgo*'s gone and bumped *Libra*. What'd she do a thing like that for?''

"*Virgo* and *Libra*,'' Kate said slowly, "that's the Hansons and the Clarkes. They're related.''

"I can tell. What their boats are doing is incestuous. Ah, *Aries* is away...gently, gently...and *Capricorn*. Are they going to hit the opposite bank? No, they're heading out to sea. How satisfying. Two of our crews have obviously sailed on a park lake before."

"*Aries* has the best boobs," said John complacently.

"Two pairs, in fact. One for you and one for me." Kate looked at them both scornfully.

"On *Aries*? You have to be joking. The Fairchild girls are far too upmarket."

Patrick was still fascinated by *Virgo*'s nautical manoeuvres. "What are they trying to do? Oh, I get it . . . I think. *Libra* can no longer steer because her anchor warp is wrapped round her propshaft, so *Virgo*'s going to push her—sideways—all the way to Port Spiglia. Very interesting . . ." The other two actually got up to watch.

"I bet the Greeks haven't seen anything like that before," said Kate.

"I doubt whether anyone has."

Behind them, another engine was wildly over-revved. John choked on his beer.

"It's all right," Patrick soothed, "Cap'n Phyllis is making up for lost time. Fingers crossed she pushes the gear lever forward not back." *Aquarius* shot across the water like a rocket.

"Please, please!" murmured John. Patrick shook his head.

"It's no good, madam. They won't take off whatever you do." *Aquarius* careered round the corner of the bay and out of sight, the echo still reverberating.

"Did you mention at the Briefing," John asked slowly, "those derelict oil tankers moored together beyond the point?"

"Damn!" The three of them listened attentively.

"Wouldn't we have heard the bang by now?"

"Or seen the smoke?" There was a hoarse cry from the quayside.

"So soon?" said Patrick, startled.

"What is?" John was nervous now.

"*Pisces* seems to have abandoned her skipper, Louise."

"She's not in the water, is she?" said Kate, "Surely we'd have heard the splash?"

"No, she's over there, look. Having one last drink at Ianni's. Oh—look what that idiot's trying to do!" On board *Pisces*, Roge was attempting to hoist the main, but the boat was still at anchor. Patrick grabbed the megaphone and forced himself to sound calm.

"I shouldn't try doing that just yet. Wait till you get under way— Oh, my gawd! His wife's gone and started the engine!" *Pisces* bucked like a stallion. Thrown off balance, and trapped under the sail, Roge scrabbled about like a ferret.

It took time and patience to sort things out. By the time *Pisces* had departed, fully crewed, neither Patrick, John nor Kate were capable of speech. On board *Zodiac*, however, the radio could not be ignored.

"Hallo—Mayday, Mayday? Are you there *Zodiac*?" John lurched across and seized the transmitter.

"This is *Zodiac*, this is *Zodiac*. Please identify yourself, over?"

"Oh, we'd rather not do that. Not with everyone listening, but it's a real emergency." John gritted his teeth.

"This is *Zodiac*, this is *Zodiac*, what's the problem, over?"

"Our lavatory pipe's completely blocked."

CAPRICORN WAS BECALMED. Mr Pringle thought it a very pleasant way to sail. The boat stayed upright, motion was imperceptible, all he had to do was go below occasionally, to recharge their glasses.

Liz was at the helm. Matthew went up front and unclipped what Mr Pringle had assumed was a spare mast. He watched with interest as Matthew fastened it to the bottom of the jib. It worked on the same principle as his granny's clothes-prop had done, keeping the limp material taut to

catch every suggestion of a breeze. Matthew then man-
oeuvred the jib in the opposite direction to the main, so that
the boat floated like a butterfly, sails akimbo, across the
glassy sea.

There was no doubt they were moving. Plastic bottles
passed them, going in the opposite direction. He was surprised to see one or two came from Tesco. Fancy them having a branch out here! The sky above was cloudless, the sun
hot and the Ionian as glorious as a sea could be. It was so
beautiful it made him ecstatic.

"My goodness," said Mr Pringle, "this is nice."

EIGHT

IT WAS GOING very well, thought Charlotte. She stretched, turning her well-oiled body more towards the sun. Matthew was watching her from *Capricorn*, the knowledge was heady. She didn't have to look, she just knew. Just as she'd understood the real reason why he'd suggested they come on this holiday, he didn't have to phone privately to explain.

Emma moved further into the shade. She burned more easily, being fairer. Charlotte pushed the sun-oil across. "Why did you and Matthew behave like strangers at Preveza?" Emma shrugged.

"I wasn't sure if he'd remember me. It was a long time ago. He never used to notice if you were around." It was said without rancour. "What d'you think of Liz now that you've met her?" she asked. Charlotte smiled smugly.

"Apart from her money, she's pathetic."

THEY WERE GAINING GROUND. She knew the others weren't yet aware. Matthew's uncle lolled beside her, his old-fashioned hat tilted over his eyes. Matthew himself crouched in the shelter of the jib as the sun burned down. He was staring at the half-naked odalisque. Elizabeth watched, expressionless, feeling with her body every movement of the water, every shift of air, aware whenever the 'tell-tale' stirred.

On *Aries*, Charlotte was the first to notice. She stiffened. "Pa won't like that."

"Mmm?" Emma was half asleep.

"Look." *Capricorn* was half a length ahead. Without meaning to, Charlotte glanced back at her father. He'd realized what was happening. He yanked angrily at the cleat, unsheeting more of the main. The gap between the two widened, *Capricorn* was ahead by a length now. Behind, they could hear sails begin to flap: *Aries* was in stays.

Elizabeth could see where the line of wind rippled the surface of the water. If they should just get that far... The main began to fill. Beneath her hand, the tiller responded and Matthew was beside her in the cockpit. Elizabeth waited.

"This isn't a race, you know." From beneath his brim, Mr Pringle listened. "Fairchild's not the sort of bloke who..."

"Who—what?" But Matthew didn't reply. *Capricorn* heeled as she gained momentum, leaving *Aries* far behind.

"I don't think we need the whisker pole any more, do you?" Elizabeth asked sweetly. There was nothing Matthew could do except go back up front and unclip it.

Mr Pringle thought it was time to act. "Anyone fancy tea? Or can we assume the sun is down over the yardarm?"

THERE WERE VARIOUS WAYS of making landfall, and on *Aquarius* Phyllis favoured the Approach Positive. She headed toward Port Spiglia at speed, overtaking the cautious, ignoring murmurs of protest.

Her crew stood-to nervously. At the Briefing they'd learned that the waters here were deep. Anchors must not be let go too soon, to trail ineffectually. Phyllis announced she would drop hers at the last possible moment, or rather Reggie would. This most dangerous task had been delegated to him.

He knelt up front, one hand on the anchor, the other cupped to his ear because something ghastly had happened: Phyllis had discovered his guilty secret. She'd tricked him into admitting it. In a nutshell, his wife now knew what made him deaf and had given him a bad back. Lurking at

e back of Reggie's mind was the uncomfortable feeling
hat Phyllis might be about to wreak revenge.

Phyllis balanced against the backstay uttering excited
ries. Her blood was up. The quarry was in sight—it was the
ast remaining mooring space on Port Spiglia quayside. Six
oats were heading for it. *Aquarius* was in the lead but
vould she ever stop?

"Let go forrard!"

"Pardon?"

On *Zodiac*, Patrick's hands joined automatically in
prayer. *Aquarius* was now on collision course at a speed
approaching five knots. Beside him, Kate moaned, "Oh,
God, no...!" and Phyllis herself began to perceive it might
be a damn close-run thing.

"Drop the wretched thing for Heaven's sake, Reggie!"
he called impatiently. The other couple threw aside the
enders they'd been holding and prepared to abandon ship.
But at last Reggie had heard. He flung the anchor overboard and raced to the back of the boat. Unchecked, the
heavy chain rasped the paintwork, flaking it off in layers.
Out in the bay, the rest of the flotilla watched apprehensively.

It was the other two on *Aquarius* who, in a desperate act
of self-preservation, pushed Phyllis aside, seized the tiller
and thrust the gear lever into reverse. Simultaneously, the
trailing anchor caught the mooring line of a stationary caique, lifting its bows clean out of the water. On board,
sleeping fishermen faced shipwreck for the first time in their
lives as *Aquarius* juddered to a halt, spun round and, with
the caique in tow, headed straight towards the oncoming
boats. There was an immediate reaction. As he saw the flotilla begin to scatter, Patrick issued staccato instructions
over the radio. On *Pisces*, Louise reached for the bottle.
"Jesus!" she muttered, "Thirteen more days..."

NINE

THE RESTAURANT was up a steep hill in the village o
Spartahouri, overlooking Port Spiglia. The only road wa
a series of hairpin bends, each tighter than the last, edge
with scrub and cypressus. A lorry was waiting to take then
up and Mr Pringle claimed a place on it, along with th
women and children.

Halfway up they juddered past a shrine. He couldn't ex
pect a Greek Madonna to watch over him after so brief a
acquaintance but the smell of hot oil from the engine made
him resolve to walk back down.

Their arrival was dramatic. As they rounded the fina
bend they were suddenly among villas, street lights and dig
nified men and women who stood aside to let them pass: a
wave of sunburnt foreigners, hell bent on enjoyment.

But the smiles were welcoming and long tables were ready
in a courtyard where children rushed up and down with
bread and wine. Mr Pringle was so anxious to avoid the
Gills, he failed to take heed of the empty place beside him
Opposite, the Fairchilds sat with Matthew and Elizabeth.

"Room for a little one?" Roge shoved a fat buttock up
against his own. "This is a bit of all right. Bring on the
dancing girls, eh?" He leered across at Elizabeth. Mr Prin
gle's heart sank. He'd forgotten to warn her that Roge was
searching for a backer.

It was mercifully brief. Roge had scarcely begun his fore
play when Patrick rose. "Ladies and gentlemen . . . I won
der if I could have your attention for a moment. I'd like to
discuss a tiny alteration to our schedule..." He paused. The
next bit was more difficult.

"It appeared to us on *Zodiac* today . . . that one or two of you . . . are perhaps—*slightly* less experienced than the rest. So we wondered if you might all *prefer* to continue sailing as a flotilla until we've completed the longest leg to Parga."

He paused to allow the wave of protests, loudest among them being Phyllis. Her dearest wish, she told him, was to get away from it all, and that included everyone here tonight. Patrick jumped in before she could offend further.

"It's only a slight change to the route, but what we thought was that, tomorrow, we should only go as far as Nidri. To let all of you have more time to get accustomed to the boats . . ."

"And to teach some people the three points of sailing," murmured Matthew, a little too loudly. Elizabeth tried not to laugh.

"Nidri's a pretty place, only a short sail. Lots of shops and restaurants." Patrick looked at Kate and John for support.

"Plenty of boutiques," Kate said promptly, "and hot showers." Some of the women began to perk up.

"What about gin?" demanded Mr Fairchild. "Supplies are running damn low on *Aries*."

"Masses of shops, supermarkets—everything."

"And the barbecue?" asked Matthew. Again Patrick looked at John and Kate.

"We could have that tomorrow too if you like. Nidri's as good a place as any. Now, are there any more questions?" Phyllis had plenty but the rest settled down to their meal. Roge sulked. His chance had disappeared. Matthew had Elizabeth's entire attention; he was playing the lover so devotedly, she'd begun to glow a little.

Mr Pringle relaxed. The slight friction between *Aries* and *Capricorn* seemed to have dissipated. He was facing Emma and Charlotte, two of the most attractive women on the flotilla, even if Charlotte looked downcast. He ordered

more wine and set himself the pleasurable task of distract
ing her.

BY THE TIME he began the descent back to the harbour, he
was in a merry mood. The girls had laughed at his jokes,
he'd had a man-to-man chat with Fairchild about tax evasion, it'd been a social whirl of an evening. Street lights were
out now. Beyond the village, the road was a mysterious
place with patches of shadow. Mr Pringle set off alone but,
to his surprise, was joined by Mrs Gill. She clung to his arm.
It was slippery, the gravel shifted beneath her feet, causing
her to lose her balance. Mr Pringle no longer wondered why
any woman should cling to him instead of her husband.
He'd even forgotten how much he disliked Mrs Gill. He'd
had enough wine to drown rational thought.

"Look at the stars...magnificent!" he burbled but Mrs
Gill had a more urgent topic: Elizabeth Hurst. Mr Pringle
stopped listening and succumbed instead to an overpowering urge to sing.

> "All things bright and beaut-i-ful
> All creatures great and small..."

"My husband once talked to Leonard Hurst—I'm sure
she'd like to hear about it," Mrs Gill persisted.

> "One man went to mow...
> Went to mow a meadow—"

There was a sudden, terrifying scream. It shattered the
night. Up and down the hillside they stood stock still, pet-
rified. Ahead, Mr Pringle could see a glimmer of light from
the shrine, he and Mrs Gill were almost at the half-way
point. In the silence came another sharp cry then a horrible
tearing noise of a body slithering through scrub. A girl cried,

"No, no! For God's sake, help!" Something, someone fell on to the road. Mr Pringle was paralysed. Voices shouted, "What's going on?" "What's happening?" and puny torch beams poked about in the darkness.

Mrs Gill gripped him so hard that it hurt. "What is it?" she whispered. From the shadows came another groan.

"Someone's lying over there," he muttered hoarsely. He tried to move forward but she held him back.

"Hadn't we better—?" There was another whimper.

"Help me!" then silence. This time he thought he recognized the voice. He thrust Mrs Gill away and moved forward, arms outstretched like a blind man.

"Hang on, I'm coming!" Behind him other feet thudded along and a beam more powerful than the rest sliced through the blackness.

"What's going on?" panted Patrick as he drew level.

"Over there, in the dark by the bend." The beam wavered then found what it was looking for. She lay very still, a fan of hair half-covering her face, her body crumpled beneath her. As she felt the beam, she stirred. Patrick got there first, followed by Kate and John.

"What happened?" cried Kate but Patrick stopped her.

"First things first. Hold that steady." He pushed the torch at Mr Pringle. Very gently, he and John moved Emma on to her back and began checking her limbs. John pushed his sweater under her head, Kate wiped away the dirt. As she did so, Mr Pringle felt sick. There were deep bloody gashes on Emma's face and arms. Her jeans had saved her legs but the shining hair was matted with filth.

When he'd satisfied himself nothing was broken, Patrick sank back on his heels. "Can you tell us what happened?" Mr Pringle shaded the beam from her eyes. He could hear people behind him whispering, calling out to one another as they made their way towards the light. When they reached it, they fell silent. Emma licked swollen lips.

"I was looking for Charlotte. She'd got our torch. Someone grabbed me in the dark. Tried to...I struggled but he twisted my arms behind my back. Then he suddenly let go...I fell. It was awful!" She began to weep. Patrick asked urgently,

"Have you any idea who it was? Did you see him?"

"It was too dark."

"Was anyone near you?"

"Char was ahead. She left before I did, I was hurrying to catch up. The only person I remember seeing...was Roge."

"Oh, no." Roge's wife, Maureen, pushed her way through to the front, "I don't care if she did see him, he and I were together all the time. Roge—where are you? Come and tell them." He moved forward reluctantly.

"It wasn't me. I didn't push anyone. I was holding on to Maureen."

Mrs Fairchild arrived and the group parted to let her through.

"My darling, what happened? Your poor face!"

"My God, Em!" Her father knelt beside her. "Who did this?"

"I don't know," she moaned. "Someone pushed me. All I know is—it was a man. He...pressed himself against me..." There was a stillness among those listening. "When I started to struggle he let go... He gave me a push to make sure I went over the edge."

She looked up at the steep incline. The rest did the same. Against the sky, jagged shapes of trees stood out menacingly. Mrs Fairchild was stunned. "My darling, you could've been killed!"

"Can you walk?" Patrick was brisk. He had to get them away from here, back to the boats. He and John lifted Emma to her feet. After a few tottering steps she collapsed into his arms and he and John carried her the rest of the way. A subdued procession followed. Louise fell in step beside Mr Pringle.

"It couldn't have been Roge, Pring. I could see him and Maureen when we left, hanging on to one another like he said. Anyway, he isn't the type," she said flatly. "Not Roge. He'd never have the nerve."

"Someone did."

"Yeah . . . Sounds more like one of the dirty raincoat brigade, don't you think?"

Quite illogically, Mr Pringle was thankful he'd been with Mrs Gill. She'd disappeared, presumably to rejoin her husband.

"One doesn't like to think there is a potential rapist in our midst," he murmured.

"No, one doesn't, does one?" The ironic tone wasn't lost on him.

"I'm sorry."

"Oh, don't worry, Pring. I know it wasn't you. But they're not nearly so rare as you think, rapists."

"I'm very sorry to hear it," he said helplessly.

"Sure. It's a great life. Night." And she went swiftly along the quay to *Pisces*. He looked after her thoughtfully then with Patrick's torch still in his hand, he climbed on board *Zodiac*.

HE ENTERED UNOBTRUSIVELY. Kate and Emma had disappeared, presumably to one of *Zodiac*'s four cabins. In the saloon, Mr Fairchild was arguing with Patrick.

"I want Emma back on *Aries* where I can look after her. Suppose this—this madman strikes again?"

"With respect, I don't believe he will." Patrick caught sight of Mr Pringle. "How about a pot of tea?" Mr Pringle automatically picked up the kettle. "The way I see it," Patrick went on, "one of our party had a skinful and took a shine to Emma. That's not to excuse what happened, but I am thankful she wasn't more seriously hurt."

"She must see a doctor."

"Let's see how she is in the morning, James." Mrs Fairchild was much more calm. Her husband still wanted his pound of flesh.

"How about finding out who did it, dammit!"

"John and I will visit all the other boats while you're having tea," Patrick replied, "and if we can't discover who it was, at least we'll put the frighteners on, to make sure he doesn't try again."

"How can you be sure it wasn't a local?" Patrick returned a level gaze.

"Because I've been skippering out here for five seasons and I'd stake my reputation that it wasn't. The villagers aren't like that—and they want us to keep coming back. No, I'm afraid it's much more likely it was one of ours. Ready, John?" The engineer was on his feet. "Please, have your tea. I know how you feel but believe me, John and I will do all we can."

The Fairchilds drank in silence. Mr Pringle took two mugs along to the sick bay. Emma was white against the pillows but already the gashes were less livid. "It's okay for her mother to come and see her," Kate murmured. He went back to the main cabin. Mrs Fairchild left and he was alone with Fairchild. The silence was intimidating, he was glad when Kate returned.

"Well?"

"Try not to worry, Mr Fairchild. Emma's asleep. I'm pretty certain there's no permanent damage." After listening to his grumbling and further gentle persuasion, she managed to get him to go back to *Aries*. As he disappeared through the hatchway, Kate sighed with relief. "God, I'm tired . . . but what a thing to happen."

"Perhaps Patrick and John will discover who did it."

"I doubt it. It was so bloody dark. *I* didn't see what happened and the three of us weren't that far behind." She yawned wearily, "I simply heard Emma go over the edge after she'd screamed."

"Try and get some rest," Mr Pringle advised, "At least you'll be safe here with Patrick and John."

"Yep." Kate managed a tired laugh, "there's enough muscle between them to frighten any rapist." Mr Pringle made ready to leave.

"I shall keep my fingers crossed that it's a good trip from now on," he told her.

"I'd keep everything crossed if I were you," Kate replied.

TEN

IT WAS PERHAPS not surprising that many had rationalized the affair by morning, particularly those ladies who hadn't yet gone topless. Mr Pringle could hear their muttered comments as he stood in the cockpit, helping Elizabeth make *Capricorn* shipshape for departure. Matthew joined them.

"I think I ought to go and see how Emma Fairchild is," he said. "Do you mind?" Elizabeth flushed.

"Why on earth should I? Go ahead. There's no need to ask my permission." But Matthew moved closer.

"I didn't want you to think I'd gone sneaking off behind your back," he murmured, kissing her discreetly, "not after last night." Elizabeth reddened even more. From where he pretended to be deaf, Mr Pringle decided the situation between the two had improved. He waited until Matthew had gone ashore before asking, "What shall I do with this bit of rope? Shouldn't it be attached to something?"

Elizabeth reacted swiftly, "Let me do that. Why don't you go below and make us some more coffee." He went, happily enough, and she checked the sheets on his side of the boat. Simply knowing Mr Pringle had fiddled with equipment made Elizabeth nervous.

Emma was in *Zodiac*'s saloon, sitting between Patrick and John. The marks on her face were still livid but her hair was once again a silken mantle. She was quite calm.

"Hi." Matthew waited diffidently in the hatchway, "How are you feeling today?" Emma tried to smile but her face was too stiff.

"Not too bad, thanks."

"She's bloody brave if you ask me," said John loudly. "Not a peep out of her while Kate was re-doing those bandages—and I bet everything still hurts." Emma gave a careful shrug.

"Only my bum. That's as sore as anything." She pulled a comical face to make them laugh, "I hope nothing's permanently scarred down there!"

"On behalf of the company," Patrick began formally, "I really am terribly sorry—" but Emma reached across and put a hand over his mouth.

"Forget it," she said pleasantly. "By tomorrow I should be feeling a lot better. The stiffness will've gone by then, I expect. Sorry I made such a fuss last night but I was so frightened, what with the dark and the shock and everything." She lowered her arm and sunlight showed them the deep raw gashes in the skin. Matthew felt sick.

"I agree with John, you were bloody brave about the whole thing," he told her. "Some women would still be having the vapours." John was suddenly jealous.

"When I discover the bastard who was responsible, I'll break his ruddy neck," he promised. Emma shook her head firmly.

"Leave it. It's over. Whoever did it is probably feeling too shit-scared of you and Patrick to try again. I wish I hadn't hurled accusations around last night, though." She paused to take a final sip of coffee, "Time to put all that right, I think. Thanks to all of you for the tender loving care." She rose, stumbling slightly. John grabbed her arm, making her wince.

"Sorry, sorry," he mumbled.

"I think I'm better on my own." She smiled charmingly then wobbled across to the hatchway, laughing at herself, "I'm as weak as a kitten this morning," and let Matthew help her up the steps. Mr Pringle and several of the others watched them emerge. Still holding on to Matthew, Emma turned and blew kisses at John and Patrick, "Thank you both again."

"Stay out of the sun with those scratches," John advised.

"I will." Matthew lifted her ashore. From both ends of the quay, greetings and questions showered down. Emma acknowledged them graciously. "This really is a heavenly place, isn't it?" Mr Pringle heard her say, then, as she looked about, "Where's *Pisces* moored?" Matthew pointed and she went forward alone. As she passed him, Mr Pringle told her what a pleasure it was to see her up and about and was favoured with a smile that made him feel young again.

Up on the quay, Elizabeth was topping up the water tank. "I hope what's happened hasn't spoiled the sailing for you," she said earnestly. "Today looks like being a good day for it."

"Yes, doesn't it." Emma sniffed the fresh dewy morning, "I hadn't noticed before but you're right—and I don't intend to let anything spoil this holiday, thanks." She walked along to the furthest boat. "Hallo there! Anyone on board?"

Roge popped up out of *Pisces* like a jack-in-the-box.

"Oh, it's you." Emma didn't hesitate. In a voice loud enough to be heard on other boats she apologized and said she'd been mistaken.

"It wasn't me," Roge grumbled.

"I realize that now. I'm sorry I thought it was. All I could remember was seeing you ahead of me." She turned to Maureen, "Weren't you wearing something dark?" One or two remembered the navy dress. Heads began nodding. "That's probably why I only remembered Roge. He had on light coloured jeans, didn't he?"

Maureen said eagerly, "It's very nice of you to come and apologize..." but Emma raised a deprecating hand. She turned to the other boats.

"Is there anyone here who feels he should apologize to *me*?" she asked pointedly. No one said a word.

As the sun rose, wasps were a welcome menace. It gave them an excuse for a rapid departure.

"Look at them all," said Patrick sarcastically, "Doing everything by the book this morning. Trying to prove what wonderful sailors they all are... Well, it's too late for that."

"Did you get anywhere last night?" asked Kate quietly.

"Nope."

"They all looked guilty," John said helpfully, "even the women."

"Who d'you suspect?" Patrick and John looked at each another.

"Not the Hansons or Clarkes, right? They were together."

"Check. Nor Matthew and his girl-friend, or Pringle. The Fairchilds are out. How about Cap'n Phyllis's better half?"

"What—old Reggie?" Kate was astonished. "He's deaf as a post!"

"Since when did that interfere with the male urge?"

"My money's on Gill," Patrick was serious, "he wasn't with his wife." Kate shivered.

"I hope to God you really did frighten him off."

"Don't worry." John lifted his eyes to Heaven, "And don't let it blow till we've got 'em all to Parga."

On *Aries*, Emma Fairchild smoothed ointment on her wounds.

"Does that sting?" Charlotte asked hesitantly.

"Not too badly. Char, did *you* see anything?" Her sister groaned.

"Don't you start! Pa kept on at me half the night."

"But did you?"

"No. And I'm sticking to you like glue from now on, and that's an order—"

"Ouch!" Charlotte flinched in sympathy.

"Shouldn't you stay below out of the sun?"

"It's so stuffy, I'd feel sick in minutes."

"I really am sorry, Em..." Charlotte flushed a little, "Pa insists it was my fault anyway... and the wrong one got hurt." Emma grinned pointedly at the bared breasts.

"Tut-tut! I shouldn't worry about it, if I were you. I'm not, any more. I don't think it'll happen again. Can you help me with this?" Charlotte eased the loose shirt tenderly over Emma's shoulders.

ON *CAPRICORN* IT WAS Matthew's turn at the helm. The sails were trim, Elizabeth was beside him. Mr Pringle sat at his usual station, one hand resting lightly on the lifebelt.

"Do you think—whoever it was last night—got the right one?" said Liz. Matthew looked at her curiously.

"What makes you say that?"

"It's the kind of thing that's always happening to me." She shrugged, "Not rape, so far, thank Christ, but cranks. They send anonymous letters, threaten all kinds of sexual harassment. My trustees intercept most of them, but from time to time one or two get through."

"How very unpleasant!" She shook her head at Mr Pringle's priggish expression.

"It'll all be different... once I get rid of the money."

"But until that happens," Matthew hugged her with his spare arm, "I'm not letting you out of my sight." She smiled enigmatically but she didn't respond as she might have done once, not now she'd met Charlotte Fairchild. The sailing therapy had worked, reflected Mr Pringle. Elizabeth was much more self-confident: Matthew would have to look to his laurels.

ELEVEN

NIDRI WAS IN SIGHT. The flotilla surged forward, past the Onassis Island with its warnings to trespassers. Closer inshore, dinghies skimmed about like dragonflies and windsurfers wobbled across their bows. They were near enough now to make out the restaurants, then they saw the line of masts all the way along the quay.

Patrick's voice crackled over the radio: "This is *Zodiac*, this is *Zodiac*. Looks as if we might be unlucky. There could be another flotilla ahead of us. Stand off please, while I investigate."

The big yacht slipped past. Mr Pringle was childishly disappointed. He was also hungry and there was no food left on board. Lunch was beginning to look like a mirage. Ahead of them *Pisces* began circling.

"Bloody maddening," shouted Louise. "What say we ask Phyllis to clear a space?" It was tempting providence.

"This is *Zodiac*, this is *Zodiac*. I'm sorry, we *are* out of luck. There are no spaces left. Make for the alternative, I repeat, make for the alternative, Tranquil Bay. Out."

At the helm, Matthew cursed, "Blast!"

"Over there," Liz pointed to where *Zodiac* was heading towards a small tree-lined anchorage that lived up to its name.

The flotilla turned disconsolately. They'd been permitted a glimpse of what they yearned for, that was all. When they'd booked the holiday, they'd promised each other it would be a chance to get away from it all, away from the rat race, but now they were faced with tranquillity, it was more than they could bear. Over in Nidri were crowds, bars,

shops, all the familiar things. Phyllis was the first to crack.
"Ice!" Reggie jumped.

"What's that?"

"I refuse to go any further without ice. Gin doesn't taste
the same without it. And a hot shower, like they promised." She pushed the tiller hard over and the yacht responded.

Over in Tranquil Bay, Kate had been about to drop anchor. She shaded her eyes. "Oh, no! One of them's turned
back."

"Which one?"

"*Aquarius*, I think."

On *Libra* and *Virgo*, Clarkes and Hansons asked each
other what *Aquarius* knew that they didn't. Kate shouted,
"Some of the others are turning back now, too!" Patrick
grabbed the transmitter.

"This is *Zodiac*, this is *Zodiac*. We are all, repeat all,
mooring in Tranquil Bay, over."

But mutiny was established. Boats wavered then fell into
line. What had been a loose formation became a spearhead
with Phyllis leading the way. Matthew hesitated then tucked
Capricorn in behind. "Might as well find out what's going
on."

Orders poured out of *Zodiac* but they turned down their
volume controls. Out in Tranquil Bay, John started the engine and prepared to give chase.

Reggie was standing in the prow. "Look," he said surprised, "there's a bloody great gap on Nidri quay. Plenty of
room for all of us— Oh, there's a sign: 'Ferry—Private'."
Phyllis was impatient.

"I can't see a ferry, can you? It probably only calls once
a week in a little place like this." The reason she couldn't see
it was because the ferry was hidden behind the Onassis Island but it was on time, heading for Nidri.

In restaurants up and down the quay, people sat up and began to take notice. They were from the other flotilla, experts every one and they scented disaster.

"That lot are surely not going to...?"

"They are, you know!"

On *Zodiac*, they already knew about the ferry. Patrick yelled into his transmitter. At the quayside, other yachts tuned to the same frequency, and his voice boomed out.

"This is *Zodiac*, this is *Zodiac*. Greek ferry boats do not, repeat DO NOT GIVE WAY. *Do you read!*"

"Not only do they not read," one old salt confided to another, "those buggers have switched their radios off. Come on." They were pouring out of the shops now, anxious for a grandstand view.

On his bridge, the Greek ferry captain sat serenely contemplating his retirement. In three months' time he would be joining his son in a little café in Potters Bar. He'd had enough of the monotonous beauty of this twice daily run. He cleared the end of the island and looked ahead, and jammed his thumb on the klaxon.

"Oh, shit!" Louise had seen it. She heaved on the tiller, pulling *Pisces* in a tight turn. Roge lost his balance.

"Hey!" Then he saw it, too. "Look at that! It's coming straight for us—it could run us down!"

"Attaboy, Roge."

Matthew reversed *Capricorn* at top speed and Mr Pringle clung to the lifebelt with both hands. They'd been close enough to see food and drink on the restaurant tables. He licked his lips, whether for hunger or terror, he couldn't be sure.

Reggie was making a professional job of tying up *Aquarius* to the large bollard. Some of the locals were shouting and using their hands but he couldn't make out what they were saying because of the ruddy din. He also couldn't make out where all the wash was coming from, forcing their yacht against the quay. Something blotted out the light. "Oh, my God!" he whispered. Phyllis rallied.

"Fore!" she cried. "Fend off, Reggie!"

THEY RETIRED TO Tranquil Bay, to lick their wounds. Still shaking, Patrick ordered them all on board *Zodiac*.

"I'd like you to know ... two of our boats—and at least three belonging to the other flotilla—have been badly damaged. We've got to make them last another eleven weeks!" He was in danger of losing control. His flock didn't like being scolded. It wasn't their fault, he'd promised them they were going to Nidri.

"What happens now?" Phyllis was far from penitent.

"We think it would be better if we carry on heading towards Parga, as far as Levkas. The wind will be behind us so it won't take long. It's a bigger place than Nidri and I'm absolutely certain ours will be the only flotilla."

They didn't take much convincing; anything was better than hanging about here, feeling stupid. Kate managed to produce enough bread and fetta cheese to dull hunger pangs and John made a heady punch. After an hour or so they were ready to leave. Patrick issued instructions.

"When we arrive we moor bows-to alongside the open-air cinema."

"A cinema?" someone asked.

"Yes, it's great. They're usually showing some old vampire movie or other. Now listen everyone, it'll be a quick passage because of the wind but I'd like us all to meet and head down Levkas canal together, okay?"

Once out in open water, there were real waves. Elizabeth deserted them. She was tired and needed a rest, she said. Could Mr Pringle take the tiller for a while? It would've been churlish to refuse.

Matthew went below, too, to plot their course on his chart, and Mr Pringle stood alone. They were hurtling along at a tremendous rate. Spray broke over the boat. Sunshine had been replaced by an opalescent haze that obscured the land.

With a panic he saw he'd allowed them to drift off course. He corrected swiftly but it would be his fault if they were lost. He looked around but couldn't see another living soul. What came next? Wasn't Albania round here, or Yugoslavia?

"Cup of tea?"

"What— Oh, thanks very much." It was amazing how much braver he felt with that in his hand.

"I can take over now if you like?" Elizabeth yawned.

"Good Lord, no. I was just beginning to enjoy myself."

"Fine. I wouldn't mind another half hour. I feel bushed," and she went below again. It was another age before Matthew appeared.

"Shouldn't we be seeing the canal entrance by now?" Mr Pringle strove to keep his voice casual. Matthew looked at his watch.

"Not yet. If you're getting impatient, I could let out the reef in the main?"

"Oh, why bother? What's another few minutes?" In his short career as a sailor, Mr Pringle had learned that a reefed boat didn't lean over too far. And what was time after all? Simply another dimension.

When they eventually turned towards the land, he was astonished how the rest of the boats appeared from nowhere. They'd been within a few minutes' sailing of each other and he hadn't realized.

One by one they began to follow *Zodiac* through the entrance and down the narrow channel of deep water. Khaki-coloured shallows stretched away on either side. Wading birds stood motionless to watch them pass. Ahead were the lights of Levkas itself and, as Patrick had promised, theirs was the only flotilla. Gently, easily, they slid into place— even Phyllis managed without a hitch—and began to prepare for a night on the town.

ON *PISCES*, Louise had mislaid her pills. "You've been waving that ruddy bottle about," Roge grumbled. "It probably fell out of your bag."

"Oh, what the hell, I'll get some more. This place surely has a pharmacy."

On *Aries*, Charlotte put on a dress, pulled the sash tight to emphasize her waist and began coiling her hair. It was bleached white-gold and her skin was the colour of honey.

"Is that for Matthew's benefit?"

"Maybe..." Emma sensed the excitement in her voice.

"You could get hurt," she warned.

"Oh, phooey. All's fair in love and war." Charlotte caught sight of Emma's face. "Don't worry—I know what I'm doing. Are you fit enough to try dancing tonight?"

"I think so."

"That engineer looks nice," Charlotte was all innocence. "He's big and brawny enough to look after you, too."

THEY WEREN'T disappointed. Despite the hour, Levkas was alive, its shops open, its inhabitants enjoying the cool evening air. Up and down the streets members of the flotilla kept bumping into one another, crying out in self-conscious recognition, boasting of bargains and exchange rates in the boutiques.

By ten p.m. most had gathered in the appointed restaurant. Mr Pringle was late. He'd decided to buy Elizabeth a present. She'd still looked so tired as she and Matthew got off the boat, he felt guilty. She'd done more than her share of the sailing. Row upon row of dresses gave him an idea. On the spur of the moment, he walked into one of the shops.

They were all the same style, finely pleated cotton gathered at the shoulder with loose wide sleeves. It didn't really matter that they were cheap, Elizabeth would look much more feminine than in the severe style she normally wore.

e remembered her dark skin framed by the straight bob
d chose a colour he thought of as mushroom which
epened to brown at the hem.

The salesgirl watched him. She hadn't seen a foreigner in
panama before. He must be rich. When he didn't haggle,
e was sure of it. She put a necklace of matching beads on
p of the dress.

"For the young lady," she said with a twinge of con-
ience.

There wasn't time to return to the boat. He hurried to the
staurant still carrying his parcel. Dancing had already be-
n. Tables once again lined a courtyard and coloured lights
the vines overhead competed with the stars. Judging by
e noise, wine had been plentiful.

Elizabeth was sitting with Emma and John. As he
tched they were joined by Patrick and Kate. There were
veral empty bottles on the table. Elizabeth's glass was full
t she looked tight-lipped. Where on earth was Matthew?
en Mr Pringle caught sight of him, dancing amorously
th Charlotte. It didn't matter that they were in a far cor-
r, they could be seen. And in Mr Pringle's opinion, they
re making an exhibition of themselves. He sought a chair
far away from it all as possible. What tiresome behav-
ur on Matthew's part!

The beat grew louder and young Clarkes and Hansons
armed on to the floor. Matthew and Charlotte returned
the big table. Mr Pringle saw Matthew bending over Liz,
viously inviting her to dance. She shook her head and
ank more wine. Beside the healthy tans of those next to
r, she looked very pale. He hoped she wasn't ill.

He didn't see her disappear but he did notice the com-
otion. Mrs Clarke got up abruptly and went after her into
e Ladies. There was a pause. People chatted to each other
vkwardly, then Emma and Kate followed Mrs Clarke.
Such a shame when you see a young girl like that . . . too

much wine. You'd think she'd know better." It was M
Gill, feigning concern.

"Excuse me." Mr Pringle brushed past her and hurrie
over to the Ladies where he waited outside helplessly. Th
sad little procession re-emerged. "Is there anything I ca
do...?" Elizabeth was leaning on Mrs Clarke's arm.

"No thanks, dear, we can manage. Now pet, let's get yo
out of here." Mrs Clarke guided her skilfully towards th
exit.

"We'll get her to bed," said Emma. "She'll feel bett
now she's been sick." Mr Pringle doubted it. He didn't thir
a stomach upset was what was troubling Elizabeth.

On his way back to his seat he saw Charlotte dancing wi
Patrick. Her happiness made him furious. Matthew wa
waiting at his table.

"Look, I'm sorry about what's happened—"

"Really, Matthew, this whole business has to stop. The
attempts with both young women... No wonder Elizabet
is upset, being publicly humiliated—"

"Now look, uncle. It was her idea that I dance wi
Charlotte. Liz said she was too tired herself. Patrick wa
with Kate, John's making eyes at Emma—there wasr
much choice left."

"There's dancing and dancing—and well you know it."

"But that's because Charlotte... Look at her now, ove
there with Patrick. She's just the same with him." Mr Prir
gle sighed. It was partly true. Patrick wasn't the danc
Matthew was but Charlotte was again the centre of atter
tion. Music electrified her. The rest had stopped and we
clapping in tempo. Even from here he could feel the excit
ment.

"I did invite the Fairchilds," Matthew insisted, "and a
ter what happened to Emma at Spartahouri..."

"Nevertheless I would strongly recommend you concer
trate on Elizabeth from now on."

"I intend to, that's what I came to tell you. I'm going ack to the boat, but you stay and finish your meal. I can anage. Patrick will stay with Charlotte." He went, paus- g briefly to speak to the Fairchilds. Mr Pringle tried a outhful of moussaka: it had congealed on his plate. Blast! Ie'd been looking forward to it, he was extremely hungry. Ie sipped his wine. Why was it on this holiday, just as he vas beginning to enjoy himself...

IE CLAMBERED ON TO the bow and made his way to the ack of the boat. Matthew met him in the cockpit en- rance, bucket in hand.

"How is Elizabeth now?" Mr Pringle felt a little guilty. Ie'd actually stopped in a café, to enjoy a couple of bran- ies and watch the world go by, on his way back to *Capri- orn.*

"Pretty rotten," said Matthew seriously, "It must've been omething she ate. I've never seen her as bad as this before. hope she manages to sleep with all that going on, too." In he open-air cinema across the quay, demons were about to estroy mankind. His nephew looked worn out.

"Are either Mrs Clarke or Emma—?"

"Emma helped Liz undress. Mrs Clarke produced some otion she uses on her own kids." Matthew indicated the ucket, "I wouldn't say it's actually helped..."

"Is Emma with her now?"

"No, she and John went to the cinema but don't worry. 'm coping."

"Is there anything I can do?"

"You could make us some tea if you liked. I wouldn't aind a cup when I've finished cleaning up."

Mr Pringle put on his pyjamas. Outside, screams of aidens being ravaged mingled with catcalls from the au- ience. As he washed their mugs he heard the climactic ausic and settled thankfully in his bunk.

Outside he heard people leaving the cinema, then Emma
and John called softly. Through the hatch, Matthew re
plied that Liz was sleeping and for a while all was quiet.

But not for long. Mr Pringle woke to the sound of ago
nized retching. Matthew hurried to and fro with glasses o
water. He wondered aloud whether he should fetch Kate bu
Liz called hoarsely that she didn't want anyone to see he
like this. Serve Matthew right, thought Mr Pringle grimly

TWELVE

T WAS AN early start because the passage to Parga was a
ong one. "I hate to ask you but d'you think we could
anage two-handed? Liz isn't fit enough this morning." Mr
ringle didn't feel particularly well either and Matthew was
ollow-eyed.

"If you think we are capable?"

"I've checked with Patrick. The wind'll be behind us
ost of the way." Mr Pringle had heard assurances like that
efore but he couldn't think of an alternative. Matthew took
iz a hot drink, made sure she was firmly tucked in and told
im to cast off. They followed the rest into midstream and
egan the slow passage back down the canal. Once outside,
e flotilla spread out. *Zodiac* with her greater sail area
eaded towards Anti-Paxos to take advantage of the wind
ut Patrick warned the rest to stay close together.

The wind followed the pattern of previous days and be-
an to freshen. Matthew staggered back from the forepeak,
 aying Liz didn't want any lunch. Mr Pringle wasn't sur-
rised; they were heeling at a most unpleasant angle.

"When we get there, there's everything we want at Parga,
ccording to Patrick: snorkelling, wind-surfing, even para-
nding if you feel like trying that."

"What is it?"

"You'll see. Only a few quid and worth every penny, ap-
arently. If we make reasonable time, we're having the bar-
ecue tonight as well." Mr Pringle decided not to think
bout that.

Matthew told him what else he'd learned at the Briefing.
arga was a mainland port in a wide bay with a small shel-

tered harbour to one side. The town itself was on the o|
posite side of the bay but caiques would ferry them acros|
"It's a very peaceful anchorage." All they had to do no|
was find it. "What's your heading?"

"Three-four-five."

"Try three-five-five for a bit." It was all terribly hit |
miss.

"What's this?" Matthew stood in the hatchway holdi|
Mr Pringle's parcel.

"A dress. I bought it in Levkas to give to Elizabeth."

"What a smashing idea—why didn't I think of it? It'll |
just the thing to cheer her up. What colour is it?" Mus|
rooms reminded Mr Pringle of toadstools.

"It's brownish. Could you take over for a minute? I nee|
to visit the heads." It was dangerous below. Clinging |
handholds he saw one row of portholes was nearly und|
water. On the other side he caught a glimpse of solid rock|
He prayed Matthew wouldn't get too close. There was |
urgent shout. He hurried back to the cockpit.

"We're nearly there—look." He couldn't see the fold |
the land that Matthew had described but they were follow|
ing two of the other boats. "Got to get the sails dow|
okay?" Mr Pringle nodded.

By the time they'd tied up in the harbour he was r|
minded of his visit to Yarmouth. Then, as now, outside w|
all wind and spray, but here was absolute calm. Land curve|
in an arm round the basin. He could see two paths, one di|
appearing through the trees, the other leading down to t|
beach. In the distance was a restaurant and thatched hu|
that had once marked the site of a holiday village. Beyor|
was the town itself. He stared at it through binoculars. It w|
in the tradition of mainland Greece and had a style ar|
graciousness about it.

"Fancy a swim?" Matthew asked him.

"That's a good idea." But Matthew himself still ha|
things to do.

"I won't if you don't mind. I want to make sure Liz has something to eat, then I need to collect wood for the barbecue. The site's up on that hill, I think."

"Oh, yes..." Mr Pringle wished he felt more enthusiastic about that. "Well, if you're sure there's nothing I can do..."

The beach was full of holiday makers, he would go in off the rocks. He found a mask and snorkel in the cockpit locker and tried them on. Carrying flippers, he stepped gingerly across the hot concrete of the quay, nearly tripping over a female, sunbathing. He could see she was female; she had on nothing but a piece of ribbon strung with beads. Immediately, his mask steamed up. He must get into the water quickly!

It was much colder than at Sivota. He got away from the rocks as quickly as he could, then floated face-down and looked at the underwater landscape. Not far below the surface were more rocks covered in sea-urchins. Between them hovered shoals of tiny grey fish. He followed, the flippers making swimming effortless.

The sun burning the skin between his shoulder-blades made him eventually turn on his back. My goodness, he was a long way out! He realized that, going back in, the rocky shoreline might be dangerous. The only safe way would be round the end of the jetty and into the harbour, which was even longer. And he hadn't eaten since breakfast.

By the time he reached the harbour, he was exhausted. He moved from one anchorline to the next until he reached stone steps and crawled up on his knees. Someone helped him on board *Capricorn*.

"You look all in," said Mr Clarke. "Shall I find you a towel?" Mr Pringle nodded, too winded to speak. The boat was empty and the doors had been left open to let air circulate. Mr Clarke re-emerged from the heads, "Will this do?" He offered him one of Matthew's.

"Thanks." He wiped away the worst of the salt and pu
on his glasses. The sun awning was up. He moved into th
shade and concentrated on breathing.

"You still don't look too clever. Perhaps you'd bette
have a drink." Mr Clarke went below again and found tw
cans of lager in the cool box. "Join you, if I may?" M
Pringle didn't care what he did so long as the pain in hi
chest subsided.

"I was hoping to see Miss Hurst." Mr Pringle's hear
stopped pounding long enough for him to speak.

"She and Matthew must've gone for a walk... I'm afrai
she hasn't been well ... Something she ate."

"Ah." Both of them remembered the scene in the restau
rant.

"I used to know her father," said Mr Clarke, "Leonar
Hurst. We were in the war together." Mr Pringle was a ma
in whom many sought to confide: in launderettes, trains
almost anywhere. This time it didn't take long. Word
weren't Mr Clarke's forte. It was a tale of small heroism a
Dunkirk in a motor boat with an engine that needed coax
ing. They were hit but kept going. As the last man wa
helped ashore, the boat sank beneath them. That was whe
there'd been a promise, over a handshake, of a job. "Th
engine was my department, see. And I kept her going." M
Pringle wondered why he'd been told all this. "Look here
That's her father, that's me."

The faded snapshot was pushed into his hand. Ho
young they were, thought Mr Pringle. "I'm afraid I don'
know when Elizabeth will be back," he apologized, "Mat
thew said something about collecting firewood."

"No matter. You show it to her when she does come. I'
like her to see it. Of course it's all changed now... Once h
got drowned. I lost me job for one thing."

Ah yes, now he remembered. The Clarke family had use
redundancy money to come to Greece. Mr Pringle couldn'
think what to say. Elizabeth wouldn't take kindly to an

appeal for re-instatement, he was sure. Nor did he think she could arrange it. But he needn't have worried. Mr Clarke was far too shy to push his case. "You just show it to her," he said. "I expect she'd like to see it."

Mr Pringle waited until his guest had left before going below to change. His knees were still shaky, he needed food, he told himself. One beer had given him the taste for more and there was that restaurant on the beach. It was annoying, therefore, as he stepped ashore, to find Roge lying in wait.

"I'd like to see Liz."

"She isn't here."

"I can wait." It was ridiculous the way everyone was chasing her.

"I've no idea when she'll be back."

"It doesn't matter. Where are you off to?" Mr Pringle was exasperated.

"I'm going paracending."

"What's that?" Mr Pringle didn't stop to explain because he didn't know, but also because he wanted another peep at the lady sunbather, but she'd disappeared. Probably scared off by Roge, he grumbled.

On the beach he saw for the first time what he'd committed himself to. High above the bay a doll hung from a parachute, as if from a gallows in the sky. The other end of the rope was attached to a speedboat which raced round the arc of the bay. How high the victim was—silhouetted against an ancient castle on the rim of hills.

On the second circuit, the doll began to fall. The parachute fluttered, dipped the body into the water then rose again as the boat picked up speed. Mr Pringle found himself trembling. Higher and higher into the sun before the boat turned, slowed and the doll finally sank into the sea, alongside the launch platform. And he'd told Roge he was going to do that! He'd need a hell of a lot more beer first.

In the beach restaurant he glanced round. There wasn't anyone he knew. Parga was obviously popular, the place was crowded. He thought about Elizabeth. Had she gone shopping? They were short of supplies in the galley. Perhaps he should've stayed to help? No, why should he—he'd done his share of the sailing today. He was entitled to enjoy himself occasionally.

"May I join you?" He rose very slowly, to indicate his feelings to Mrs Gill but she still sat down. "That looks refreshing, I think I'll have one too. You haven't seen my hubby, have you? He was hoping to speak to Miss Hurst."

Pent-up annoyance threatened to choke him. He swallowed the first beer and ordered a second. He pretended to be deaf but that didn't worry Mrs Gill. She simply carried on, telling him of school fees and worries about hubby's future, "Which is why he has to speak to Miss Hurst." She gave him an expectant smile. He remembered how unkind she'd been in the restaurant.

"Look here, Mrs Gill, Elizabeth is out here on vacation. She's already told me how people pester her for money at home..." Let Mrs Gill blush, he didn't care any more about being rude, "Out here, she's entitled to be left alone. I suggest you go back to your boat and tell hubby that from me." He raised his hat to make a dignified exit but found he wasn't wearing one.

Back on *Capricorn* he discovered he'd missed Matthew and Liz a second time but they'd left a note.

"We've explored the town and collected some wood. See you at the barbecue. The dress looks great." Underneath, Liz had added, "Thanks for my lovely present XXX". He felt a little hurt, he'd wanted to be there when she'd opened the parcel. Oh, well ... He searched for a clean shirt. The boat wasn't so tidy now, there were clothes strewn about. He wished they'd waited.

In the heads, Mr Pringle combed his moustache so that it curled under at the corners, which he always did when he wanted to look younger. He thought about the girl with the beads: red ribbon with green beads. Or were they blue? He'd check tomorrow. He hummed one of his happy songs, "Ten green bottles... Hanging on the wall..." And that reminded him.

The last duty-free bottle was in the galley. He was surprised there was so little left in it until he saw Matthew's scribble—"Sorry!" Mr Pringle poured what there was into a glass. He didn't really need to hurry. He wasn't that anxious. His only experience of barbecues so far was eating half-raw chicken in a drizzle. He went up on deck and looked hopefully at the night sky but it was cloudless.

Several of the women were setting off from *Zodiac*, he noticed, carrying sacrificial offerings wrapped in cling film. He settled to watch the sunset, there was no need to rush. The measure of whisky must've been larger than he realized, his legs felt wobbly.

When finally he set off, he told himself he'd overdone the swimming. And he needed food. He'd scarcely eaten anything all day. He'd steer clear of the Gills this evening, he didn't feel strong enough to deal with them.

It was dark under the trees. By the time he reached the site, he'd stumbled often enough to feel anxious. As usual, he'd forgotten a torch. He could see Patrick and Kate doling out food and, not far off, John in charge of the bar. The aroma of roast chicken made his mouth water and he joined the end of the queue.

There was a stereo blaring. One or two were dancing in the firelight. Gill walked past and Mr Pringle moved further into the shadows. As soon as he'd had his chicken, he'd go back to the boat. An early night would be a luxury. Then he caught sight of the dress and shouted "Elizabeth!" but she was too far away to hear and continued her headlong rush up into an olive grove.

"Did you see which way Liz went?" Matthew came hurrying towards him with two glasses of wine. He thrust one in his hand, "I've lost sight of Emma, too. You haven't seen *her*, have you?" Mr Pringle felt suddenly uneasy.

"Isn't she with John?"

"He'd got his hands full with the bar. I said I'd keep an eye on her while he was busy. Now I've lost both of them."

"Elizabeth went that way, I think." Mr Pringle indicated the dark hillside. "Perhaps she knows where Emma is."

"Thanks," Matthew disappeared.

"Want a top up?" It was Reggie, a bottle in either hand. "Red, white or rosé?" he gestured. Mr Pringle held out his glass. The taste wasn't too awful once you got used to it.

An hour or so later, Louise and someone else helped him down the hill. He tried to thank them but the words were difficult to get hold of. It hadn't been a bad party, really. In fact, come to think of it, it was the best barbecue he'd ever experienced, but he couldn't tell either of them because he was having such trouble with his legs. The other woman shone her torch so he could see the way but it didn't make much difference. Maureen, that's who she was. Roge's wife. He wanted to ask why on earth she'd married a silly fellow like that but Louise kept shouting, "Watch where you put your feet!"

They were on the jetty with ropes criss-crossing everywhere. He went to step on to *Capricorn* but it moved away. He was in a cat's cradle, dangling over the water. They got him on board eventually. Louise thought it would be a good idea to have one for the road but the bottle was empty. Anyway, he was awfully tired. Maureen understood. She helped him into his pyjamas. And Louise pushed him into his bunk.

THIRTEEN

MY GOD, he was thirsty! He must've slept with his mouth wide open to be in this state. His lips felt chapped. When he closed them, they rasped like sandpaper. Some fool had left the hatch open. It was already hot outside.

He thought he wasn't too bad until he started to move. After that, he knew he was very, very ill. He kept his eyes shut—it was safer—and groped for his spectacles. And found them! That was lucky. He opened the eye furthest from the light. It must be morning. He'd assume that and not bother looking for his watch.

The thought of lying down and letting it all go away was irresistible, then he considered what might happen if he were horizontal, and stayed where he was.

His tongue wouldn't work. He couldn't wiggle it about, which was a pity. He was fond of his tongue. Perhaps if he gave it a drink of water? He'd never realized before what a complicated business it was, trying to fill a glass. His feet were wet by the time he'd finished. Should he climb Everest next to try and find the Alka Seltzer? Oh, Lord...

The bulkhead door was shut—good. He didn't want to wake them. They might want to talk, or make breakfast. He clung to the sink at the thought of food. Outside a towel hung on the rail where he'd left it yesterday. He would put his shorts on, walk along the beach and have a shower. That would make him feel better. Why on earth hadn't he thought of that before?

He moved carefully. Even so, the sun scored a direct hit on his eyeballs before he got sunglasses on. There was some money in the cockpit stowage; he helped himself to it. He might feel well enough to have a coffee at the beach restaurant afterwards.

It was quiet in the harbour. Some were sleeping on deck. Emma was fast asleep in *Aries'* cockpit. He sidled past.

On the beach an old man offered him a paper-bag full of apples as shrunk and wizened as his head. Mr Pringle felt sorry for the apples. He bought them and wondered if he'd the strength to find the donkey he'd seen tethered in the olive grove. It might like them.

Half-way along the beach someone hailed him; the ferryman who took customers out to the platform. He was pointing at it now. Two people were already there, unpacking the parachute. Mr Pringle walked along to explain that he'd changed his mind: today he was too ill.

The ferryman overflowed with kindness as he helped him on board. Mr Pringle pointed to his chin and tried to translate "unshaven". They were heading for the platform, it was ridiculous!

The girl had lustrous brown eyes. She wore a tight sort of top and a bikini bottom. Mr Pringle wondered if she were sister to the girl in red string? He began to tell her why he couldn't take up her offer.

Her companion helped him step into the harness. It fitted under Mr Pringle's crutch, round his waist and over his shoulders. The two of them adjusted each part so that it was snug, then fastened the buckle across his chest. The girl reached round Mr Pringle's waist to check the tension. Her breasts were warm, she was delightful.

"Is okay?"

"Very nice." For some reason she obviously thought he was referring to the equipment. Her companion was showing him how the parachute was attached at the shoulders, his hands were free—he could move like a bird. The girl was tying a rope to the harness with a double knot. The other end disappeared into the ferryboat—it wasn't a ferry at all, it was the speedboat he'd seen zooming round the bay yesterday! The girl was demonstrating something.

"Lean back, let the boat pull you forward. Three jumps, okay?" As she leapt from foot to foot, her breasts bounced. She shouted a question above the engine noise. "Which your boat? You over there?" She pointed to a yacht the size of *Britannia* out in the bay. He wished the noise would stop, it was cracking his skull!

"No, over there," he bellowed. "Inside the harbour." The girl nodded and smiled indicating the speedboat. "He will drop you in the water by the rocks so flotilla friends can see you—okay?"

"No!" He'd seen what was beneath the water over there—jagged rocks. "Absolutely not!"

The boat went like a bullet from a gun. His feet touched once, twice and he was off the edge without putting a toe in the water, scooped into the air. Up, up, up! The white and yellow canopy filled, lifting him. He was thousands of feet up, soaring beneath a white and yellow cloud.

He was sixty feet up at the end of a thin piece of string!

Suppose he bumped into something? He looked round nervously for gulls and accidentally let go with one hand—but he didn't fall! Very cautiously, he let go the other. He could fly! The parachute was keeping him aloft. Arms spread wide above Parga Bay, Mr Pringle warbled in a thin baritone, "What's the use of wearing bra-a-ces... Hats and spats and boots with la-a-ces—!"

The speedboat had swerved to avoid *Britannia*. Mr Pringle ceased singing abruptly. Feet curled in fright, he stared at someone on the sundeck below. A female person. He could see this quite clearly because she was nude—not a single bead! "Coo-ee!" he called, and waved. He nearly emasculated himself turning upside down in his harness to see her reaction. She waved back! Wait till he told Mavis Bignell about that!

The speedboat turned in a wide arc inside the bay. They were passing the ruined castle on the hill. Mr Pringle spread his arms and banked like an aeroplane. "Brrmm, brrm, brrm!" he shouted happily, cocking both guns at the sentries, "Rat-atat-tat!" Good Lord, he hadn't had as much fun as this since that day out with his father at Burnham on Crouch.

The platform slid past underneath, then the beach restaurant. They were nearing the harbour. He had a moment's panic about the promised dip in the water but remembered that would come on the second circuit. He would worry about that later. On the flotilla, one or two tiny figures looked up. He wanted to shout but already they were at the place where he'd snorkelled yesterday and there, her dress billowing round her, was another female person who didn't wave because she was lying face down in the water.

Mr Pringle shouted himself hoarse on the second circuit. It dawned on him gradually that no one could hear. He was as tiny as they were and none of their sounds reached him. The beach went past for a second time, then the harbour. There were more people on the boats now. Several stared up as his shadow passed over them but Mr Pringle no longer waggled his arms. He hung, limp as a sack, dreading what was coming.

He heard the change in engine note. The driver looked back at him, estimating his rate of descent, one hand on the throttle. G. D. H. Pringle prayed aloud, "Dear God, please don't let it happen!" but of course, it did.

In slow motion, he came down out of the sky and plopped gently into the water. The dreadful thing rippled away but the speedboat driver had seen it and cried out in shock. They tried to reach it but waves swept it away, crashing it again and again against the rocks.

They took Mr Pringle back to the beach. He tried to run all the way back to the harbour, forcing one foot in front of the other, sobbing for breath. His varicose vein ached, tears half blinded him and when he reached the flotilla he could tell they already knew. They stared at him: he knew each of them by name but they were all strangers now. They stood aside but he couldn't manage the last few steps to *Zodiac*, his knees buckled. Kate knelt beside him.

"One of the locals spotted her. The police are on their way. Patrick and Matthew have gone to bring her in."

He waited on *Capricorn*: he lost all sense of time. People tried to help. Mrs Clarke put a towel round him, he was shivering despite the heat. From time to time, tears still ran down his cheeks.

Mrs Clarke brought him tea. Her husband helped him dress but, most of all, Mr Pringle wanted to be left alone. He felt numb. Then *Zodiac*'s dinghy returned and he saw they'd wrapped the corpse in a blanket. Seeing her like that, shocked him back into consciousness. There was no denying it now: Elizabeth was dead.

FOURTEEN

THE DAY SEEMED ENDLESS. He lost all sense of time. He stayed where he was until bidden to board the police caique. No one spoke as they were taken to Parga. As they walked through the streets, a few tourists turned to stare but Mr Pringle wasn't aware of them. Inside the cool grey-green building he waited his turn. He was the last to be summoned.

It was a bare room but one thing comforted him. On a high cill was a plant like the one Mavis kept in her hall. He gazed at it while the police inspector noted down details from his passport.

"May I offer my condolences, Mr Pringle, and explain what is to happen. There will be an inquest, probably tomorrow."

"Yes." He'd expected that.

"Today we enquire into the circumstances."

"Yes."

"When did you last see Miss Hurst?"

"Last night at the barbecue."

"How did she seem? Was she distressed in any way?"

"I don't know. She was too far away. I called but she didn't hear."

"Did you see her again, after that?"

"I'm not sure." It was painful to confess. "Last night I drank too much wine. I know that at one point my nephew was searching for both Miss Hurst and Emma Fairchild. Whether he found them or not, I'm not sure. I remember asking him at the barbecue but I can't recall his reply." He felt more embarrassed than ever.

"And yesterday? You and Matthew Shaw sailed to Parga with Miss Hurst?"

"Yes. Elizabeth was ill. She'd been taken poorly the previous evening in Levkas so Matthew and I sailed the boat."

"And when you saw Miss Hurst last night, had she fully recovered from the—upset?" Mr Pringle wondered if his use of the word was deliberate. He decided it was.

"My nephew looked after her while she was being sick. What happened between them then, I've no idea. Elizabeth was certainly very ill. None of us got much sleep."

"And when you observed her in the restaurant at Levkas, was she emotionally distressed?" Mr Pringle considered the question carefully. He must get the emphasis right.

"I met Miss Hurst for the first time last Easter when the three of us went sailing. She was still recovering from the deaths of her parents, she depended on Matthew rather a lot." He paused and the Inspector nodded he'd understood. "On this holiday, I thought she'd progressed, become more self-reliant."

"More independent, perhaps?"

"Yes."

"But when your nephew was with Miss Charlotte Fairchild, was this new self-confidence shaken in any way?" The Inspector *had* learned a lot. Mr Pringle returned a level gaze.

"I think Elizabeth was angry. It was certainly thoughtless of Matthew, although I'm afraid Charlotte Fairchild is a bit of a flirt." It was said mildly enough but he felt he'd been too censorious. "Miss Fairchild is very beautiful of course."

"Of course." The Inspector was equally serious. "And was the distress caused by this beautiful woman sufficient to make Miss Hurst throw herself off a cliff?"

"Good Heavens, no!" He'd spoken involuntarily but he was confused. Surely the intelligent man behind the desk didn't think it was suicide? Hadn't Elizabeth's death been accidental?

THE CAIQUE WASN'T available to take them back immediately. Emma, John and Matthew were waiting for him. "Please come and eat," Emma begged. "If you do, I'm sure Matthew will make the effort. You both need food." She tucked an arm under his, her blue eyes full of concern. Mr Pringle discovered he was very, very tired. He needed to think. Perhaps lunch would help. Emma's small hand with its tapered fingers was warm and comforting, but in an instant he remembered Elizabeth's capable hand on the tiller. Tears came unbidden. He followed blindly as Emma led the way to the restaurant.

He waited until the waiter had taken their order before asking, "Would one of you tell me what happened after I went back to *Capricorn* last night?"

"What don't you already know?" said John, surprised.

"I haven't told uncle about the row," Matthew admitted.

"None of it?"

"No."

"What—row?" asked Mr Pringle quietly. He looked first at Matthew then Emma.

"You'll have to tell him," Emma urged, "It's bound to come out."

"I know it is but it was the very last thing I wanted," Matthew protested, "and I still think Liz was bloody unfair."

"In what way?" asked Mr Pringle. Matthew sagged in his chair.

"She accused me of chasing after Charlotte," he said helplessly, "which when you remember how you and I had spent a day and a night looking after *her* . . ." He turned to Emma and John, "It wasn't all that easy for uncle and me, sailing *Capricorn* without Liz. That's why I felt so tired last night. I know I probably wasn't patient enough but I think Liz was unreasonable."

"When did it all begin?" asked Mr Pringle gently.

"On our way up to the barbecue. Liz suddenly came out with all kinds of accusations. Told me I had to make up my mind once and for all who it was I really wanted. I said I already had—and had told her dozens of times but that wasn't good enough. Liz insisted I mustn't have anything more to do with the Fairchilds." Matthew paused while the waiter served them with Mezedes. "I tried to calm her down. I explained that it wasn't possible to avoid seeing them because we'd already arranged to do our free-sailing together."

"It was the obvious pairing," John observed. "Patrick and I had assumed you and *Aries* would be together. The Clarkes were with the Hansons, the Gills could have teamed up with *Pisces*. Everyone knew *Zodiac* would have to shadow Cap'n Phyllis."

"So what was Elizabeth's reaction when you told her?"

"Impossible," Matthew answered flatly, "She was determined to pick a fight." He swallowed, then mumbled, "I just wish to God it hadn't happened like that. The last things we said to one another . . . so awful!"

"Try not to let it get out of proportion," Emma murmured.

"How can I get away from it, though? The police made me go over and over it. Think what it's going to sound like in court! Honestly uncle, I did try and make Liz see reason . . ." He looked at him with swollen eyes, "I did love her, you know."

They were so horribly exposed in this restaurant. Mr Pringle sipped water to cover his embarrassment. Only John appeared to be unaffected by it.

"If *we'd* done as you asked last night, we might have prevented the whole business, so don't go blaming yourself for it."

"How was that?" Mr Pringle was curious.

"Well, after Liz had dashed off and Matthew couldn't find her, he came back and asked Patrick to organize a proper search party."

"I'd already been after her," Matthew explained. "A couple of the Hanson kids helped me. We'd been up the hillside, shouting her name but Liz refused to answer."

"But John and Patrick couldn't leave the barbecue when Matthew asked them, so I offered to help," said Emma.

"And did you find her?"

"Oh, yes, it wasn't difficult. Liz was quite pleased with herself, hiding up there among the trees." Emma pushed her plate away irritably, "She was still het-up of course, but boasted how the others hadn't managed to find her."

"Did she agree to come back with you?"

"No, she didn't." Emma looked at him gravely. "To be frank, she behaved like a bitch about the whole thing. I told her it was over between Matthew and Charlotte but she refused to listen."

"So then what happened?"

Emma shrugged. "I'm afraid I gave up. I came back to the party. Charlotte was helping John with the bar. She asked what was going on—I told her the whole story."

"Did you go and speak to Elizabeth again?" Mr Pringle asked Matthew.

"No. After hearing what Emma had to say, I knew it was useless. I thought Patrick and John might succeed—"

"But before they could do anything, Charlotte ran off to tell Liz not to be silly," said Emma. "None of us thought it would work but Char wanted to try."

"What happened?"

"She said she couldn't find her," Emma replied shortly.

"What about Patrick? Had he anything to suggest?"

"Not really..." John answered reluctantly, "You see, Mr Pringle, this wasn't the first time this sort of thing has happened. I don't mean the accident," he added hastily, "we've never had anything like that before, thank God, but rows... bust-ups... they're very common on boats. It's the effect sailing has on some people. They come out here on holiday—sometimes it's the first occasion they've been so close for years. Cooped up, you know what I mean. Things get out of proportion. I think a boat is worse than a tent for finding out what people are really like. We've had quite a few divorces. I know after Spartahouri we should've been more careful but, last night, Patrick and I didn't do anything because we thought it better to let everyone cool down." He helped himself to more wine before adding, "We assumed Liz would take herself off to a hotel in Parga and would be back this morning to kiss and make up." He sighed. "How wrong can you be. I could kick myself for not listening after Charlotte had told us Gill was up there."

"Oh?" Mr Pringle was alert now.

"He made a pass at Char apparently," said Emma, "She was in a dreadful state when she got back to the barbecue."

"Are you quite sure it wasn't Gill at Spartahouri?" John asked Emma seriously, "I know we've been through this before but try and think about it quietly. Could it have been him?" Emma closed her eyes then shook her head slowly.

"I honestly don't know. I wish I did."

"Your implication being...?" Mr Pringle asked John.

"That the same bastard attacked Liz. After all, we know she was still up there when he was having a go at Charlotte. Liz didn't come down—the path would have brought her past us. Charlotte went to look directly after Emma came back, remember. She was gone for ages but that's because she was so busy searching for Liz."

"Nevertheless," Mr Pringle looked round at the three of them, "Charlotte got away from Gill—why didn't Elizabeth do the same? She was a strong, healthy girl. Surely she could have dealt with him, particularly if she'd already seen what was happening. Are you three suggesting Elizabeth was so terrified that when Gill accosted her—assuming that he did—she rushed blindly over the edge of the cliff into the sea?''

There was silence, then John answered, ''Well we all know that's what she did, Mr Pringle. Because of where we found her this morning. And if you'd seen her injuries, you'd realize she must have bashed her head in as she fell. Sorry, mate...'' He'd turned to Matthew who couldn't speak but simply shook his head. ''Anyhow,'' John continued, ''no one's suggesting Liz was so upset by anything Matthew or Emma said to her, she did what she did. Now listen, Matthew. When we get back to the harbour, Patrick and I are going to have a little chat with Gill, only you're to stay right out of it, understand? It's going to be strictly private. We'll make him tell us what really happened up there last night.'' Something dawned on Mr Pringle.

''Why isn't Gill here in Parga? He wasn't on the caique— why didn't he come and make a statement with the rest of us?''

''Because from what the police let slip,'' answered Matthew impassively, ''Gill denies even being up on the hill last night. It's Charlotte's word against his, unfortunately. After she'd made her statement, that's when the police told her what he'd said.''

''Poor Char,'' sighed Emma. ''She got quite hysterical when they told her. She couldn't face lunch. Pa and Patrick took her off to calm down. They're meeting us back at the caique.''

All the same, wondered Mr Pringle privately, if Gill was telling the truth, and Charlotte had been away a considerable time before returning to the barbecue in a distressed state, what had she been up to?

Emma and Matthew walked slightly ahead of him through the narrow streets. Emma was a sensible girl, he thought absently. Lunch had been what they all needed after the first dreadful shock. At the pierhead he could see Fairchild and Patrick, with Charlotte standing listlessly between. What happened next was almost imperceptible, Mr Pringle nearly missed it. Charlotte started in their direction and stiffened. Mr Pringle wondered why. On the edge of his vision, the couple that was Matthew and Emma separated and became two people. Emma moved forward swiftly. He heard her calling, asking anxiously how Charlotte felt. They were close enough now for him to see the streaky lines of tears and hear her reply, "Oh Em, what a bloody nightmare!"

As THE CAIQUE CAME alongside, Mr Pringle waited at the back of the group. Charlotte gravitated to stand beside Matthew, her hand resting where Emma's had been but Matthew appeared unaware of it. He was listening as Patrick repeated John's question, "Do you think it could have been Gill at Spartahouri, Emma?"

"I'm very sorry, I just can't be sure." Her father frowned. "Isn't there any little detail, Em? Nothing at all?"

"I made an accusation once before," she replied worriedly, "I daren't risk being wrong a second time, particularly now. But I agree with the rest of you, I think the police should question him. If Char says he was on that hillside last night—"

"He was!" Charlotte insisted excitedly, "The dirty pig— he put his filthy hands on me—"

"Okay, okay, calm down." Patrick spoke authoritatively, "We'll deal with Gill when we get back. If necessary, I'll bring him over to Parga myself and make him tell the police what happened."

But the Gills had gone sailing. As Kate pointed out, there'd been no reason to stop any of them: the police hadn't placed any restrictions, had urged them to enjoy their stay in Greece in fact. Apart from *Zodiac* and the empty boats, the harbour was quiet. Any questioning would have to wait. Mr Pringle and Matthew walked along the jetty to *Capri-*

corn and then saw that *Pisces* had remained. Roge was standing there, apparently waiting to speak to them.

"I wanted to tell you—I managed to see her yesterday," said Roge. For a moment Mr Pringle looked at him blankly, his mind still full of Charlotte and Gill, then he realized.

"What's that?" Matthew asked.

"Roge was here yesterday afternoon," Mr Pringle explained. "He wanted to talk to Elizabeth." He felt a sudden wave of anger. "No doubt when she got back here you badgered her for money. That's what you wanted, wasn't it? If that girl had been born penniless, she'd have been allowed to live her life in peace." Roge stared at him. "Well, was she upset when you left?" asked Mr Pringle but he didn't reply.

"She was certainly in a state when I got back from having a shower," Matthew said coldly. "Now I'm beginning to understand why." The two stared at each other. Roge dropped his gaze and shuffled awkwardly.

"That was nothing to do with me," he muttered. "I only wanted you to know I'd managed to see her, that was all."

Roge looked nervous, thought Mr Pringle. All the bombast he'd shown at the airport had evaporated. But if Elizabeth had been left in peace, how much better her state of mind would've been yesterday evening. He followed Matthew on board *Capricorn*.

"Every Tom, Dick and Harry was hanging about here yesterday," he fumed, watching Roge wander off along the jetty. "First Clarke, then him—"

"What on earth did Clarke want?"

"The same as Roge. To see Elizabeth. Or rather, to talk to her and show her something. Here..." Mr Pringle rummaged in the Nav-table stowage, "He wanted to show her this. That's him with Leonard Hurst, taken during the war. At least Clarke wasn't asking her for money." Matthew took the snapshot and looked at it curiously.

"I don't suppose this would've done Liz any harm."

"You're probably right." Mr Pringle's anger was fading as quickly as it had arisen, "Elizabeth had got over her father's death. She might've found this interesting."

"Perhaps she saw it. Did Clarke return later, as Roger did?"

"I've no idea. We'd better ask him."

Virgo and *Libra* arrived back together. By the time they'd tied up, the tea was made. Mrs Clarke fussed over Mr Pringle and Matthew and insisted they join them. When questioned, Mr Clarke shook his head. "I wish I had gone back yesterday," he admitted. "I thought about it but we were all getting ready for the party by then. I'd have liked Miss Elizabeth to have seen it." The crowd in the saloon fell silent as he slid the photo back inside the cracked plastic wallet. "Never be another opportunity now, will there? They were cursed, I reckon, because of the money. First Mr Leonard and his wife, then Miss Elizabeth..." He paused and looked accusingly at Matthew. "You should've taken better care of her," Mr Clarke said quietly.

IT WAS NEARLY DARK when the Gills returned. Mr Pringle and Matthew watched as Patrick and John went on board *Scorpio*. It wasn't long before they came ashore and walked round to *Capricorn*. From the set of Patrick's shoulders it was obvious what had been said.

"He refused to answer any questions...won't even discuss it. Denies attacking Emma at Spartahouri and said he was damned if he'd talk to us about last night."

"To be fair..." John spoke reluctantly, "he did say he hadn't seen Liz at all yesterday evening." Patrick nodded.

"All I can do now," he said, "is ask the police to reconsider questioning him again. I'll emphasize that we believe Charlotte's version of events is the true one—and I'll try and see them before the inquest starts tomorrow."

FIFTEEN

MOTES OF DUST danced in front of his eyes. Mr Pringle lost concentration as he gazed at them. When he tried to refocus, the man's face was blur: the pathologist was finishing his evidence. Translation had become laconic but perhaps this was just as well.

"She is dead . . . before being in the water." Mr Pringle jerked awake. Beside him, Matthew failed to comprehend the significance and still sat, nursing his head in his hands. Had the fall killed Elizabeth outright?

"There was no sea-water in her lungs," the translator went on. Well that obviously confirmed death prior to immersion. The next bit sounded full of medical terminology and the translator hesitated before saying, "Her head . . . smashed by big rocks . . . on the way into the sea." Was that it? There was something more about the contents of the stomach containing food and wine, then the doctor sat down.

Mr Pringle waited while there was more discussion and the occasional sympathetic glance in their direction. The intelligent officer appeared to be answering further questions but these weren't translated either. Eventually they were given one further morsel of information: Elizabeth had injuries to her arms and legs, also caused, it was assumed, by the rocks.

He thought wildly of Gill. Why not subject him to forensic examination? Surely particles of hair and skin might still be trapped under his fingernails? A sturdy girl who could handle a boat so competently would've put up quite a fight . . . Mr Pringle had a sudden sharp memory: Elizabeth eaning through the spray and smiling, "Isn't this marvellous!", the dark straight bob plastered against her cheeks, then he remembered how the blanket had covered her head on the stretcher.

It was over. People were standing up, waiting for him and Matthew to do the same.

"That's it then," Patrick heaved a sigh of relief, "Thank God they didn't find it necessary to say the balance of her mind was disturbed—it always makes everyone else feel guilty they hadn't done more to help."

"Didn't you tell them about Gill?" demanded Mr Pringle.

"Yes, but they weren't interested. They'd got the result of the post mortem by then—you heard it. Death caused by the fall, not by drowning, which wasn't surprising when you consider those rocks." Patrick paused, uncertain they might be upset by what he'd said, but Mr Pringle didn't appear to be listening any more. Patrick spoke to Matthew instead. All the necessary arrangements had been made, he told him, the two of them were to fly back to England that afternoon from Corfu airport. Matthew nodded that he'd understood. Liz Hurst's body was being returned to England as soon as possible and the relevant authorities had been notified.

"I've been told there will be another inquest over there," Patrick explained, "it's mandatory. You'll be told about it by the police once you're back. Sorry—are you okay?" Matthew looked very pale.

"Yes...lack of sleep, I expect. And I keep thinking about Liz...and those rocks."

"But she was dead by then." It was Mr Pringle who spoke. The other two stood looking at him. "Wasn't that what they said? Or did I imagine it?" Patrick decided he must stop them brooding.

"I'm afraid this does go on but there's more paperwork to be completed before we can leave. D'you think you can face it?" Matthew roused himself.

"Best get it over with. Will you be all right, Uncle? You can wait outside until we're finished."

IN THE COOL grey-green entrance hall, Mr Pringle's head was in a whirl. There were so many questions he wanted to ask. Elizabeth had been dead before she reached the water—why was no one surprised? He wanted to speak to the doctor but the man wasn't there, neither was the interpreter. As he sat, the police officer in charge of the case walked past.

"Excuse me!"

"Yes, sir?"

"Did I understand correctly this morning? That Miss Hurst was dead before her body entered the water, there was no doubt about that?"

"No doubt at all. Miss Hurst did not drown."

"What I wanted to ask you, is it also possible that she was dead *before* she fell over the cliff?" The officer looked at him steadily. Mr Pringle's eyes were earnest behind his glasses as he tried to explain his theory. "Perhaps there was a scuffle in the dark, like that other time? Whoever it was may not have intended to harm Elizabeth. When he realized what had happened, he panicked. Pushed the body over the edge? Could it have been like that?"

The officer thought he understood. "You have no reason for saying this?" he asked gently, "It is speculation—yes?" Mr Pringle reddened.

"I'm sure Charlotte Fairchild met Gill up there as she says she did—I'm not making any accusations of course, but he must've been up there, lying in wait."

"If that is so," the officer replied patiently, "and we accept those two persons met each other, I must remind you both of them have denied seeing Elizabeth Hurst. Now if we believe one, why should we not also believe the other? And why should either of them harm Miss Hurst?" Mr Pringle put aside thoughts about Charlotte's possible motive because it made him uncomfortable, but he had to admit he wasn't being fair to Gill. The officer was speaking again. 'Try not to distress yourself. We know the girl was unhappy. She was more than that, she was in what you call 'a state'. And she had had too much wine. Perhaps that was why she didn't notice her danger? We have examined the ground very thoroughly—you are welcome to look at it yourself. The bushes and trees where someone has rushed past, the rocks where they were dislodged—it is very clear to see where Miss Hurst went over..." Or where a man pursued a terrified girl, thought Mr Pringle.

"Please," the officer looked at him sympathetically, "do not distress yourself further. It is a sad, sad end of a young life but..." He shrugged because there was nothing more to say.

"Thank you," mumbled Mr Pringle. "Most kind..."

BACK AT THE HARBOUR, Mrs Clarke was waiting for them on board *Capricorn*. "I hope you don't mind, either of you, I took the liberty of packing Miss Elizabeth's bits and pieces. It was Kate's idea. The police said they'd finished and we thought you'd want to take everything with you. The thing is, d'you know what needs to go on the labels?"

"Oh, yes." Matthew forced his voice to remain steady and fished in his pocket. "There are forms and things...with the address on. Everything gets returned to England with the—the body."

"I'll leave you to do the necessary then, shall I?" Mrs Clarke was full of concern. "There's a cup of tea any time you want it on our boat."

Mr Pringle decided to pack his own sailing-bag. When he'd finished there were still two hours to fill before they could begin the journey to Corfu. To be on the boat stifled him. "I think I'll go for a swim off the beach. D'you feel like joining me?"

"I'd rather stay here if you don't mind," Matthew sounded dangerously near to tears, "I'd like to be on my own for a bit."

AMONG THE HOLIDAY-MAKERS on the beach, Mr Pringle saw Louise. She waved, indicated he should sit beside her, but didn't speak. He was grateful. He fiddled aimlessly with pebbles, wondering whether he ought to go back up to the olive grove instead, but dismissed the idea. He'd no wish to see the track through the undergrowth, nor the gash in the rocks. The police might learn much from it but he knew he wouldn't. Elizabeth had fallen to her death. She'd been dead before she hit the water. If there had been another person there, the police had obviously found no evidence of it: they were satisfied she hadn't been pushed. But why hadn't she screamed the way Emma had done that night? Or maybe she had, and no one had heard above the noise of the music at the barbecue or the waves?

"Was it bloody this morning, Pring?"

"Not too bad, thanks."

"How's Matty boy taking it? Is he okay?" Mr Pringle thought of the haggard face.

"He's coping, just."

"Had Liz been raped?"

"Goodness, no! What makes you ask that?" Louise clasped her knees and stared at the sea.

"It's more common than you know nowadays. And it makes a girl feel so goddam **dir**ty—you go crazy. Do stupid things like—throwing yourself off a cliff. Me—I drink. But the pills help."

"I'm so sorry," he said humbly.

"Pring, don't apologize. A nice guy like you isn't to blame. I just thought it might be what happened last night to Liz."

"Nothing was said at the inquest. If there had been any evidence at all..."

"Sure." But again Mr Pringle found himself thinking of Gill. Suppose it had been attempted rape and Elizabeth had broken free?

"Listen Pring, you're off soon. Come for a swim first."

The sea washed over him, easing tension in his mind and body. Above the bay another figure dangled from the parachute. All around them children were having the time of their lives.

"Isn't it dangerous, taking those pills of yours and drinking?" he asked quietly. Louise was floating beside him.

"Only if you take them in the wrong order—take them with the booze and you end up legless. I have one last thing, after I'm pissed, with plenty of water. That way they relax me. I used to get nightmares, wake up in a real sweat. Now I guess I'm getting over it. Maybe one day I can even give up the booze."

"I hope so." He'd embarrassed her.

"Yeah, well... C'm on—race you to the platform!"

FAREWELLS WERE BRIEF. He and Matthew hurried past sympathetic faces to the waiting ferry-boat. Emma gave him an affectionate hug and told Matthew to keep in touch. As he stepped on board, Mr Pringle caught sight of Charlotte watching her sister. It gave him the same momentary unease he'd had yesterday at Parga: Charlotte looked unaccountably jealous.

During the flight, he asked Matthew if he hadn't been surprised by the medical evidence.

"Not really. The police had told Patrick and me privately about it before the proceedings began and I'd had time to think it over. It seemed to both of us it was much more likely Liz had been killed by smashing her head against the rocks than by drowning. I'm thankful you didn't see how bad that was." Mr Pringle swallowed.

"It was a mercy I didn't, I agree. But I fear I may cause you further distress, Matthew. You see I have this nagging doubt about the whole business."

"In what way?"

"I find it unbelievable that Elizabeth would kill herself."

Matthew groaned. "Oh, God! That means it was my fault because of the row!"

"Nonsense," said Mr Pringle stoutly, "You're not suggesting Elizabeth was a hysteric who got carried away in the heat of the moment. She was a sensible girl even if she had lost her temper over Charlotte—"

"But, as Emma pointed out, she had had too much wine."

"Matthew, I cannot accept that would change her very nature. In my view, remembering her behaviour under similar circumstances in the Levkas restaurant, she would become more belligerent."

He'd obviously touched a raw nerve, reminding Matthew of that. His nephew looked very white. "I gave Liz no cause to complain," he whispered, "not after Levkas."

"I'm sure you didn't, my boy. Try not to distress yourself. What I want to suggest to you is that there must've been someone else there in the olive grove. I accept what Charlotte said about Gill but—why should he have been the only one?" The thought was slow to percolate but eventually Matthew said,

"You mean—someone killed Liz?"

"Not exactly. It could have been accidental if it happened in a scuffle as it nearly did with Emma—"

"But that would be murder!" Matthew's voice rang out above the noise of the aircraft jet engines. Mr Pringle cringed as he imagined the reaction of the other passengers. He lowered his voice and without looking round murmured, "I think technically speaking it would be deemed manslaughter, if it were accidental."

THEY AGREED HE SHOULD tell the police his theory, the problem was how. Gatwick arrival terminal was thronged but none of the uniformed men on duty looked approachable. After further discussion it was decided Mr Pringle would visit his local police station in the morning. They at least would know where to direct him. After that nothing remained but to make the journey home in the rain.

His cold house was so depressing, Mr Pringle took himself round to The Bricklayers. Events had caught up with him: by the time he arrived, he was full of misery. Although surprised to see him, Mavis assessed his mood and steered him into a quiet corner.

"Now then, dear, what on earth's the matter? Why are you back so soon?" He told her the whole story. Despite her natural resilience, it took Mavis a considerable time to recover from the shock. "Poor girl, poor thing..." she kept repeating and her hand trembled as she sipped her port and lemon. "How's Matthew taking it?"

"Badly, as you'd expect. One minute he seems to be recovering, the next he's weeping."

"Poor lamb. You'd be the same in his shoes, dear. How terrible for him. And you say it might've been someone on the flotilla?"

"That is only my theory," said Mr Pringle cautiously, "but I do not see any other explanation is possible. Not once you accept that Elizabeth did not kill herself."

"I expect you're right," Mavis answered pensively, "You'll have thought it through before committing yourself. You'll have to go and tell the police in the morning. I expect they'll be glad of a bit of help." From past experience, Mr Pringle doubted it. Mavis finished her drink and said shakily, "It's been a terrible shock for both of us. And I don't suppose your bed's properly aired. You'd better come back to my place tonight." In the darkness, thinking about death, they cuddled each other in gentle consolation.

SIXTEEN

NEXT MORNING IN THE police station, two women were ahead of him. One had mislaid her dog, the other her husband. Of the two he judged the former felt her loss more keenly. Eventually it was his turn. "Yes, sir? What can we do for you?"

"I'd like to report a suspicious death. That is to say, suspicious circumstances surrounding a death." Already he was flustered.

"Oh, yes?" The desk sergeant had grown a couple of feet and was staring at him through narrowed eyes. "And where will we find the body?"

"It's on its way back from Greece in a lead lined casket." The technical details failed to impress. There was an unpleasant silence while the sergeant decided whether or not Mr Pringle was mentally disturbed. He came down marginally in his favour. "If you'd like to take a seat, I'll see if one of our CID officers is free." After all, he thought as he picked up the phone, Christie had been an inoffensive little bloke like this one and he'd had over a dozen bodies stashed away in cupboards.

"HOW DID YOU GET ON?"

"Not very well, Matthew!" His nephew was in a callbox and the line was bad. Mr Pringle had to shout. "They kept telling me how busy they were and of course there isn't a body, not yet." He didn't like to add that the CID man was obviously determined there never would be a body, not on his patch anyway. "Have you any idea when she...when Elizabeth's remains will arrive?"

"No. I've been doing what you suggested, though. I've written out an account of everything that happened that night beginning with us leaving the boat for the barbecue. Can we go through it?"

"Yes, of course. Will you be at home this evening?"

"Ah, yes I will but there is one small snag. Mother's very upset about the whole thing."

"Oh." Mr Pringle knew precisely what he meant. And he didn't feel like facing up to Enid, he wasn't strong enough. "Can we meet in a pub instead?" he asked hopefully.

"I think it would be better if you came round here. Then she could get it off her chest. It would give the rest of us a break." Mr Pringle sighed.

ENID HAD PUT ON weight. Mr Pringle had a weakness for soft feminine plumpness but this was pure fat and gristle.

"How the pair of you let it happen to Elizabeth I do not know. Criminal carelessness, I call it. Especially after that other poor girl—what's her name?"

"Emma Fairchild."

"After what happened to her, you both knew there was a rapist about."

"Emma wasn't raped, Enid," said Mr Pringle. It was a mistake to argue with her.

"Rubbish! What else was he after? I know men..." Mr Pringle put down his cold cup of tea. Enid never offered him a drink; he wasn't important enough. He could see she was about to launch into one of her interminable accounts of how a patient in male surgical once assaulted her honour. Anything but that!

"D'you think we could go through your notes?" he asked Matthew hastily but Enid wasn't prepared to let him escape that easily.

"You're not to let whoever it was get away with it. You owe it to Matthew and me to find out who it was—and deal with him."

"I'm afraid I couldn't, Enid." It was a mistake to give her an opening like that.

"Oh, don't be so spineless! You're retired, aren't you? Nothing to do all day but twiddle your thumbs? And you were there when it happened so it can't be that difficult. Besides, the police are far too busy nowadays chasing drug traffickers. And you're always boasting about being a private detective." Mr Pringle had once foolishly let slip details of his new hobby in a Christmas letter.

"Fraud, Enid," he insisted desperately. "I told you I intended to specialize in figures." She gave a contemptuous sniff.

"Excuses! I might have known. Now listen to me, you're an amateur so you can't pick and choose. If it's murder instead of fraud, who are you to complain? And if that's all the tea you want from this pot you'd better get on with it."

They retreated, Enid's words following them up the stairs, "He should be castrated, whoever he was..." Mr Pringle kicked shut the bedroom door to vent his feelings.

"Your wretched mother regards castration or the gallows as a universal remedy. Matthew, it's no good. I never could stand her. I refuse to step inside this house again. When we need to meet, it'll have to be elsewhere."

"She's upset because she thought it would be a marvellous marriage for me, because of Liz's money," said Matthew baldly.

His nephew didn't look any better, thought Mr Pringle. The golden glow, the vividness had disappeared. The eyes were red-rimmed in the tense face and he didn't look as if he'd slept at all.

"Shouldn't you see the doctor, Matthew," Mr Pringle began...

"I'm all right. Don't worry about me." It was brusque, so his uncle took his cue from it.

"I have a few questions of my own before we look at your account." He opened his notebook, "They're not in any particular order. Was Elizabeth drunk that night?"

"I told you, she'd had one or two."

"I meant was she in as inebriated a state as I was?" asked Mr Pringle candidly.

"Oh, no. Nothing like that. We'd had a couple of drinks at the beach restaurant, then quite a bit of wine at the barbecue. Liz had had enough to get worked up but she was coherent, not sloshed."

"I didn't realize you'd been along to the restaurant?" Matthew shrugged.

"We hadn't intended to, particularly. There wasn't enough booze on the boat so we decided to leave what there was for you."

"I see," said Mr Pringle thoughtfully, "that was kind of you. It made a hefty measure, I fear, and I'm not used to whisky. I'm afraid it was the beginning of my downfall that night." He sighed apologetically. "Did you take the path up from the beach to the site?"

"Yes, I thought I'd told you that?" Matthew was surprised.

"If you did, I'd forgotten. I'm sorry. Now, where did the row take place?"

"It began as we walked along that path," said Matthew slowly. "I kept trying to stop her but, as I told you before, Liz definitely wanted to pick a fight that night. By the time we arrived at the barbecue, she was being very loud about it. Here, you can read what happened next..." Mr Pringle went carefully through the account, surprised as always by Matthew's obsessively neat script. It never seemed to fit with the handsome exterior, it was an older finicky man's fist.

"That's all very clear," he said when he'd finished. "Have you also had time to write down what you remember everyone else was doing?" Matthew handed him another sheet of paper. He'd listed each of the crews and added a couple of sentences about them. When he got to *Pisces*, Mr Pringle looked up. "Nothing about Roge?"

"He wasn't at the barbecue. At least if he was, I didn't see him."

"You're positive?"

"Yes. His wife Maureen was there, and Louise. They took you back to *Capricorn*, didn't they?"

"They did." Mr Pringle preferred to forget about that. He waved the two sheets of paper. "To summarize: up to the time Elizabeth rushed off, the only men you don't list as being there were Gill and Roge. Afterwards...? After you'd exhausted your searching?"

"I'm not sure," Matthew said uncertainly, "I really can't be certain who was or wasn't there. Or who came and went. I kept seeing faces I knew—"

"Roge or Gill's?"

He shook his head slowly. "I don't think so. I know Patrick and John stayed on the site the whole time."

"I think we can safely cross them off any list of suspects," said Mr Pringle, "I know I have."

"The Fairchilds stayed together. After Liz had disappeared, Mr Fairchild was very anxious about Charlotte. He really pitched into her when she got back to their boat that night. She didn't tell him about Gill then, though. Emma persuaded her to keep quiet about it, I think. Of course it all had to come out after Liz was found next morning."

"Quite. Now can we assume the Hansons and Clarkes stayed together?"

Matthew shrugged helplessly. "I'm sorry, Uncle. I really can't be sure of anything. I went up the hill several times that night, trying to find Liz. I kept coming back to the boat to see if she'd slipped past in the dark. In the end, I decided Patrick was right and she'd gone to a hotel in Parga. I came back to *Capricorn* to get some kip. It was just beginning to get light."

"So what we're left with," Mr Pringle reminded him, "is Roge missing and Gill in the olive grove before Elizabeth disappeared, with no certainty about Hanson or Clarke?"

"That's about it," Matthew agreed. "It was possible that either of those two nipped off on the pretext of going for a pee, and chased after Liz. Neither family would suspect anything when they got back." Mr Pringle nodded thoughtfully.

"What about Phyllis's crew?"

"All four of them were pissed," replied Matthew shortly. "By the way, did I tell you I had a phone call from the Fairchilds last night?"

"No?"

"It was Charlotte who rang. She and Emma decided they didn't want to carry on with the holiday and their parents agreed. They were hoping to catch a flight back today or tomorrow."

"Very sensible in my opinion." Mr Pringle shifted in his chair. From where he sat in Matthew's small bedroom, he could see Enid out in the garden below. She was waving a watering-can labelled "Poison" over a weed that had had the temerity to defy her. "Despite what your mother said," Mr Pringle went on, watching her, "there is very little more we can do at present, either of us, except try and resolve the most obvious question of all."

"Which is?"

"Why did it happen? What possible reason had anyone to kill Elizabeth, albeit accidentally?" Matthew replied curiously,

"Surely it was simply a repetition of what happened at Spartahouri? As you suggested?"

"But why was there no struggle, no scream?"

"There may well have been," said Matthew sadly. "It was a fair distance from the barbecue. We had the Hansons' ghetto-blaster pumping out music for dancing by then. Liz could've been screaming her head off and no one would've known.''

''Poor girl!''

''As for a struggle, Liz had plenty of injuries to her arms and legs I promise you. I saw them.''

''But were those inflicted before or after death, during her fall? The evidence didn't make that clear.'' Mr Pringle hadn't been taking sufficient notice: Matthew was as white as a sheet. ''I'm so sorry, my boy. Thoughtless of me. Let's consider another aspect entirely. Assuming there was a struggle, what about the other person. He would've had torn clothes, scratches, that kind of thing.''

''But we didn't see anyone until late the following morning,'' Matthew pointed out. ''Plenty of time to dispose of torn clothing and cover any injuries.''

''Disposing of clothing implies collusion by the man's wife.''

''So?'' Matthew shrugged impatiently, ''wouldn't any woman stand by her husband? It might not have been the first time, remember.''

''Perhaps the second post mortem will reveal more than the first, particularly if the police pay attention to our theory.''

''The only person I can remember with torn clothing at all,'' said Matthew carelessly, ''was Charlotte when she came back after the episode with Gill. And you surely can't suspect her? By the way, Liz's trustees have asked me to go and see them tomorrow. You wouldn't come along too, would you? To give moral support?''

THE TOWERING office-block presented a blank impersonal face with darkened glass at every level apart from the soaring atrium. The only sign at the entrance, in discreet gilt lettering: Hurst House. They waited in the tropical forest of the atrium like two midgets. The lift that bore them skywards was a perspex bubble. They looked out on so many evels of sophisticated businessmen, it was a surprise to be met at the penthouse level by a harassed looking individual n a tweed jacket. All the same, Mr Pringle was glad he'd vorn his best suit. He was even more thankful that there was 10 way Matthew could have committed any crime. The bower that Hurst House represented would surely be used o seek out and crush any wrong-doer?

Mr Pringle sat while the tweed jacket and two lesser min-ons exchanged condolences with Matthew, marvelling at he thought of what Elizabeth's wealth had represented. Had she lived a few more months, all this would have been 1ers. Would Matthew have ever agreed to give it up as she 1ad wanted? Mr Pringle sighed inwardly. Perhaps one benefit of the sorry business was that his nephew wouldn't 10w be subjected to that temptation. As it was, no one brofited by Elizabeth's early death, at least as far as he knew.

He asked Matthew about the Trust Fund on the way back to the tube. "I suppose it gets broken up," Matthew an-swered. "D'you think I should have told the Trustee what Liz intended? Give him the names of the charities she wanted to give to?"

"Plenty of time for that," said Mr Pringle from experi-ence. "The CTT on that little lot will take years to sort out, I should think." They arrived at the station entrance.

"What happens next?" asked Matthew.

"We wait, I suppose. The police will get in touch when they want to see us." In fact the phone was ringing as he unlocked his front door. But it was the Press not the Law. Elizabeth's corpse had arrived at Heathrow and the news-men wanted a statement.

SEVENTEEN

CHARLOTTE HAD THE window seat and was gazing down at the fountain in Lake Geneva. "Em, d'you think *she's* in the hold?" Emma was horrified.

"What a truly ghastly thing to say!"

"It's possible though, isn't it? What a thought—weird!" Emma shuddered.

"I don't want to talk about it." She closed her eyes.

"All the same," said Charlotte softly, "it does change everything, now she's gone. You can't pretend that it doesn't." But Emma's eyes stayed shut. "And are you going to carry on with your little act? The caring little woman bit . . ." Emma was wide awake now, staring at Charlotte. "Oh, don't think I haven't noticed . . . I'm not stupid, Em. Not as far as you're concerned. You might fool Pa with your pretty little ways, but you've never fooled me."

"You're jealous," Emma said coldly. "Pa admires results and at university I got them. You didn't. That's all there is to it. And as for what's happened to Elizabeth Hurst, if you think you've only got to snap your fingers and Matthew will come running back . . . ! You're pathetic, Char." If she'd sought to needle her sister, she hadn't succeeded. Charlotte simply grinned.

"It's no good, Em. As far as Matthew's concerned, it's me he's interested in, not you. And if you think he's going to sit at home mourning that stupid bitch, you're wrong. He needs someone. I'm going to make sure he knows I'm around when he realizes that."

"I've never understood before how callous you really are," said Emma steadily.

"Come off it!" Charlotte was angry now. "Don't you call me names. I meant it when I said you fooled Pa. What if I tell him how you and John were at it every single night!"

"He probably already knows," replied Emma coolly, "and no doubt he heaved a sigh of relief about it. John and I were discreet. And Pa knew no one else was likely to attack me when John was around."

"No, they went for Liz Hurst instead."

"Jesus, Char, what a thing to say!"

"I'm sorry!" This time Charlotte had lost her poise, "I didn't mean her any harm!" Charlotte was frightened now, "Em, please . . . don't look at me like that!"

"The police are going to want to question everyone all over again, Char. They're likely to be much more thorough."

Charlotte put her hand up as though to ward off the very idea.

"It's no good pretending you can avoid it," Emma insisted. "There's no way any of us can dip out this time, not even Mr Gill."

"But I told the truth last time," Charlotte pleaded, "when I said I didn't see Liz Hurst in that olive grove, only that pig, it was the truth!" Emma stared at her in silence for a moment then she said,

"That's all right then, isn't it?"

EIGHTEEN

HE'D DEALT WITH the Press; he'd been interviewed by th
police, who actually came round to the house this time s
that Mr Pringle wouldn't be inconvenienced. He appreci
ated that. He also basked in the attentive way the office
listened to his theory. In the end, Mr Pringle got so carrie
away, he mentioned previous occasions when he'd actuall
assisted the police with their enquiries. This time he went to
far. He didn't notice the way the man's eyes glazed over no
did he hear subsequent remarks made in the privacy of th
police car. As far as Mr Pringle was concerned, it had bee
a remarkably successful morning.

The sun was shining so he went and did his shopping. O
his return, Mavis was waiting for him, standing in the hall
Perfect! He wondered why she was still wearing her coat bu
advanced eagerly for a kiss. "Hallo, hallo!" She offered
cheek. "Oh, dear. Have you been waiting long?"

"Long enough. Your sister Enid rang. I answered it."

"Oh." He could see now, Mavis was swelling visibly.

"What that woman said to me, I will not repeat. It woul
be demeaning myself to use her filthy words—and she's o
her way round."

"Oh, my Lord!" Did Mavis intend staying? It would b
the clash of Valkyries! Between the two of them, he woul
be annihilated.

"The woman called me such names!"

"Mavis, I am sorry—"

"Don't ask what I said in reply—it was forced out of me
I have never been reduced to the level of the gutter be

ore!" Mavis was so magnificent, he longed to throw his
arms round her but he was far too frightened to try.

"Enid used to work as a nurse in a hospital. I fear it
coarsened her tongue," he babbled. "She's much younger
than I am. We were never very close."

"You won't get round me with that." He could see that
he wouldn't.

"Renée loathed her," he offered.

"I'm sure your late wife and I would've got on very well
indeed. It's your sister I can't stand. So when you've finished helping Matthew and completed your investigation—
and got rid of Enid for good—you can phone me. But not
before you've made sure she never visits here again, right?"
It was final, irrevocable, and he knew it.

"I'll be as quick as ever I can be." He stood out in the
street to watch her go and waited until she'd turned the corner before retreating behind his front door and kicking it
shut. Twice in a week, Enid had forced him to do that, and
now she was coming round. Blast, damn and hell! But by
the time she arrived, some of his courage had evaporated.
It was the effect she always had on him.

"Is that harlot still here?"

"Don't be silly, Enid!" Where on earth had she got hold
of that word?

"When I remember poor, poor Renée..." She walked
inside without being bidden and he followed her angrily into
the kitchen.

"As you could scarcely bring yourself to be polite to my
wife during her lifetime..."

"The police have been round," she interrupted. "They
were pestering Matthew. Asking him questions for over an
hour."

"Of course they were," he snapped, "it's all part of the
routine. They've been here as well. What is it?" Enid had
filled the kettle and lit the gas. Now she was searching for
something, "What do you want?"

"The biscuit barrel." No wonder she was fat. Mr Pringle emptied out his morning's shopping recklessly and flung a packet across.

"Help yourself and get out of my house."

"I told the police you were dealing with the matter, not Matthew. They didn't take any notice. These aren't very nice, haven't you got any creams?" Memories of childhood flooded back. Enid finishing a pound of custard creams at a sitting, Enid with spots on her chin.

"Matthew will have to answer questions for himself. So will everyone else on the flotilla when they get back."

"They are back. At least, some of them are. One of them phoned Matthew last night, a girl. Apparently they'd all decided they'd had enough."

Presumably the Fairchilds had returned. Enid leaned forward, resting her elbows on his table. He resented seeing her like that, taking over his furniture. "I want to have a serious talk about this woman you've been harbouring," she said.

"I've been—what?"

"You've let yourself go to seed. It's not real affection, it's only lust and at your age, that'll soon pass—"

"Enid!"

"It's what happens to old men when they're lonely. They're a pushover for predatory women like her. You don't want to do anything stupid. She's only after you for what she can get." Enid looked round disparagingly. "I know this place won't fetch much but Alan and Matthew are entitled to think of it as theirs, one day."

"Enid, for the last time finish your tea and get out of my house. It is still mine, however shabby, and will remain so until my last gasp. After that, I wouldn't count on anything if I were you. Both you and your children might be very disappointed. As for my friend Mrs Bignell, she is a lady—"

"She's a trollop!"

"Enid, until you make a proper apology to her for the way you spoke to her today—"

"I'll do no such thing!" But Mr Pringle had had enough. He jerked his sister to her feet and stuffed the remaining biscuits in her bag.

"I've never liked you, Enid. When we were youngsters you made my life a misery." He tugged her out of the kitchen, "You were deliberately sick over my twenty-first birthday cake. Granny saved her coupons for months for that cake." He pushed her ahead of him down the passage, sustained by fury, "You were rude to Renée even when you knew she was dying—"

"I went out of my way to be civil to her, fool though she was!" Mr Pringle had got the front door open. He shoved Enid down the steps.

"What about Matthew?" she demanded, clinging to his arm, "He's relying on you."

"I shall do my best for him, on condition you never come here again!"

ENID COULD WALK AWAY but Mr Pringle was drained. He sank to the floor and stayed there for a very long time. When he finally managed to get to his feet, he tottered into the kitchen and poured himself a brandy. Eventually his hands stopped shaking and he reached for his notebook and set to work. The new Lysistrata in his life, Mavis, meant what she said, he was certain. She wouldn't be back until the case was finished and the police declared themselves satisfied. He sighed again, remembering the current success rate of the force, and set to work. Wild oats had to be so carefully husbanded nowadays, not to be able to sow them was a tragedy.

He worked late into the night and began again early the following morning. He needed to consult Matthew about the long list of questions. He wondered if the police would be interested but the officer he'd spoken to remained elusive. He was about to dial Matthew's number when his own phone rang: it was Charlotte.

"Is Matthew there? I've just spoken to his mother. She thinks he may be on his way to see you."

"I very much hope he is. Is there any message or would you like him to call?" Charlotte hesitated.

"The police have been here, asking us all questions."

"Yes, they're visiting everyone."

"The trouble is, I don't think they believed me."

"Oh dear."

"I told them the truth!"

"Of course." Mr Pringle waited.

"Can I come round and see you?"

He'd done his best to please her by the time she rang the bell. He'd prepared coffee and a glass of sherry. His favourite picture was on an easel so that she could admire it to advantage. Charlotte walked straight past it and stared out of the window. "Where is he, d'you know?"

"Matthew? I'm afraid I don't. Perhaps he'll still come." Charlotte recollected her manners and went over to the easel. The humdrum northern scene meant nothing to her; she tried to find suitable words.

"A bit different from Greece."

"Yes, indeed. I doubt whether that artist ever visited the country."

"I wish we hadn't!" She was so lovely in his shabby room, he hadn't noticed how tense she was. Now he thought she looked as if she were about to crack, her face was so thin and sharp. He longed to offer comfort but didn't know how. "Is Emma—improving? Are the wounds fully healed?"

"Oh, Em's fine. She acts as if she didn't believe me, so do Pa and Ma. They all behave as though I was breaking up— they listen then look at one another. It's bloody frightening! Have you got any vodka?"

"I'm sorry, Charlotte." He looked sadly at the tray. He'd flattered himself he'd thought of everything: he'd even decanted the sherry. She took a glass of it reluctantly.

"They all assume I *should* have seen Liz, but I didn't. Only Gill."

"Would you mind telling me what you did that evening? Earlier on, I mean. Did you and Emma go up to the site together?"

"No. She went with John because she was helping him with the bar. They didn't need me so I went for a stroll along the beach."

"Did you see Matthew? I understand he and Elizabeth went for a drink." Charlotte flushed.

"I was looking for him, I admit," she answered. "They must've been ahead of me. When I finally got to the barbecue, Matthew was already chasing round trying to find Liz. At the time, I thought he was making a stupid fuss." Mr Pringle looked at her primly. "Oh, forget all that stuff about speaking no ill of the dead," Charlotte said angrily. "That bitch and her money took Matthew away from me!"

"Was it as simple as that?" asked Mr Pringle quietly, "And is Matthew such a venal creature?"

"Oh, shit! I don't know," Charlotte pulled savagely at the frayed edge of a cushion. "I keep telling myself it was only because of her money. Now I keep thinking Matthew prefers Em to me—it's all perfectly bloody!" He refilled her glass and waited for the emotion to subside. "D'you think Matthew's avoiding me?" she demanded.

"My dear, how can I possibly answer that?"

"He could've had my money if he'd waited," she cried. "Pa's making each of us a settlement when we marry. Anyway, maybe Matthew and I will get married now. He can't go on grieving for Liz for ever."

"Possibly not," said Mr Pringle warmly, "but I certainly expect Elizabeth to be laid to rest before Matthew even considers attaching himself to anyone else." Charlotte jumped as though he'd slapped her.

"I'm sorry!" she whispered. "I don't know what's got into me lately. It's the way they stare at me at home, as though I'm lying. I *did* go up the hill to try and find her, I swear that's what I wanted to do. When Emma came back and told us what a state Liz was in, I didn't hesitate. I even tore my dress, I was in such a rush."

"You were helping John with the bar when she told you?"

"Yes. Patrick was there, then Matthew came up. Emma said Liz was screaming all kinds of things about me. She thought someone should go and calm her down. I said I would. If I was the reason for the row, why shouldn't I go? You see, I wanted to help, truly..." Tears splashed on to her skirt. "I know you all thought I was trying to get Matthew back—and I was for a while. But that night at the barbecue, I went to tell Liz I was sorry...and ask her to come back down. I don't think I realized the consequences until then, about dancing with Matthew and that... I loved him, you see that's the truth." Mr Pringle could tell that it was, he had no doubt about it at all. "D'you think he still cares for me a little bit?" she begged.

"I really can't say," he answered sadly. Tears continued to rain down. "Can I get you a glass of water?" Beautiful women hadn't dampened his study before; he was at a loss.

"Can I have some more of this? It's not too bad once you get used to the taste."

"I've no wish to upset you further," Mr Pringle said, setting the decanter back on the tray, "but do you think you could describe what happened when you met Mr Gill?"

"He was up there, under the trees. It was pitch dark so he gave me quite a fright. When someone grabs hold of you like that, your heart nearly stops beating. I screamed. It was ages before I got away from him, I kept tripping over things in the dark and he kept trying to help me up. Ludicrous, really.''

''Did he say anything?''

''Oh, only the usual crap... all about how he'd been fancying me ever since he first saw me. The sort of thing men like him always say.'' The beautiful face had an ugly sneer now. ''He kept trying to grope me... it was all pretty pathetic, looking back.''

''After the initial fright—did you think he was going to harm you?'' Mr Pringle peered through his spectacles; Charlotte hesitated slightly.

''Thinking about it... I don't believe I was terrified, not for my life, or anything like that. I was angry. And I felt dirty because he was pawing me—I was filthy, too, from falling over so many times—''

''But you didn't believe he was going to kill you?''

''No,'' Charlotte answered flatly. ''Now that you ask me like that, I don't believe I did.''

''What happened to Gill?''

''God knows. I left him up there, crashing about. I hoped he'd break his neck but he didn't. They all made such a fuss when I got back and they saw the state I was in, that made it worse. And I'd had a fair amount to drink, of course.'' Mr Pringle nodded.

''Do you think Elizabeth was somewhere nearby while it was going on?''

''If she was, she was a fool,'' said Charlotte indignantly. ''I mean she'd know what she was letting herself in for by staying there. Why not get clear while she had the chance?''

Perhaps, thought Mr Pringle, because Elizabeth was no longer in any position to help herself. ''How long before Gill reappeared at the barbecue?''

''He didn't,'' said Charlotte, confirming Matthew's account. ''Patrick went chasing after him to thump him but he couldn't find him. I'd had enough of it by then. Matthew was trying to organize another search but I went back to our boat."

"Is it possible," asked Mr Pringle carefully, "that someone else was there in the olive grove?" Again she looked a little surprised.

"I suppose it was just possible..."

"You see, supposing it wasn't Gill who attacked Emma at Spartahouri."

"No. She's not sure anyway."

"Quite. Then it was possible—assuming it's the same person—that it wasn't Gill who attacked Liz." Charlotte shivered.

"How spooky! Someone else up there, watching it all going on. Or rather listening. Like I said, it was dark."

"I was wondering about—Roge Harper?" Charlotte stared as though she hadn't heard properly then shrieked with laughter.

"You're not serious? He's a joke!"

MATTHEW ARRIVED full of indignation about half an hour after Charlotte had left. Mr Pringle had been about to sit down to a lamb chop.

"It's incredible..." Matthew strode ahead of him down the passage towards the kitchen. "Oh—were you about to eat?"

"It doesn't matter."

"Guess what—Gill's done a bunk!"

"What?"

"Is there anything to drink?"

"You'd better come up to the study." There wasn't much left; Matthew emptied it into a tumbler.

"Charlotte was here."

"Oh, was she. Listen, you remember we agreed I'd get the addresses and phone numbers of everyone on the flotilla. Well, not surprisingly, the travel firm was a bit sticky over the phone so I went along to chat them up. While I was there, the police phoned twice. First to check the Gills' address, the second time to ask if there was any other number to contact.'' Matthew paused to pull a soggy piece of paper from his pocket, ''Sorry about this, it's been raining most of the afternoon.''

''I'll get you a towel.'' When he got back, Matthew had stripped off his wet clothes and draped them over the furniture. His eyes burned with excitement. ''You do see what this means? About the Gills?''

''The inference isn't immediately clear. If the family aren't at home, perhaps they're visiting relatives?'' Matthew shook his head violently.

''Something else I learned while I was with the travel firm. There have been two lots of police looking for Gill. The ones investigating Liz's death and two other men from a different department altogether.''

''What for, do you know?'' Matthew flopped back in the chair.

''Don't know, sorry. The receptionist wasn't very bright, she couldn't remember. Anyway, there's the full list although I don't suppose you'll need it now.''

''I wouldn't jump to any conclusion, Matthew. Let's wait until the inquest first.''

''Oh, that's next Monday, did you know?''

''No.''

''You'll probably hear in the post tomorrow—God, I'm starving! What did Charlotte want?'' Mr Pringle sacrificed his chop and listened. Whether because of the disappearance of Gill or the impending inquest, Matthew needed to talk. It was as though a dam had burst. First about Charlotte, how he'd been attracted but never really sure of her. ''She's so gorgeous to look at, you don't realize how it's all on the surface. There's no depth, she changes with the moon. Liz was so different, you could always depend on her.''

''Do you not think Charlotte has changed?''

"Perhaps. It's embarrassing the way she's always phoning me. When we were going out together, I had to fend other blokes off. Now it's as if there's no one else..." he shrugged impatiently.

"I think she's very fond of you, Matthew."

"Why can't she understand—I'm still numb inside!" he burst out. "You can't simply ignore what's happened and move on... not immediately. Liz was such a terrific person to be with, you know." Again, Mr Pringle listened. To how he'd met Liz on a sailing weekend, how tentative his first approach had been. "I mean with someone rich, everyone's going to point the finger—and they did. That's why it was so marvellous when Liz said she wanted to give all the money away. We weren't going to tell anyone until after the wedding, that's when we were going to make an announcement, to have the pleasure of proving everyone wrong," he said defiantly. "It was going to be our secret." Mr Pringle felt ashamed. He'd underestimated him. "It's all happened so quickly," Matthew muttered, "that's what I find most shattering."

"I fear it's rather late. Would you like to stay here tonight?"

"No, I must be going." Matthew yawned. "D'you think I should give Charlotte a bell first?"

"Why not leave it until tomorrow? She told me she wasn't going home but staying with a friend in town. I think it would be a kindness if you could persuade her to return to her parents, though. She looked very lost when she left here."

Matthew looked at the number on the paper. "That's Susie's place. Charlotte uses it as a bolt-hole when she's in bother... okay, I'll see what I can do." He sounded impatient.

"All those phone calls may be an indication of her concern, Matthew, nothing more. Like Emma, Charlotte probably only wants to help." Matthew looked blank for a moment.

"You could be right. And it is possible we might get together again, eventually. As you say, she has changed...we all have. So who knows?"

Mr Pringle held open the front door. "See you in Court!" Matthew called. It echoed back along the sleeping street.

NINETEEN

"ASPHYXIA BEING consistent with this internal haemorrhaging in the pericardium?"

"Yes."

"And this asphyxia was the cause of death."

"In my opinion, yes."

"These other injuries to the limbs and skull?"

"Occurred after death and were aggravated by the action of sea water." Which, thought Mr Pringle, was a euphemism for what jagged rocks could do when waves lifted a body and crashed it down on to them. Coroner and histopathologist paused with their copies of the post mortem report. He swallowed. He hoped there wouldn't be much more of this. Next to him a woman listened avidly, her mouth hanging slack.

The coroner had begun that morning by telling the court of his decision to order a post mortem following the arrival of the body of the deceased within his jurisdiction. Looking round the closely packed faces, Mr Pringle thought he'd been wise. If this lot had been denied their spectacle, there could've been a riot. He shifted slightly. These benches weren't intended for comfort, they were designed for a passing trade.

As the case progressed, he'd grown more and more dismayed. A picture had built up which, for Mr Pringle, was distorted. An extract of Patrick's report was read out: summing up the meal at Levkas in a sentence made it appear Elizabeth was taken ill instantly. Even if, like Cassio, she'd had "poor and unhappy brains for drinking", it hadn't been as quick as that.

"As to what caused the asphyxia, Dr Morgan?"

"There were no signs of external pressure. Vomit lodged in the oesophagus was insufficient in my opinion—"

"But, when considering the emotional condition of the deceased?"

"The airway had not been completely blocked by the vomit."

"I see." In the courtroom, the atmosphere changed perceptibly.

Earlier, Emma had been taken through her report and, like all the witnesses, sat close to the coroner, facing him, with her back to the court. Mr Pringle hadn't been able to see her face, he could barely hear her answers. Quiet monosyllabic replies which described her attempt at discussion with a woman in a rage. The only time Emma hesitated was when she said she didn't know how much wine the deceased had consumed.

Charlotte was tearful but Mr Pringle's heart went out most to Matthew. He heard the voice tremble as it described the terrible journey back to the harbour with Elizabeth's broken body. Now the courtroom was equally hushed.

The coroner lowered his voice as he asked the histopathologist, "In your report you say there were no signs of violence prior to death?"

"Apart from slight bruising to the hands, which could have occurred several hours beforehand, none whatsoever, sir."

"So there was nothing to indicate the deceased had been attacked or had defended herself during an attack?"

"Nothing." The pathologist hesitated slightly. Mr Pringle could sense a responsive quiver within the court.

"Yes?" asked the coroner.

"I was going to add, the deceased did not *appear* to have attempted to save herself during her fall." And that Mr Pringle found most odd.

The solicitor representing Miss Hurst's Trustees had no further questions so the summing up began. There was a guarded reference to the deaths of the deceased's parents—which gave the Press their lunchtime headline: The Curse of the Hursts—but which had been intended to illustrate Elizabeth's possible depression. Another reference to society's most pernicious drug, alcohol, especially its effect on young women and a résumé of the medical evidence which appeared to exclude foul play. Finally, praise for foreign authorities for completing their investigations promptly, and sympathy for those who had done all they could to dissuade the deceased from her—presumed—headlong rush. It was the emphasis placed on this word which led the coroner to give the only possible verdict: an open one. Mr Pringle felt an enormous sense of relief.

"IT'S ALL SO bloody unsatisfactory," Matthew complained bitterly. "And why no reference to Gill? Despite what the coroner said, everyone will blame us for not preventing Liz's death."

"Nonsense, Matthew." Mr Fairchild was confident, "Of course they won't. Why should they? It was perfectly obvious you'd done everything possible." He turned to Emma and squeezed her shoulder, "I was very proud of you this morning." Again Mr Pringle thought he glimpsed jealousy in Charlotte's look.

She cried out, "Gill was there that night, I didn't imagine him."

"No one said he wasn't," her mother soothed.

"But even if he made contact with Elizabeth," Mr Pringle pointed out, "we must all remember there was no evidence of foul play."

"You've not changed your mind?" asked Matthew urgently. "You're not saying now Liz killed herself, are you?"

"No." The group in the café listened to him attentively. They'd all gathered for coffee following the verdict and had pushed two tables together so that the Fairchilds were at one end, Enid and Matthew at the other and he was sandwiched in the middle.

Enid turned on him angrily. "You're not trying to suggest Elizabeth threw herself off that cliff because of Matthew? I hope you know where your loyalties lie?"

"They lie with the truth, Enid, they always have."

"So what are you saying?" she asked.

"Everything reported in that court this morning sounded correct, but the sum total of the evidence appeared to me to be wrong. I cannot believe Elizabeth threw herself off that cliff and died from shock or vomit stuck in her throat. The impression of an unstable, grieving woman was not the person I knew."

"She'd had plenty of wine," Emma said quietly.

"But that surely wouldn't have changed her whole character? We know how she reacted to wine at Levkas, it made her belligerent." Emma's gaze dropped.

"I'm sorry, I'd forgotten that."

"So what d'you intend to do, Pringle?" asked Mr Fairchild. "Are you prepared to carry on with your enquiries, to get to the bottom of it?"

"There's nothing he'd like better," Enid snapped viciously, "then he can pretend he knows more than all those experts—"

"Mother!"

"What I must do," said Mr Pringle, ignoring them, "is find everyone who visited the olive grove that night and discover precisely what they heard or saw."

"You still believe, do you," asked Fairchild, "that Gill could be involved?"

"He was there!" Charlotte said passionately, "I know I didn't see Liz, but that filthy old man was real enough!" Gill was probably more than ten years younger than Mr Pringle but he hadn't time to think about that now, they were pressing him on all sides with their questions.

"Consider the facts for one moment," he said, topping the gabble. "There was plenty of time. Anyone could have gone up there—the medical evidence didn't state precisely when she was killed. Elizabeth could have been alive quite late that night, and we were all in and out of the firelight. None of us was in full view all the time after Elizabeth disappeared, were they?" Matthew and Fairchild shook their heads in agreement.

"Nor can we say about anyone else," said Matthew thoughtfully, "as we weren't there the whole time ourselves."

"The police will be pursuing their enquiries, of course." He was feeling tired now, the enormity of questioning so many potential witnesses was weighing him down, "I shall also make my investigation. Not because of anyone here," he stared at Enid, "but because I want to eradicate the impression given this morning of Elizabeth being an unstable drunken young woman. She was a fine person..." To his horror, Mr Pringle found himself near to tears. "Something terrible must have happened. Maybe it nearly made her choke, I'm sure it terrified her, but she was not suicidal. And as she made no effort to save herself when falling, I must point out the most obvious fact of all: dead women do not jump off cliffs. Now Matthew, I shall need plenty of help with all this. Could you telephone me this evening, when you're free?"

BUT MATTHEW CAME round and brought Emma with him. "We're on our way to collect Charlotte," he explained. "We don't think she should stay in that flat on her own."

"We thought we'd take her for a curry," said Emma. "She never bothers to cook when she's at Susie's."

"That's a kind thought." Mr Pringle took her anorak and hung it up in the hall. Emma shook the raindrops from her hair. The flaxen silk settled again round her shoulders.

"We can't stay long," she apologized, "but we wanted to tell you something. It was after you left this morning, what you said set us thinking. You see I don't remember *seeing* anyone when I was with Liz."

He was surprised, "Not even Gill?"

"No. I *heard* someone. There was definitely one other person moving about up there—I presumed it was Gill after Charlotte came back and told us about him."

"But that's exactly what I meant," Mr Pringle said excitedly. "Don't you understand—that could've been someone else."

"Yes, but who?"

"Look at this chart for a moment." Mr Pringle pulled his file across and took out a sketch. "Does this tally with what you both remember?" It was a diagrammatic drawing of the barbecue site with the olive grove beyond. He'd marked everyone's position with a cross. Matthew examined it carefully.

"That's beautifully clear... and that's definitely how I remember it. What about you, Em?"

"Yes." She pointed to a track leading to a cross that represented Elizabeth. "Is that me going up the hill?"

"Yes, and this line is Charlotte. Now, consider, is anyone missing who should be included here?" They studied it again.

"I can't think of anyone."

"Which proves my point. There's no cross for Roge Harper because no one remembers seeing him. So where was he? It was very unlike him to pass up the chance of a free meal."

"Mrs Gill wasn't there either," said Emma. "At least, if she was, I don't remember seeing her all evening." Mr Pringle frowned.

"I was intending to concentrate on the men but you're quite right, my dear, one must be thorough. Heigh-ho! I hope you can give me a hand, Matthew. The list's getting longer not shorter. Now can we assume Mrs Gill was either on their boat or helped with the food?— Ah, I can check that. Mrs Hanson will know that.''

"Mrs Hanson?"

"They are neighbours of the Gills, they live in Hounslow." Mr Pringle waved the list Matthew had given him. "This is proving invaluable, my boy. I've made an appointment to visit Mrs Hanson tomorrow, to see what I can learn about the Gills." He smiled grimly, "After all, what was it your mother said—that I was idle, with nothing better to do all day than twiddle my thumbs?" Matthew grinned.

"That sounded quite a punch-up between the two of you? I've only heard her version, of course."

"It was very silly, two people of our age carrying on like that. I shouldn't have brought it up. Now, don't keep Charlotte waiting. We'll discuss what you can do to help another evening, Matthew. It's more important to see that she eats. I don't think she should be left on her own at present."

Emma went back into the hall and took down her anorak. "We're both concerned about her..." She pulled up the zip, "And we wish she was more—more reliable."

"She's so pretty," Mr Pringle had been thinking the same about Emma. He realized this must sound fatuous, "No doubt she was spoiled?" Emma pulled a face.

"I expect we both were. Charlotte's pretty all right. The trouble is, she fantasizes. What she tells you is usually what *she* wants to be the truth, d'you see what I mean? It can make life difficult."

As THE FRONT DOOR closed behind them, Emma said thoughtfully, "Roge Harper...?" Matthew shivered and pulled up his collar against the rain.

"I don't think there's any possible connection. Come on. I'll unlock the car—you jump in."

AFTER THEY'D GONE, Mr Pringle sat for some time looking at his diagram. When he'd shown it to them, he'd hoped that one or other would spot what had been worrying him all day: why, when she'd been frightened, had Elizabeth rushed *up* the hill? It was steep, pitch dark, so why hadn't she gone down, to the light and safety of the barbecue?

The phone rang. "I see from the papers it's all over then?"

"Mavis! How delightful to hear your voice!"

"Was it an accident after all? Is that what an open verdict means?" The temptation of winning Mrs Bignell back nearly overcame his resolve, but what of his declaration to Enid?

"Not quite. That is to say, it wasn't entirely accidental." There was an ominous pause.

"Does that mean you haven't finished?"

"Mavis, I cannot give up half way. But I assure you there's not the slightest possibility of my sister coming here again, at least not while I'm alive. And she has already made her assessment for purposes of disposal after my death. Please . . . I've missed you so much." But she wasn't prepared to let him off the hook straight away.

"They're short-handed at The Bricklayers. I've agreed to work extra tonight."

"May I come round and take you home afterwards?"

"I don't think so, not tonight. I'm feeling a bit tired. It's my age, it catches up with me nowadays." As indeed it did with Mr Pringle. Time was short for both of them so why waste it?

"What about tomorrow? I have to go to Hounslow but I should be back here by the afternoon."

"Well . . . I'm not promising." But in his heart he knew she was. He went joyfully to bed but he dreamed, and his dream turned to a nightmare. As he fell down and down, Mavis

reached out her arms to save him but her face dissolved to
Elizabeth's, rising up from the waves. He woke in a lather
of sweat. Time might be short for him but for her it was
over, and the sooner he discovered why, the better.

TWENTY

T WAS A STREET where all the houses were the same. Outside the Hansons' was a newish-looking car. Further proof of the premium bond win? Mrs Hanson opened the door. 'Hello, come in. Nice to see you again—mind the bike! Sorry. I hope you don't mind the kitchen, I'm in the middle of baking. Would you like a coffee? The police were round there again this morning.'' Mr Pringle looked up at the empty windows next door.

"It's very kind of you to let me call. Still no sign of the Gills, I assume?"

"No. I reckon they've gone for good. In here. Take a seat. There's a rumour down the street their house is up for sale, too. And it wasn't the same police who came asking about Miss Hurst, it was another lot."

"Have they been before?"

"Yes. As soon as we got back from holiday. He'd been fiddling money at the banks. He'd done it before, apparently, but this time it was with the Greek banks—"

"You mean fraud!" A whole new vista opened up for Mr Pringle.

"I suppose I do, yes. Frank was really pissed when he heard. We'd lent them fifty quid, you see. We can kiss that goodbye I told him, when I knew."

But if it was fraud, then it couldn't be a thousand other things. Mr Pringle didn't know much about attempted rape, or how dead girls came to fall off cliffs, but he did know an awful lot about human depravity over money. And he didn't think it would be combined with either of those other crimes. Or had Gill been so desperate for money, he'd attacked Elizabeth? Mr Pringle waited until Mrs Hanson had pressed out the last pastry circle with her upturned cup "Did the police drop any hint as to what he'd done?"

"Yes, but I didn't understand very well..." She concentrated on filling the two dozen jam tarts. "It's Jason's birthday tomorrow. He's got six friends coming round." Mr Pringle's hand was already in his pocket.

"Perhaps he could treat himself... A few sweets?"

"Oh, you don't have to... Well, all right then. Thanks very much. Now let me think what they said." She pushed the baking tray into the oven, set the pinger and leaned against the worktop. "Mr Gill had been to prison once, which is why they moved here from Kingston. *She* was always toffee-nosed about living in Hounslow—I was livid when I found out. I mean, what call had she...? Anyway, what he used to do was buy something, pay by cheque, take the thing back to a second shop for a cash refund, then cancel the cheque before the first one could pay it in. You have to do it somewhere with branches, like Marks and Spencer's, for it to work."

"Yes." It was disappointing, he'd expected more imagination.

"They caught up with him, which was when he was put inside the first time. On this holiday, he did it differently. Something like getting shops to cash his cheques, then going to banks to change the drachmas for English money." Mr Pringle thought it all sounded pathetic. "He changed the figures on the cheques as well," she added.

"Ah, I see! Did he visit many banks?"

"Yes, in Levkas and Parga, they said. He was dead keen to get back home. You remember when Miss Hurst died, when the police were asking questions—how they collected all our passports?"

"I remember."

"Well Mr Gill had been using his when he cashed those cheques, that's why he was scared he'd be found out. He'd been sacked by Freezers just before the holiday—never told anyone, of course, the police told us that—but that's why he was doing everything he could, while he was out there, to raise money. Did he try and borrow off Miss Hurst then, is that why you wanted to see him?"

Mr Pringle told her he was anxious to speak to anyone who talked to Elizabeth at the barbecue. Mrs Hanson frowned.

"I couldn't tell you, I'm afraid. I don't remember either him or Mrs Gill being up there. She didn't help with the food. Kate asked her but me and my sister ended up doing it. Never did a hand's turn if she could avoid it, that one." And Mrs Hanson cleared away the remains of her pastry making to make room for ingredients for a chocolate cake. Once he'd confirmed that none of the Hansons or Clarkes had spoken to Elizabeth that night, Mr Pringle took his leave.

At Hounslow Central tube station, he sat and considered the case against Gill. It was certainly possible he'd been the man to attempt rape at Spartahouri, but what would be the reason? Surely all Gill's efforts were directed at raising money, and his wife's, at meeting Elizabeth? And as for that booming, arrogant manner, designed to intimidate, to prevent diffident bank clerks asking awkward questions. Would such a man, however desperate for money, use force? But no force had been used—there hadn't been any sign of violence. The pathologist had made that plain. He must remember that. He was almost downhearted, then Mr Pringle remembered something else: Mavis might be at home waiting for him. After that, the train couldn't get there quick enough.

"THE THREE OF US were chatting when Emma said something we'd never heard her say before. We think it must have been in her subconscious, from when she was attacked."

"At Spartahouri?"

"Yes."

"Well?" Mr Pringle was being curt on the phone because Mavis had been in while he was out and had laid the table for two, with a candle!

"Poppet."

"Pardon?"

"That's the word. Emma remembered that during the struggle the man called her something that sounded like 'poppet'."

So what was the significance of that? Downstairs Mr Pringle heard a key turning in the lock—"Look, Matthew, can we discuss all this tomorrow—"

"Yoo-hoo!" Mavis was in the hall.

"Charlotte thinks Reggie used to call Phyllis poppet."

"Coming, coming!" Mr Pringle cried eagerly, then to Matthew, "You don't mean Phyllis's husband—'Fend off Reggie'?"

"That's the one."

LATER, MUCH LATER, after the candle had been snuffed, he told Mavis.

"Well dear, you've always said to me that nine times out of ten, when there's been suspicious circumstances, a death was either Domestic, Sex or Money, right?"

"Correct. It certainly wasn't domestic. Elizabeth hadn't any relatives or family left. No one on the flotilla, apart from Matthew and myself, knew she would be there in Greece, either."

"And it wasn't money, was it, dear? Elizabeth hadn't inherited her fortune and nobody gained anything?" Mr Pringle sighed.

"Not as far as I'm aware."

"So that leaves the other." Mavis stretched luxuriously, both arms behind her head, leaning against the pillows. "Although it makes the world go round for you and me, I'm glad to say, it does make some people quite nasty if half you read in the newspapers is true. Especially if they're not getting their share.'' Mr Pringle was momentarily distracted. Mavis's Titian tresses were curling delightfully across her creamy skin—ah, if only he were younger, he might begin all over again! She was speaking seriously. He tucked his hands under the sheet.

"When you first got back from Greece, I remember you saying there had to be a connection between that business with Emma at howsyourfather and Parga. Maybe it was sex?''

"Possibly.''

"I've been thinking—Elizabeth and Emma—they're about the same height, aren't they?''

"Yes. Quite a different shape, though. Emma's slimmer, smaller boned.''

"But it was dark. Suppose it was the same chap. He wouldn't be able to see which was which under those trees, would he? He'd hear them both *talking*. When Emma left, he grabbed Elizabeth and found he'd got the wrong one. That's when he panicked.''

"And did what? There were no signs of violence on the body, remember?'' Mavis shrugged voluptuously. Mr Pringle gave a little moan of delight.

"You'll have to put your thinking cap on, dear. This Reggie, what sort of a person is he?''

"He's a solicitor in Warlingham.''

"Oh, well then. There's your answer.'' Mavis reached up to switch off the light and the curve of her breast stroked his ear. "We get them in The Bricklayers sometimes, solicitors—''

"Mavis, don't switch that off for a moment—''

"Oh, no. I know what's in your mind—you've had quite enough for one night. I don't want you complaining about your lumbago tomorrow. You think about this Reggie person instead. It's going to be quite tricky, asking him questions. Solicitors have a way of wriggling out of anything unpleasant."

In the dark he snuggled up, wrapped himself round her thighs and started to nibble her ear. After a while Mrs Bignell spoke to him severely; "You're not concentrating on that list of questions, are you?"

"No, I'm not." Seldom had Mr Pringle been more positive. Ten minutes later she said, "Have you got any intention of going to sleep?"

"Not yet."

All the same he thought, when he did give his mind to it, it wasn't going to be easy.

TWENTY-ONE

IN THE END he had plenty of time to think about it. Mr Pringle's was the sort of car they don't make like that any more. The mechanic confirmed it when charging him for a new set of plugs after he'd broken down. What was worse, he'd no certainty when he got there of meeting Reggie. The phone number on Matthew's list was Reggie's business one and, when Mr Pringle rang, the secretary told him gloomily that as the weather was fine, her boss might be on the golf course all day.

And how did you ask a man if he'd attempted rape, twice? The second time with fatal consequences but without inflicting any signs of violence? Nor did it comfort Mr Pringle when he arrived at the office to learn that Reggie was the senior partner.

The man was in but he was furious. Holidays were one thing but this was an invasion of privacy, it was outrageous! A casual acquaintance—on a boat—wasn't entitled to presume—hadn't Mr Pringle any sense of professional etiquette! Reggie swelled with anger, blocking the entrance to his office, prepared to repel all invaders. Outside, in the reception area, the gloomy secretary wound fresh paper into her typewriter. "I checked your diary before I told him he could see you. There's nothing written down for today except lunch with the Rotarians."

"I shall not take much of your time." Mr Pringle was extremely apprehensive and wished himself anywhere but here in Warlingham.

"There's always Mr Ridgway in an emergency." The secretary looked pointedly at the clock. "If he remembers to come in."

Inside the office Mr Pringle was given the least comfortable chair. He decided to get the interview over as quickly as possible, there was no point in attempting to soften up Reggie first. "May I ask if as a term of endearment you are in the habit of using the word—'Poppet'?" To his surprise, Reggie turned pale.

"Phyllis put you up to this, didn't she? Are you from an agency? My God, what a way to earn a living—you're part of the snooper society, aren't you? I should've known. First time I spotted you out there, I knew you were the type! So she's really going through with it this time, is she?" Reggie snarled. "Well, you can tell her from me—I don't bloody care!" He leaned forward so threateningly, Mr Pringle was apprehensive for his own safety.

At the same moment, the door swung open and the secretary marched in carrying a tray. On it were two cups of coffee. She handed Mr Pringle the one with a chocolate biscuit balanced on the saucer. Reggie's saucer contained only Rich Tea. Mr Pringle settled back in his chair knowing he'd gained time: the ground rules had been established. It was against every unwritten law of hospitality to eject a man before he'd finished a chocolate biscuit. He fired his second barrel. "Was it you who attacked Emma Fairchild?"

"No it bloody well wasn't!" Reggie mopped coffee off his pinstripes. "Of all the damn cheek!"

"Emma has remembered hearing the word 'Poppet' spoken by her assailant during the incident—"

"I don't care if she remembers hearing heavenly music as well—it wasn't me and I can ruddy well prove it! That road down from Spartahouri was so blasted dangerous, the four of us stuck together the whole way—we'd only got one torch. Walter held it and I had the girls on either side of me.'' Phyllis, a girl? Mr Pringle sighed. Among the Rotarians, paunchy balding Reggie probably described himself as 'one of the lads'. Nevertheless, it had to be faced that his was a solid alibi. Mr Pringle remembered the sliding gravelly surface. Reggie certainly wasn't agile enough to have slipped away in the darkness, done the deed and returned without his group noticing, particularly the watchful Phyllis.

Mr Pringle chewed on his biscuit as Reggie blustered about his wife having no business interfering with his private life, and a man having a perfect right to have a friend in Horsham.

During a pause Mr Pringle asked, ''On the night of the barbecue, did you speak to Elizabeth Hurst at all?''

''Why should I do that? I didn't know the woman. I'm not one of those who goes round trying to pick up with people simply because they've chosen the same holiday venue. Anyway, the police have been round about that.'' Reggie looked at him sarcastically. ''Stop trying to pretend that has anything to do with your enquiry. You're here because of Phyllis, we both know that. I suppose she discovered your mucky trade while we were in Greece?''

''I've never had the pleasure of speaking to your wife,'' Mr Pringle protested mildly, ''and when I retired from the Inland Revenue, I began making the occasional investigation, more as a hobby. At present, I am doing so on behalf of my nephew—''

''If that young man had kept an eye on Miss Hurst, none of this would be necessary. I was brought up to believe a man had a duty to protect his womenfolk,'' said Reggie pompously. In Horsham as well as Warlingham, wondered Mr Pringle? ''As for that Fairchild girl, taking her clothes off all the time,'' Reggie continued, ''she deserved what she got. You wouldn't catch Phyllis behaving like that.''

''No, indeed!'' Mr Pringle tried not to shudder.

"Your nephew was a blasted pest that night. Came whining to Walter and me at one point. Wanted us to join his ruddy search party."

"And did you?"

"Certainly not. Nothing to do with us. Not our boat. How were we to know the girl had fallen off a cliff? Anyway the booze was running low so we toddled off to that other place on the beach. Phyllis needed to eat, she loathes barbecued chicken."

"Did you go back to the party afterwards?" Reggie looked at him in surprise.

"What on earth for? I've told you—they'd run dry. There was only red wine anyway. We needed a decent drink so we all went back to *Aquarius*."

As Mr Pringle rose to leave, Reggie returned to his idée-fixe. "What's Phyllis actually said about my friend? How much has she told you?"

"Nothing. I've told you, I haven't had the pleasure of speaking to your wife."

"I wouldn't put it past Phyllis. She's made threatening noises in the past, you know."

Mr Pringle doffed his hat to the secretary. "Thank you for the refreshments." He could see past her into Mr Ridgway's empty office and found himself glancing automatically at the clock. It was only twelve fifteen.

ON THE WAY HOME he became more and more depressed. His enquiries had been so superficial. He hadn't even demanded corroboration from Reggie, he was simply judging the man by his reactions and behaviour. A proper investigator would've gone to see "Walter", presumably he lived in the vicinity? And as for avoiding an encounter with Phyllis, that was simply cowardly. If Reggie appeared to be genuine, how was that an excuse? Several women had found Dr Crippen very charming.

In the old days, Mr Pringle commenced every investigation with a set of forms. A natural reaction, perhaps, for a former civil servant. But over the years, as in his former occupation, he found the answers were often misleading. And on this occasion, he had no official status. No one had employed him to investigate a crime. Indeed, there was as yet no suggestion of one. Simply an open verdict and an atmosphere of general unease.

He ate the sandwiches he'd bought for lunch while waiting for his radiator to cool. Why had Elizabeth died? There was no evidence of rape, no one benefitted and if it had been a drunken panic attack, why had no one else shown signs of injury? Surely Elizabeth would've defended herself? He shook his head, angry with himself: there had been no sign of injury before death on the body itself—he must remember that. And where had everyone been at the time? Apart from Gill, had Roge been there? It was all most unsatisfactory. He'd even tried out the puzzle of why Elizabeth had run up, not down, the hill on Mavis.

"I don't know, dear, it does sound very odd. If it had been me..."

"Yes?"

"I'd have screamed blue murder and run like hell. Mind you, I couldn't do that nowadays but I could still yell."

"Elizabeth could run. I suppose the music was very loud—they were dancing to it at the site."

"I'd have still made them hear me," Mavis said stoutly. "Whatever it was must have been terrifying to stop her shouting. Did you see what Matthew said, after the inquest, to the newspapers?"

"No?"

"'Death still a mystery but heiress may have choked. Boyfriend says "We are all bitterly disappointed. We had hoped today to find out the answers. Why did such a wonderful girl have to die?"''" Mavis quoted. "It was something like that. There was a very nice picture of Matthew. I've cut it out for you."

That was last night. This morning's papers hadn't been any more helpful. Now, as he locked the car, he remembered he'd forgotten to be methodical yesterday, too. He'd relied on Mrs Hanson's word that her family and the Clarkes had stayed together all evening. He hadn't been to her sister's to check. He couldn't face another journey to Hounslow, perhaps he could do it by phone? He rang Mrs Hanson again, to ask for the Clarkes' number.

"I'm afraid my sister's had to have it taken out. What with Jack being made redundant, they couldn't afford the rental. Is there any message? I usually see her on Thursday." Wearily, he asked for the address.

It would mean writing to ask for an appointment, then travelling out there, and he felt so tired! When Mavis rang to say she'd bought more candles he could no longer stiffen the sinews, summon up the blood. "I'm not feeling very well," he said pathetically, but she wasn't sympathetic. She laughed.

"I warned you you were overdoing it, didn't I. Have an early night. I'll see you tomorrow." He felt badly done to. At the very least he thought she'd offer to come round and cook his supper.

HE SLEPT FITFULLY and woke after a couple of hours feeling chilly. Because it was July he'd foolishly sent off the electric blanket to be serviced. Now he couldn't find his hot-water bottle. This irritated him so much he didn't bother making a hot drink.

By dawn he was feverish. His throat hurt. He wanted to tell Mavis he was a real invalid but this time she was out. He was flabbergasted—only 8.15—where on earth did women go so early in the morning? He checked the calendar: Friday. Mavis did her shopping on Fridays.

Disgruntled, he took two aspirin and got his breakfast ready. He'd run out of cornflakes. There was a tired old tea-cake in the bread bin. He tried swallowing stale titbits washed down with coffee. Nobody cared. He could die here and lie decomposing until his neighbours noticed the smell. There weren't any clean matching socks, either, so he put odd ones on.

There was no real excuse now for delaying a return visit to Hounslow. He had to be thorough, he owed it to Elizabeth to discover the truth, apart from satisfying himself. Mr Clarke no longer had a job therefore it was extremely likely he'd be at home. There was no need to write for an appointment, Mr Pringle would simply present himself at the front door. He refused to admit the real reason for going was that anyone else's house was infinitely more appealing in his present state than his own.

But Mrs Clarke didn't invite him inside. Her husband was on his allotment, only fifteen minutes' walk, you couldn't miss it. Half-way there, the depression the weatherman had forecast came to pass and Mr Pringle didn't have an umbrella.

Mr Clarke made room for him in the flimsy shed and offered to share his thermos of tea. They sat on upturned boxes and contemplated the redundant man's kingdom: a patch of earth roughly fifteen foot square. "I come here most days to get out of the wife's way." The increasing downpour pleased him, too. "Just what the doctor ordered." Mr Pringle sneezed. Strips of foil tied on lines of string to deter birds shivered in sympathy.

"You remember that afternoon, when you hoped to see Miss Hurst? Roge Harper came back later and managed to catch her but did you see her at all later on? Not to speak to but while she was up at the barbecue?" The name was an automatic trigger. Out came the cracked plastic wallet and snapshot.

"I never saw her again. Roge Harper must've been one of the last to talk to her." Mr Pringle knew he should press the man but the voice was so full of regret, the face so open, he didn't bother. As far as he could judge, Mr Clarke was either a consummate actor—which was unlikely—or he was telling the truth.

"Did Elizabeth have any brothers or sisters?" Mr Pringle knew the answer already but felt he should probe a little.

"She was the one and only. Her mother couldn't have any more, you see. Mr Leonard was disappointed naturally but he accepted it. There was a nephew. The younger brother went to Canada when Mr Leonard took over the firm, and there was talk at one time of the boy joining the company but I don't think anything came of it."

Mr Pringle felt stirrings of excitement. "Is it possible that this nephew will inherit the Trust now? Or a part of it?" Mr Clarke looked bewildered.

"I don't know. You'll have to ask somebody else." Such simple apathy annoyed Mr Pringle. Mr Clarke hadn't asked why he was here, nor was he interested. He assumed Mr Pringle wanted nothing better than to talk interminably about Leonard Hurst. "He was always good to me, Mr Leonard was . . ." And Mr Pringle knew they were about to embark again on the one occasion when his companion had been called upon to prove himself. For Mr Clarke, the voyage back from Dunkirk was as fresh as if it had been yesterday.

This time a few more details were added about peacetime work. A job had been found to act as chauffeur but Mr Clarke couldn't cope. "I was good with engines see, not the driving. But he found me a place in the workshop which was good of him." Mr Pringle felt he must check at least once more about the barbecue.

"You didn't have an opportunity to help search that night? For Elizabeth?"

"I was helping Kate and my wife. They wanted me to look after the fire while the kids helped Matthew." Mr Clarke was a hewer of wood, a drawer of water—would such a man even think of harming the daughter of his idol? And to what purpose? Reinstatement in his former job? Mr Pringle doubted if it had occurred to Mr Clarke to ask.

"Did any of the children manage to speak to Elizabeth?"

Mr Clarke looked astonished. "If they did, they never said."

"Could you be kind enough to ask them for me, and let me know? Here's my card." Mr Clarke turned it over in his hand and said stubbornly, "They would've told me...but I will ask, to make sure." He turned to face Mr Pringle more squarely, "You're trying to find out, aren't you? Why it happened. Why she fell like that?"

"Yes, I am."

"Her father wouldn't have stood for it—I told the wife, an open verdict wouldn't have satisfied Mr Leonard. He'd have wanted to get to the bottom of it." Mr Pringle opened his mouth to speak but a fit of sneezing overcame him. Mr Clarke looked at him critically. "You all right? I reckon you shouldn't be out."

On the train back from Hounslow, Mr Pringle promised himself a hot toddy, a hot bath, a hot anything that would stop him shaking like a leaf. By the time he reached his front door, he felt delirious. He picked up the phone. What a blessed relief, Mavis was back home! "Can you come round? I'm feeling light-headed."

He let her scold and hustle him into bed. He tried not to mind when she wrapped a woolly shawl on top of his pyjamas. He drank an egg whisked in warm milk with nutmeg on top, closed his eyes and waited for oblivion.

"They've caught him. I heard it on the radio."

"What?"

"That Mr Gill. He was trying to pass a cheque, it said. They didn't mention anything about Elizabeth." Mr Pringle forced his eyes open again.

"Were there any other details?"

"Not that I can remember. It was only a little item at the end of the news. They'll probably have it in the papers tomorrow."

Yes, they would. He burrowed under the blankets. It could wait.

TWENTY-TWO

BUT ON SATURDAY morning there was no reference to Gill. Mr Pringle stayed where he was and let Mavis cosset him. By supper-time when he felt well enough to eat, she had another development to report. "They've just said he's been remanded in custody."

"Ah."

"They mentioned the sailing holiday this time. The Greek police want to talk to him—something to do with cheques at a Greek bank."

"Anything about Elizabeth?"

"No."

"Perhaps they're keeping their cards close to their chests." But he wasn't convinced. "I think, in the morning, I should get up. There's rather a lot still to do."

SUNDAY PAPERS made the connection and were less inhibited. The news spread rapidly. Charlotte and Emma arrived unannounced and full of excitement. They burst upon him in his drab bedroom. Charlotte, in bright yellow, glowed with hope. "This is it, isn't it? You're going to see him, aren't you? And make him say what happened?" Mr Pringle was dazed by the sight of two beautiful women perched on the foot of his bed. He pulled the covers modestly over his chest.

"Charlotte is convinced you can make Gill confess," Emma explained, "and when he does, everyone will know she was telling the truth." Emma had abandoned her perpetual jeans and wore a dress. Renée had once had one with the same colour flowers, he remembered, larkspur blue.

For Charlotte, it was simple. "He'll have to confess everything, won't he? I mean, what's the point in holding anything back? If he doesn't say why he frightened Liz into jumping, he'll only make it worse for himself—"

"But he may not have done so," Mr Pringle managed to interject, "Mr Gill may be innocent of that."

"What!"

"And please understand, Charlotte, I am not entitled to see him while he is in custody, only his solicitor can do that. Moreover, if Gill has been remanded on a charge of fraud, his custody could last for months—"

"You've got to do something!" Charlotte was outraged. "You can't let fraud interfere with sorting out that open verdict! Can't you pull a few strings? Pa would. There must be something you can do?"

He was irritated, first by her bland assumption that all doors would open as soon as she desired them to be, secondly because he realized he still hadn't shaved.

"There may indeed be a way once I've had an opportunity to study the papers. As yet, I know very few details." Mavis swept in to the rescue.

"Now, my dears, you must let him have a bath and get dressed. You'll only do his temperature no good if you stay here, not to mention giving him ideas. Coffee's ready downstairs." As she shepherded them out, she hissed, "Put your striped shirt on and the fawn trousers. Your others have got a mark on them."

HE TOOK ONE PAPER into the bathroom. In soapy steam he read the relevant paragraph. It added little to what Mrs Bignell had reported. Gill had been arrested in the Midlands and, from the way it was phrased, it was obvious the police had been following a trail of dud cheques.

Mr Pringle added more hot water. This paper had one of those bosomy girls inviting him to enjoy the fruits of summer. Now he'd survived the spring, perhaps he ought to consider doing just that. He and Mrs Bignell hadn't been on one of their little outings recently. A weekend in Bournemouth might be the very thing to speed his recovery. He wondered where the bosomy creature went for her holidays, and turned the page.

"Lovers bequeath each other everything": beneath the headline was a blurred photo of Elizabeth and another smaller one of Matthew. Mr Pringle read the article carefully. Following the publication of Elizabeth's Will, Matthew had been interviewed. He told the reporter that he and Liz had been advised to make their Wills before the Easter sailing trip, as a temporary measure. Elizabeth was due to make a more comprehensive one on her return from Greece.

What followed emphasized how much the Trust was worth and by how much Matthew would have benefited, had Liz reached her birthday. Mr Pringle was astonished by the figure. He read the final paragraph: a list of the charities Elizabeth had intended to endow together with expressions of regret from their representatives. Throughout the article there was no mention of any Canadian cousin as a possible beneficiary.

NEITHER EMMA nor Charlotte was surprised by the article. "Matthew told us he'd be getting Liz's bits and pieces," Charlotte said.

"It's not that much," Emma pointed out, "when you think what it might have been, after she'd inherited."

How relative such things were, thought Mr Pringle. An inheritance dismissed as trivial by these two would appear a fortune in Mr Clarke's eyes. He asked if either of them had heard of the cousin but drew a blank.

"We hadn't even met Liz before the holiday," Charlotte reminded him, "And for obvious reasons we didn't get to know much about her." She flushed, "I know that was partly my fault. Anyway, it's too late now." She shrugged. For her the living were more important than the dead. She handed Mr Pringle all the reports of Gill's arrest in other newspapers. When he'd read them, he looked up.

"I'm afraid it's as I suspected. He's in custody and there's no way I can insist on seeing him."

"But—"

"Hear me out, Charlotte. What I can do, in view of my former employment, is ask to see one of the officers investigating the fraud. If Gill has admitted anything concerning Elizabeth—" but this was all too vague for Charlotte, she wanted action.

"That could drag on all summer."

"Possibly longer, I fear. Fraud requires meticulous investigation—"

"We can't wait for ever!"

"What can't, dear?" Mrs Bignell was surprised. Mr Pringle put it more succinctly.

"Did you say 'we'?" Charlotte flushed.

"Matthew and I... We plan, eventually... You know..." He frowned.

"I'm afraid I don't?" She went even redder.

"What's happened is tragic but Matthew can't go on mourning Liz for ever."

"Perhaps not, but for a little while longer, surely?" Mr Pringle protested, "Until results of the police enquiries are known."

"You've just told us how long they're likely to take. Why can't they ask Gill about that first, then charge him with fraud?"

"I apologize on behalf of my sister," said Emma drily. "She has never been known to wait more than five minutes for anything in her entire life—"

"Oh, shut up!" Mrs Bignell and Mr Pringle raised their eyebrows. Charlotte didn't seem to care. "It's all very well for you—Matthew and I love each other!"

"Do you?" Mr Pringle was startled, he'd heard no mention of it from Matthew. Emma looked steadily at Charlotte.

"What my sister means," she said slowly, "is that she wants to marry Matthew—"

"Bitch!"

"Ladies, ladies!"

"But unfortunately, Matthew hasn't yet asked *her* to marry *him*."

"I should hope not!" Mr Pringle was shocked at the exchange across his own dining table, "It's scarcely a month since—"

"It's nearly five bloody weeks!"

"As long as that, Charlotte? My, my!" Mrs Bignell was heavily sarcastic. In the fraught atmosphere, Mr Pringle found himself trembling.

"I think you should try and remember, Charlotte, Elizabeth's death is still a mystery. Until Gill, or one of the other members of the flotilla, admits seeing her that night, you may have been the last person in that olive grove..." And the implication hung in the air. Charlotte shrank back as though he'd slapped her.

"You don't think it was me? You can't!"

"I simply beg you to consider the circumstances and not do anything precipitate, for Matthew's sake and your own. Consider how it could appear to an outsider—" but Charlotte was on her feet, demanding where she might find her coat. The other three stayed where they were, listening as she rushed through the hall and slammed the front door. Outside an engine started, revved and drove away.

"Oh, great!" Emma sank back in her chair. "She's taken my car. Can either of you give me a lift?"

IT WAS Mavis who thought of summoning Matthew. He walked into the house on a wave of optimism. "Isn't it fantastic about Gill? And it didn't take them all that long to find him in the end, did it? I'm so relieved—the whole mess will soon be cleared up now."

"Not—quite," Emma warned. Matthew looked at her and crumpled.

"Oh, no! I thought all the police had to do was find Gill!" Emma told him briefly what Mr Pringle had said. Quieter now, Matthew asked, "Can't they question Gill about Liz while they investigate the fraud?"

"They're bound to, but they may take things in order, not simultaneously and he was wanted for fraud first."

"Shit!"

"There's something else," Emma knelt in front of him, "But don't let it upset you. Charlotte made a declaration."

"What?" Matthew looked at Mrs Bignell. "You said on the phone she'd been up to something?"

"She wants to marry you," Emma held both his hands in hers, "She told us she still loves you." Mr Pringle watched to see the reaction. It was disappointing—Matthew shook his head in mild surprise.

"Did she really . . . ? What d'you think we should do?"

"Go after her," replied Emma decisively. "You know how volatile she is just now."

"I'd better take you home first then go over to Susie's place. Char will've gone back there."

"Fine." Emma got to her feet. Matthew turned to Mr Pringle.

"What's your next move, Uncle? D'you think there's a chance the police will talk to you about Gill?"

"Not yet," he replied, "but if I can eliminate everyone else first, I'll have a stronger case for asking for an appointment."

"Who have you still to see, dear?" asked Mavis. "I thought you'd visited most of them?"

"Roge Harper. Apart from us, he was the last to see Elizabeth."

Matthew was helping Emma into her mac. "I'm sure he was the reason Liz was in such a state," he said, "Uncle, can I help in any way? You seem to be doing all the leg work." Mr Pringle had a brainwave.

"You know the Trustees. Can you ask them about the boy in Canada?" He could see Matthew hadn't heard of him. When he explained, Mr Pringle asked tentatively, "Do you think his existence could affect your inheritance?" Matthew shrugged and shook his head.

"The Trust perhaps, not the Will. The solicitor rang a couple of days ago when they were about to publish it. He said everything was in order," Matthew replied.

"I didn't realize you stood to inherit?" Matthew went crimson.

"I feel pretty bloody, I can tell you. It was such a trivial thing at the time, just a temporary measure."

"Whose idea was it? Making a Will?"

"Frank's." Mr Pringle looked blank. "You remember at Easter—Frank's boat. He said anyone hiring the thing had to make a Will first. Typical bloody Australian. Didn't trust the stupid Brits not to drown themselves, I suppose."

"It was very sensible in my opinion," Mr Pringle reproved. He stood on the step to watch the two of them get into the old Mini. "Let me know what you discover about the cousin."

"Yes, I will. I'll do it from the office tomorrow and phone you tomorrow night." Emma wound down her window.

"Give our regards to Roge and Maureen."

Back inside, Mrs Bignell was making gravy. She'd left the kitchen door open and the house was suddenly full of wonderful odours. "I'm glad they've gone. The Yorkshires are just about ready and there wasn't enough to go round, not if you want second helpings."

He set the table, helped bring in the dishes and settled to enjoy himself. Sunday lunch with Mrs Bignell sitting opposite, and the thought of what might happen later... "Is there a pudding?" he asked innocently.

"Of course there is. Spotted Dick. You need to get your strength back." Paradise was made up of simple things, he decided philosophically, and wondered if Mavis was wearing her lavender silk underwear. Then he remembered he had to visit Roge. Blast!

TWENTY-THREE

HE WAS EVEN MORE annoyed when he checked his file and discovered Roge Harper lived in Isleworth. "I could have combined this with one of my other visits to Hounslow!"

"What a coincidence. D'you think he's friendly with the Clarkes or the Hansons?"

"I've no idea. There was no sign of it before. If I'd been his neighbour, I'd have wanted to get away from Roge, not go on holiday with him." Mr Pringle was all gloom. There'd been no answer to his telephone call. "Look, suppose this is his business address, not his home? Why don't I leave the whole thing till tomorrow."

"No, go now while you're in the mood. Fresh air will do you good." Besides, Mavis wanted a little rest. She usually did after a big lunch, but if she told Mr Pringle she was going to bed he thought she meant something else. He was a bit of a terror that way nowadays. And Mavis intended to have an hour's kip without interruption. "We could pop round to the Nag's Head when you get back this evening, if you like. I feel like a bit of a sing-song." It was the last thing in the world that he wanted but he remembered he was fond of her.

"That would be nice."

HE WAS RIGHT, it was a business address. He studied the shop for a moment or two before crossing the road. On a bend with double yellow lines, parking was impossible. The next-door shop was empty but had, by the look of it, once been a general store. No doubt when they first opened, it and the hardware business had supplied the necessities of life

for the community round about. Now both had been
superseded by hypermarkets.

To try and call at a shop on a Sunday afternoon in England was a waste of time. Before going back, he'd try the
bell on the door between the shopfronts. Perhaps someone
in the upstairs flat would know where Roge lived.

"Roge!" The light in Maureen Harper's eyes faded even
as she opened the door. "Oh, it's you. Hallo. How nice to
see you again." But it wasn't. Mr Pringle dithered.

"I'm sorry... I don't wish to intrude."

"It doesn't matter. I didn't really think it could be..." She
looked past him instinctively, searching the road in each direction and the light in her eyes died altogether. "You'd
better come upstairs."

She waited until they'd climbed the narrow flight before
telling him. "It's over four weeks since Roge went. Four
weeks and two days." Her eyes were full of tears.

"I'm most terribly sorry. I'd no idea."

"Why should you have. Would you like some tea?"

"If it's no trouble—can I help in any way?"

"No, thanks. If you'd like to come through here." The
flat consisted of a large room directly above the shop, with
what appeared to be a kitchenette in an alcove beyond.
There was a square bay and in it a chair which was where
Maureen obviously kept her vigil. She went through an arch
hung with a bead curtain, with a wooden parrot clipped to
it, into the kitchenette. Mr Pringle could hear cups and
saucers being moved about.

As she spoke to him, he looked about at further evidence
of Roge's handiwork. Woodchip covered the walls un-
evenly and had a thick layer of emulsion paint. This was
supposed to conceal the overlapping joins, Mr Pringle knew,
because he'd tried to do the same thing himself. It didn't
work, it hadn't done so for him.

"Nobody knows why Roge disappeared," Maureen said
sadly, "I certainly don't. We hadn't quarrelled but every-

one assumes we had. You can tell the police think so. They'd made an appointment to see us both that evening, to go through our statements, but Roge had gone by then.''

"They visited every member of the flotilla.'' On the walls were narrow fretwork shelves, model boats and other useless shapes of wood. Roge had certainly left his signature even if he'd removed his presence. But where had he gone?

"Did they ask *you* about Miss Hurst?'' she called.

"Yes.'' Beads clashed as Maureen returned.

"Is that why you're here?''

"Partly. I believe Roge may have been one of the last people to speak to Elizabeth.''

"No,'' Maureen spoke with conviction, "You're wrong about that. He saw her during the afternoon on *Capricorn* but he didn't see her at the barbecue.'' She went back inside the alcove and he heard her making the tea.

"Are you sure of that?''

"I heard him tell the police at Parga. We were interviewed together.'' She poked her head through the beads. "When the man said, 'You must've seen her on the boat?' Roge said, 'What if I did?' Afterwards he said he hadn't intended telling him but it popped out.''

"I don't see the harm as it was the truth. Most people knew Roge, Mr Clarke and Mr Gill were waiting at one time or other to speak to her. I think Roge was the only one who succeeded.''

"Was he really?'' She didn't sound particularly interested.

"Unless Gill did also,'' Mr Pringle called cautiously.

It was a few more minutes before she emerged with the tray. Outside, lorries changed gear for traffic lights beyond the bend, then revved up again. There was a constant level of noise which made him uncomfortable.

"It didn't make Roge a liar because he didn't want to talk about it,'' said Maureen defensively. She set the tray down on a table with a wobbly leg. "None of it matters, anyway, because he wasn't at the barbecue very long. I don't know where he got to that night but he told me he didn't go up the hill and I believe him.''

"Had he asked Elizabeth for a loan? I think that was the reason he wanted to see her, wasn't it?''

"Yes,'' Maureen sighed, "it was no secret. Mr Miller, who owns the shop downstairs, wants to retire. Roge is—was—his assistant. We've known it was in his mind for a while and Roge made plans. He thought if we bought this shop and the one next door we could combine hardware with chandlery. That's things for boats,'' she explained kindly, as it was Mr Pringle.

"Yes, I see. But . . . ?'' Why go to Greece, why spend all that money on a holiday was what he was thinking and Maureen could see it in his face.

"I know,'' she sighed, "but Mr Miller only told us he'd finally decided to sell up the night before we left for Greece. He's a bit like that, now, I'm afraid. A bit mean. And he was jealous about our holiday. But you see when Roge's aunt left him this little nest-egg, he thought we should treat ourselves. We've never been on a holiday like that before. And we thought there was plenty of time to raise a mortgage when we got back. But when Mr Miller sprang it on us like that, Roge panicked and said he must try and raise a little capital where he could. We don't normally meet many rich people, not in this part of Isleworth.''

"No.'' He could see that.

"Roge says you only get one chance in this life. Now he's disappeared!'' She'd begun to weep quite openly.

"Did you gather that Elizabeth had been unable to help?'' Mr Pringle asked desperately.

"I've no idea. Roge was a great one for secrets. And Louise had been teasing him, you know. She used to when she'd had too much to drink. Roge is terribly sensitive underneath but he made the mistake of telling her all about his plans.''

"Oh, dear." There was no way of stopping her tears. "Would you like to tell me what happened? Roge didn't leave a note?"

"All I know is he rang someone before he went downstairs, the day he disappeared. Mr Miller doesn't like us using the phone in the shop so Roge used ours in the bedroom. Then he went out. I thought he was going to the wholesalers, he often does on a Tuesday..." Maureen broke off. "If he doesn't come back soon, I shall have to find somewhere else to live. Mr Miller's had a firm offer and he wants to sell with vacant possession—but we've been here for nearly eleven years!"

Her voice had reached a high wail of despondency. Mr Pringle reached out and patted her hand, then, as he hadn't a clean handky to offer, poured her another cup of tea.

"On his way out, did Roge say anything?"

"He said he was going and would I open up and hang on till Mr Miller arrived. I've done it before. Then Roge got in the pick-up and drove off. That was the last I saw of him."

"Was he cheerful?"

"He seemed to be." The tears had stopped. Maureen mopped her face and said earnestly, "Honestly he was more cheerful that morning than he'd been for ages. I said so to the police but you could see they didn't believe me. They thought we must've quarrelled because people who leave home *do* quarrel. That's what they think and you can't change their opinions."

"Have they not come up with any information? A man surely cannot disappear..."

"They said they'd checked the missing persons file but he's not on that. As if he would be."

"They must find him eventually. It can only be a matter of time—"

"But where is he now!" Maureen was on her feet shouting, a shy woman made desperate, hugging herself as if afraid her hysteria would spill over. "We haven't got relatives or close friends. We've always been with each other and that was enough. Where is he!''

Mr Pringle had a sudden inspiration. ''What about your boat? If he wanted to get away for any reason, might Roge not go there?'' Maureen was stunned by his stupidity. ''It's in the yard leaning against the wall,'' she said. ''No one could hide in it, it's only a little dinghy.''

MAVIS RAISED HER VOICE above the cheerful noise in the Nag's Head. ''Is there any significance about the date Roge disappeared?''

''None that I know of. I've looked at my notes. It was a Tuesday just over four weeks ago, after everyone had returned, obviously, because Roge came back with the rest.''

''And there's no connection between him and the other two families in Hounslow?''

''I forgot to ask,'' Mr Pringle sighed, ''but I can't think why there should be. There was no evidence they recognized one another when we were out there.'' Mavis helped herself to his remaining chips.

''It's another coincidence, though, isn't it? You keep saying you don't believe in those.''

Of course these events must be connected. It was simply that he couldn't think of the reason!

''Matthew phoned,'' Mavis went on placidly. ''He wanted to know how you'd got on but I told him you weren't back. He'd managed to get in touch with one of the Trustees. The man would like to see you when it's convenient. I've written the number on the pad. Now...'' She wiped her fingers and gave him a big beaming wink, ''Why don't you and me go home. After you've bought me another port.''

TWENTY-FOUR

"Do you know Miss Hurst's cousin personally?"

"No, indeed." Mr Pringle gave a brief account of his conversation with Mr Clarke. It was a much younger Trustee this time, in a much smaller office in Hurst House, far away from the glorious atrium. Mr Pringle noted the immaculate shirt and dark grey suit. This chap might be a high flyer but today he'd been given the disagreeable task of checking a gossipy old duffer.

"You have no reason to think there might be a claim on the estate from a hitherto unknown source?"

"Good gracious, no. I simply wondered whether this cousin stood to gain by Miss Hurst's death, since the reason for it still baffles me." The young man glanced up sharply.

"Police enquiries are continuing, as I understand."

"Good, good." Mr Pringle was at his most mild. "An open verdict is most unsatisfactory." This time the young man stopped pretending to read the notes in front of him and faced him across the desk.

"Are you trying to tell me something, Mr Pringle?"

"If I may put my cards on the table...? No doubt my nephew told you I've been making my own enquiries into Miss Hurst's death. Several odd and apparently unrelated facts have emerged—which I intend passing on to the police—but I still haven't established any satisfactory *reason*."

"It could have been accidental," but even the Trustee sounded doubtful. Mr Pringle ignored it.

"When chatting to Mr Clarke, a former employee of Freezers, he mentioned this relative who at one time was supposed to join the firm—"

"Not 'supposed', joined, Mr Pringle. Some time ago."

"Indeed?"

"Mr Peter Hurst, son of Mr Francis Hurst, works for the Australian office of our company. He began over here but didn't find living in London congenial, preferring the er, wide open spaces." This young man obviously thought Clapham Common quite wide enough. "As far as I know, Mr Hurst is still happily settled over there. I am at liberty to tell you he has made no claim either on Miss Hurst's estate, or on the Trust. He has in fact stated he wishes to make his way..." Mr Pringle could see the Trustee found this very Quixotish.

"Then that answers all my questions, thank you." The other man began shuffling his papers together. "May I ask, was anyone surprised that my nephew was the beneficiary of Miss Hurst's Will?"

"No, because we already knew the contents. We had a copy, of course."

"Of course."

"We thought of it simply as a temporary measure and had no objections. Preparation was in hand for a much more complex document which Miss Hurst was due to sign on her next birthday."

"Yes, I see." There was a pause. The Trustee slipped an elastic band round his folder.

"We satisfied ourselves before agreeing to publication of that Will."

"You mean you spoke to the police?" The younger man looked reproachful.

"Where Miss Hurst was concerned, we had a moral obligation."

"Of course."

"You yourself must have been relieved when there was no evidence..." The Trustee couldn't think how to put it pleasantly.

"I satisfied myself that Matthew was not the last person to see Elizabeth alive and that he was in company with several other people at the presumed time of her death."

"Exactly. Well, let us hope the police bring matters to a speedy conclusion."

"Let's hope they do, yes. Because dead women don't jump off cliffs." At least he'd shattered the Trustee's complacency.

MRS BIGNELL flexed her ankle. It was the only exercise she approved of in the slimming manual. "You weren't really worried about Matthew, were you? I mean, you didn't think he had anything to do with it?"

"He was the first person I had to check up on, naturally. One cannot let oneself be blinded. I was upset to find he hadn't told me about the Will."

"It's a different generation, dear. Young people don't think of these things as important—would you mind letting me have a bit more sheet?" Mavis adjusted the bedclothes. She plumped up the pillows on her side and began rotating her other foot. Mr Pringle watched, fascinated. "You're quite satisfied now though, aren't you? You don't think Matthew could've been responsible in any way?" For the umpteenth time, Mr Pringle ran through his summary of events:

"After quarrelling, Elizabeth rushed off and Matthew returned to the barbecue. He didn't leave it during the period when Emma, then Charlotte, went after Elizabeth. When organizing and during the search, he was in full view of other people. Patrick and John both confirmed that. They spoke to those who'd helped, and certainly Matthew was with some of them after Emma had parted from Elizabeth, and for a considerable time afterwards."

"And you don't suspect Emma of anything?"

"Certainly not. People heard the shouting. Emma was back at the site almost immediately, she didn't have time to climb the hill, apart from having no reason to do anything wicked."

Mrs Bignell felt a tingling in her toes. She stopped the exercise; one should never over-do things. "It's a pity you can't say the same for Charlotte. Such a pretty girl but very silly. Fancy throwing herself at Matthew like that." Thinking about a pretty woman made Mr Pringle mellow.

"I fear she's very much in love."

"Humph!" Mavis adjusted the flounce on her bed-jacket, "It's stupid to let them know it. A girl should hold a bit in reserve, be mysterious. It stops a chap becoming complacent." Mr Pringle tried not to look smug. Mrs Bignell hadn't kept much in reserve tonight.

"I certainly need to know more about Gill," he sighed, remembering, "not simply for Charlotte's sake but in view of this other business. It's very worrying. Roge's wife was nearly out of her mind, she was so distressed."

"You don't think, dear, the police are right and it was simply what they call 'Domestic'?" Mavis was leaning on an elbow. He was almost distracted by the view.

"I'm convinced she was speaking the truth. Maureen Harper isn't a devious creature, she's a nice ordinary woman whose husband has disappeared. She hasn't the least idea why—she doesn't know where to turn. Her grief was genuine—I felt guilty at leaving her in that state, but what could I do?"

"Nothing," said Mavis firmly. "And if you start thinking about it, you'll never get any sleep."

Mr Pringle sank back against his pillows. "The thing that keeps going round and round in my head is why. Every time I begin a new line in questioning, more unexplained coincidences occur. Every single occurrence must have a reason and may be connected but I cannot fathom it."

"I think you need a little break. Why don't we take ourselves off for the day. Brighton would be nice. Sea air would blow away the cobwebs, help you think straight."

"We might even take two days? How about a naughty weekend?" Even the prospect made him feel better.

"I'm not sure that I can spare two days," Mavis was more reserved.

"I must try and see the police first about Gill. Then I'll have done everything I can to check the entire flotilla—at least everything I believe to be relevant."

"That might take about a week? Before we could leave?"

"Quite possibly, why?" he replied, mystified.

"Well, you see that crack in your ceiling? Over there, above the wardrobe. I'm sure it's bigger than it was. I've been thinking, it might be a good idea to ask my Mr Kelly to come and have a look at it. He's a bit of an alcoholic but he's a good workman if you keep your eye on him. After he's replastered, you could get the decorators in..." It was a conversational topic guaranteed to send Mr Pringle off to sleep. Mavis was still going through the list of essential repairs when she heard gentle snoring from the other side of the bed.

TWENTY-FIVE

IT TOOK LONGER than a week because of Mr Gill's second appearance in court. This was again in the Midlands and led to another remand on a further charge of fraudulently obtaining credit. Mr Pringle read the details wistfully. He would've enjoyed investigating that. To wander through a labyrinth of figures without the pressure of reaching a climax before the end of the financial year would have been bliss.

As it was, the officer who interviewed him originally, finally agreed to see him. It was on a rare hot afternoon when the humidity doesn't lift from London streets. Mavis remarked pointedly how much fresher the air would be in Brighton and Mr Pringle promised to be as quick as he could. He meant it, too. The alcoholic Mr Kelly had hacked quite a chunk out of his bedroom ceiling.

At the police station it was shirt-sleeve order. The constable leading the way down the corridor smelled of sticky sweat. He opened a door. "Mr Pringle."

"Thanks. Come in. Take a seat." In the interview-room there was a table and two chairs but very little air. "Cup of tea?"

"Could I have a glass of water?"

"One tea, plenty of sugar, one glass of water." The constable withdrew. "Well now, Mr Pringle... You've got something to tell me?"

"I fear it may not be relevant." He pushed the neatly written sheet across the table. The CID man went through it quickly.

"We knew about this of course, 'Disappearance of Mr R Harper—how does it concern the other enquiry?"

"I don't know but I don't believe it can be coincidental. You see apart from Gill, Roge Harper also needed money. Mrs Harper believes her husband approached Miss Hurst for a loan—of course we won't know whether he did until he reappears."

"If—he reappears."

Mr Pringle said sadly, "Yes, I'd reached the same conclusion, after such a long period of absence."

"Look, Mr Pringle..." The CID man leaned in a friendly way across the desk, "I appreciate what you're trying to do but don't read too much into this—not with the Harpers." He tapped the paper with a stubby finger, "Don't think me callous but nine times out of ten in a case like this, the bloke's done a bunk because he can't face up to some crisis in his life. For instance— Oh, thanks John. Put it here, will you."

There was a pause. The tea was red hot but the CID man finished half a cup in a gulp. "Great . . . Now, we made enquiries, of course we did. And as you say, Harper was trying to raise a loan. He knew he'd have to, to carry out the big plan, but he didn't actually *do* anything, did he? He was a little man, Mr Pringle. Talked big in front of the neighbours but hadn't organized himself. Then he was given this ultimatum just before his holidays, right? Now you've been round and seen their place—would you lend those two the sort of mortgage money they need? Of course you wouldn't. It doesn't need a genius to know those shops wouldn't pay. And I reckon Roge Harper knew it. So what does that ultimatum mean—crunch time. His dreams are shattered." The officer leaned back in his chair the better to expound on the little man's defeat, "His day-dream—finally owning his own business—disappears. He knows it, he can't face it. So what does he do? He tells the little woman to open up the shop and he vanishes. Maybe they had a row, maybe they didn't.

The neighbours don't know but some people yell at each other in whispers. Anyway, he's gone. And frankly, we think we know why. As to whether it's connected? Well, if he asked Miss Hurst for money that night and she turned him down—''

"He spoke to Elizabeth during the afternoon, I heard him say so."

"And did he look cheerful about it?"

"Not particularly."

"So maybe she'd just turned him down. And then he decided to ask her again during the barbecue—''

"But that's my point. Suppose Roge did approach Elizabeth again after Emma Fairchild had left her?'' The CID man considered this for several moments.

"I don't know that it'll affect the outcome, do you? If by some miracle Harper is still alive, well obviously we can question him. And it's possible—I'd have thought unlikely—that he got so fierce, he terrified her into jumping. But as we'll probably never see the man again..."

"The open verdict will remain?"

"Our enquiries are continuing, of course." It was automatic and lacked conviction.

"It's affecting all of us, particularly the young people, not knowing what happened."

"Do what we do, sir, put the whole thing behind you. If further information comes to light, well and good."

"But what about Gill?" This time, the CID man looked at him warily.

"What about him, sir? The matter is sub judice."

"Yes, I'm perfectly aware of that. But surely only on charges of fraud? What about Miss Hurst, hasn't he been questioned about that?"

"If he has," the man replied guardedly, "the answers will be confidential." Mr Pringle trod more carefully.

"Can I assume Mr Gill did not deny encountering Miss Charlotte Fairchild that night?" When the officer didn't

eply, he added, "I saw her that evening in Parga—she
ooked like a ripe peach. I can well understand Gill losing his
ıead even though it was reprehensible." The CID man gave
ı non-committal grunt. "Someone attacked Emma Fairchild at Spartahouri."

"As I understand it, Gill has denied that absolutely."

Mr Pringle decided to concentrate on the main business.
'Can I assume Gill also denies meeting Miss Hurst?"

"Now you know that's a question I can't answer, Mr
Pringle."

"But if he did meet her, surely it would be to his advan-
age to admit it? Medical evidence has shown there was no
violence, if there was some kind of accident and he con-
fessed rather than risk a separate charge later...?"

"Exactly. And with what Gill's already got facing him,"
said the officer with a rare burst of candour, "he might as
well confess to killing the Pope. He'd get a concurrent for
t with all the rest. There's a string of charges—forget I told
you that."

"Certainly," Mr Pringle bowed with dignity, "but I appreciate the inference." He stared bleakly across the table at
the officer. "The only possibility remaining, then, is that
Roge Harper may have threatened Elizabeth in some way,
after her argument with Miss Emma Fairchild?"

"It's a possible assumption." The officer maintained his
level gaze across the table. Was he inviting him to reach a
conclusion?

"During my years in the tax inspectorate, I met many
such as Gill and Harper. Some like Gill had committed
fraud; one or two were successfully prosecuted..." He
waited for praise for his endeavours but none came. "Men
like Harper generally came because their affairs were in a
mess, they had perhaps been over-ambitious. Quite a few
threatened violence but very rarely, I'm glad to say, did
anything come of it."

"As you know, Mr Pringle, we deal in facts. However if we do succeed in questioning Mr Harper, I would be surprised to discover he had terrified Miss Hurst in any way..."

"Which brings us back to Mr Gill?"

"Assuming Miss Charlotte Fairchild is telling the truth and of course, as I said before, our enquiries are continuing."

It was said as the officer rose to his feet to indicate the interview was over but the phrase stayed in Mr Pringle's mind. Had Charlotte's hysteria been the result of grappling with Gill? With Elizabeth's death, the one obstacle to her happiness had been removed, and Charlotte was not only beautiful, she was athletic. He'd been uneasy about her role from the beginning. On the way home on the bus he told himself not to be silly, how could Charlotte, however distraught have lured Elizabeth to the cliff edge? But once he was home, he had no time to brood about it; Mavis had been out and bought the train tickets.

THEY DIDN'T HAVE a naughty weekend because midweek travel was cheaper, but Mavis entered into the spirit of the occasion whole-heartedly. Even more so after Mr Pringle revealed his daring plan. "I've booked us in as Mr and Mrs Smith. You will remember when you sign the register, won't you?" He was more embarrassed when they signed in as Pringle and Bignell but Mavis was enchanted with the new idea.

"I shall tell them I've retired from the stage and you've been defrocked." As a final touch, she bought a black nightie. "Lots of lace but not much else," she winked.

It wasn't a real hotel, more a bed and breakfast, but they didn't mind. Mavis declared the sheets were very well aired. "We've time for a walk along the prom before lunch if you fancy it?" Their eyes met across the double bed. She smiled. Mr Pringle knew the next move was up to him.

"We could do as the French," he said, "and take a late lunch."

"I've always said the air down here is very bracing."

What followed was...and Mr Pringle's lumbago scarcely troubled him at all.

THE WEATHER continued hot. Mavis left him to paddle while she made expensive forays round the shops. For lunch they patronized various pubs so that she could compare them with The Bricklayers. Together they enjoyed the glorious folly of Prinny's Brighton Pavilion and at night, they redoubled their efforts.

On the final morning, exhilarated but with shakey knees, Mr Pringle suggested a final walk as far as the Marina. They stood looking down the curving concrete road, past the parked cars to row upon row of pontoons. Moored alongside, bow to stern, were the boats.

In the basin immediately below was an eccentric collection of small craft, mainly motor boats, some home-made with lace curtains and geraniums, not destined to go to sea, perhaps, but representing the height of modest ambition. Further on, craft were larger and definitely sea-worthy. Expensive and streamlined, heavily subsidized by tax evasion or intricate business machinations that might appear incredibly complicated to little men like Roge Harper but not to Mr Pringle. One or two boats might have been paid for out of honest toil and sweat but he thought the percentage was probably small.

In pride of place, spaced out along the largest pontoon, were the ultimate in sleek ocean racers: serious yachts that didn't pander to human frailty—there were no portholes or guard rails—these boats were designed to conquer the elements, at greater and greater speeds for men who would never be content, whatever they achieved.

And was there, among all these hundreds of boats, one owned by a girl like Elizabeth? A girl who leaned through wind and spray to shout excitedly, "Isn't this marvellous!"

"What a lot of money that lot represents," said Mavis. "I've been told sailing's like standing under a cold shower tearing up ten pound notes."

"Something like that." Elizabeth owned her own boat, why couldn't he get the words out of his mind?

"Those looked very cramped," Mavis pointed to the homely ones, below. "Where d'you put your belongings?"

ON THE TRAIN, an idea began to take shape in his mind. It was the most appalling idea he'd ever had. Mavis misunderstood his expression. "If you've got indigestion, you'd better stay off fatty things for a bit."

"It's not indigestion. I need to see a pathologist."

"Oh, dear Lord! You're not that bad yet!"

But there was another matter to distract him. In one of the newspapers stuffed through the letterbox, because he'd forgotten to cancel them, was a small paragraph describing how a body in a burnt-out truck found on waste land was thought to be that of Mr Roger Harper of Isleworth, Middlesex.

"I must go and see her, Mavis. That poor woman, waiting and hoping."

"Not tonight, dear. Leave all that till tomorrow. You don't want to go careering about too soon. It'll undo all the good the Brighton air did for you." And Mavis blushed as she remembered what else had been good in Brighton.

The next day, when there was no reply from the phone, he made the journey out to Isleworth and found the shop shut with the "Closed" sign still in position.

A neighbour watched him knock three times. "She's gone away."

"Where to, do you know?"

"No. Mr Miller won't be opening up either, not for a bit. They took him to hospital with a heart attack." But Mr Pringle wasn't going to give up that easily, not after coming this far.

In the next group of shops he found a newsagent. Yes, the shopkeeper knew the Harpers, nice woman Mrs Harper. Nasty business about her husband though, wasn't it. No, he didn't know where Mrs Harper might be found now, but she had been in to cancel her order for *Woman's Weekly* and if the gentleman would just hang on a sec, "Sheila! Any idea where 23 Main Street's gone?"

"Who wants to know?"

"Never mind shouting. Come here right this minute. There's a customer waiting." A girl emerged from the back of the shop and stared.

"She said the Council had offered her a place at the other end of Hounslow."

"But what's the address, that's what this gentleman wants to know."

Mr Pringle waited patiently while the young lady asked her father if he thought she was a bloody mind reader or what, when, in mid-sentence, she turned and said, "Tell you what, though. Mrs Harper did say she was leaving a forwarding address with the police."

It took Mr Pringle several hours to convince a desk sergeant, a WPC and the officer who'd had to break the news to Maureen, that all he wanted to do was visit the widow to offer his condolences. By late afternoon he was on his way.

It was a very unpleasant part of Hounslow. He walked along, half-deafened by low flying jumbos on their way in to Heathrow.

"Yes...?" Maureen's voice was muffled by the entry-phone.

"G. D. H. Pringle, Maureen, from *Capricorn*." It seemed in another age, quoting that.

She was moving much more slowly. She stood back in the shadows, having opened the door.

"May I come in?"

She'd barely closed it again before she said, "I had to go and identify him. He'd been lying there such a long time.. And he'd been burned." Emotion filled the narrow hall.

"Can we...may we sit down?"

"Yes. It's upstairs again but I had to take it. There wasn' any choice."

The noise of the traffic didn't bother him here because of the aircraft overhead. How on earth could Maureen stick it? The small room felt musty and was full of packing cases. Everywhere was as bare as her other home had been crowded. She read his thoughts.

"I don't feel settled...that's why I haven't bothered. I keep thinking something will turn up. It won't. Not now." Her voice was low and monotonous. She'd stopped weeping but her face was so haggard, it was worse. Her hair had been scraped back behind clips and her creased acrylic cardigan hung in folds. "I know I've lost weight," there was a pathetic defiance in her attitude, "I can't help it, I don't feel like cooking."

"Would it help to talk about it?"

"They kept asking if Roge had got any identifying marks. I didn't know what they meant. What they should have said was had he got any on his body. Then I wouldn't have needed to look at his face, see. But Roge hadn't any..." She began to shiver uncontrollably, "So I had to look at his face..."

Mr Pringle was very frightened. Outside in the noisy rackety street was a neon sign, a doll-like face in a check cap advertising a café. "Look," he said. "Why don't you put the kettle on—you've unpacked that haven't you—and I'll get us some food. Let me see if I can read the menu..." He peered through the bare window at the poster opposite,

Beefburgers, hamburgers, chick-o-burgers—Good Heavens, what are those?''

"I'm not hungry.''

"Well, let me tempt you, my dear. And forgive me if I buy some for myself, I'm feeling peckish. Now, can you find plates and some knives and forks. I shan't be a jiffy.'' He went quickly down the uncarpeted stairs. Perhaps the shaking would stop by the time he got back.

He dashed first to an off-licence then demanded from a startled girl in the café, "Two of your most nourishing takeaways, large helpings please. Quickly.'' He saw a cona machine, "And two large black coffees.''

"They only come in one size.''

"Then I shall take four. Piping hot.'' He went back triumphant. Maureen had managed to find one plate.

"I'm really not hungry.''

"Yes, you are, just a little bit. I'll have mine out of the box. Here, take plenty of chips. Now, hold out that coffee.'' He splashed brandy into it generously. After a few minutes, she began to look less pallid. Her voice was steadier, too.

"The inquest's at ten o'clock next Monday. They've warned me what the verdict's likely to be. But I don't believe he killed himself.''

Neither do I, thought Mr Pringle. "Where was he found?''

"In an old culvert. They were laying a new gas pipe...it'd been raining, it was full of water...and there'd been rats. They did warn me before I saw him.'' Mr Pringle refilled both cups.

"If it hadn't been for the pipe, he might never have been found. Not for years, anyway.''

"There were no witnesses?'' She shook her head.

"There were still bits of rubber tube round the exhaust and a paraffin can like the sort we sold in the shop.''

Mr Pringle satisfied himself that Maureen would not ▌
attending the inquest alone. When she was out of the room
he tucked a couple of ten pound notes under some books c
the mantelpiece. He made her promise to have hot tea b▌
fore she went to bed then he left. There was nothing more ▌
could do. If forensic science couldn't prove otherwise, Ro▌
Harper's death would obviously be pronounced suicide.

AHEAD, PARKED outside his own front door, was a famili▌
looking Mini. Mr Pringle hurried along the pavement, the▌
were several things he wanted to discuss with Matthew. B▌
it was Enid who was in the kitchen.

"How did you get in!" He was thunderstruck that h▌
home could so easily be violated.

"I told your neighbour I was your sister. Naturally sh▌
unlocked the door." He'd once given the woman a key o
the strict understanding that if ever his curtains remaine
drawn and she surmised the Dread Visitor had called du▌
ing the night, she was to notify the police and hand the ke▌
to them. Using it to admit Enid was a breach of trust. H
had another unwelcome thought and looked round instinc
tively. Enid understood. "You needn't worry," she told hir
coldly, "your—friend—isn't here." And for the first tim▌
ever, Mr Pringle prayed Mavis wouldn't turn up.

"I don't know what has prompted this visit, Enid—"

"How you've got the nerve to stand there and say that!"

"I beg your pardon?"

"The way you've been upsetting people," Enid loosed of
her ammunition in every direction. "You've been sayin▌
things to people you'd no business to, you've been upset
ting my son. You've not sorted anything out, you've onl▌
made matters worse."

"What are you talking about?"

"Did you or did you not visit Miss Hurst's Trustees?"

"At their request, certainly I did. There were questions
also needed to ask."

"And while you were there, did you or did you not say that she had been murdered?"

"No, I didn't. I pointed out that dead women do not jump off cliffs." Enid came at him belligerently.

"Exactly. You're always going round saying that, Matthew told me."

"But it's perfectly true."

"That girl fell because she wasn't looking where she was going. I know she was in a state but that was hardly Matthew's fault. He'd done all he could to calm her down. But in the dark she ran, tripped over the edge and fell. Now no one suggests it happened differently, except you of course. Elizabeth goes headfirst on to those rocks—her face was knocked to pieces, her skull was smashed. Matthew said her right eye was torn out of its socket, you could even see her brains—of course she was dead when she reached the water. So would you have been." Mr Pringle steadied himself against the kitchen table.

"Now if anyone's to blame it was that man who attacked Charlotte and then went chasing after Elizabeth, that's what you were supposed to find out, not go making allegations. But what have you done about that? Nothing."

"Enid, all that you've just said is pure speculation. You weren't there."

"Neither were you because you were dead drunk inside that boat of yours! I've heard all about that. And you had to be carried back to it that night. You've been at it today too, haven't you? Don't deny it because I can smell the alcohol on your breath. It's disgusting, a man of your age, with your background." She was annihilating him, soon there wouldn't be anything left.

"Enid, I must protest—"

"Be quiet and listen to me. What happened was tragic, but nothing will bring Elizabeth back. Matthew was just beginning to get over it when you started interfering. I thought you were going to *help* him. Now Charlotte's been driven frantic, all because of you.''

"How is Charlotte?" Apart from the need to divert Enid, Mr Pringle knew he was partly guilty of causing the girl's distress.

"She and Matthew are fine. And unless I'm mistaken, I've heard the chime of wedding bells."

Such a coy phrase coming from Enid's ugly square-jawed face was an obscenity.

"Already?" He was genuinely shocked. His sister looked at him pityingly.

"Just because your life is nearly over it doesn't mean other people don't want to get on with theirs. George and I were very sorry about what happened. It would've given Matthew a marvellous start in life but George says Mr Fairchild is very important in the City. It's just as good an opportunity." Mr Pringle felt nauseated.

"I'd like you to leave my house now and please don't come back." Enid picked up her solid black handbag.

"I can't stop you poking around, I know that. I don't suppose I can prevent Matthew coming here if he has a mind to—''

"I should hope not!"

"But I don't want you upsetting things any more. If you can't be helpful then keep quiet—''

"Get out, Enid."

He sat there long after she'd slammed the front door. First thing tomorrow he'd go round to his neighbour and demand the return of his key. Never mind if his corpse rotted here for days and lowered the level of property prices in the area, he was past caring. Which reminded him, he still needed to speak to the pathologist.

TWENTY-SIX

THAT WASN'T AS EASY as he'd hoped. Apart from natural suspicions about unknown men who telephoned the department of pathology, the secretary had her own problems tracking down her boss. Dr Morgan was currently in Belfast, appearing for the Crown. After that, she'd heard a rumour, he was intending to take several days' leave. She promised Mr Pringle she would do her best but she couldn't promise. He had to be content.

Maureen phoned the day after the inquest. "They said there was insufficient evidence about the state of Roge's mind but that he must've done it himself. Did you read about it in the papers?" Her voice was so tired he had to strain to hear.

"I'm terribly sorry."

"They found some money on the floor of the pickup. The coroner read me bits from a report—'microscopic particles'."

"A pathologist's report?"

"I don't know. I expect so. He said he was filing it as evidence."

"Maureen, can we meet? If you're feeling well enough, I'd like to invite you for a meal, anywhere you like." Except Mabel's Pantry, he thought, then had a brainwave, "May I bring along a friend, Mrs Bignell? She is a widow and understands your position." But he must brief Mavis thoroughly. Her recollection of the late Herbert had changed in emphasis over the years and with constant repetition. Gone now were once favourable traits; nothing but the bare bones of Herbert's deceit were held up for inspection nowadays. She must therefore be made to understand how deeply attached Maureen had been to Roge.

They rendezvoused at a Berni. It was Mavis's choice. She knew Mrs Harper would need cheering up, she said, and it was comfortable even if the Jacobean beams were plastic. Also, they had a special offer on this month, for Steak and Strawberries at £4.99, which wasn't to be sneezed at. Mr Pringle kept his misgivings to himself but after two schooners of sherry he could see Maureen was beginning to perk up.

She'd made an effort. Her hair, newly washed, was soft and it curled round her face. If it made her look vulnerable, that was no bad thing. She wore one of the pretty dresses he'd seen her in in Greece. Mrs Bignell broke the ice and Mr Pringle settled back to wait. Lots of female chatter was probably welcome.

At £14.97, he could afford to be reckless with the house red. By the time the strawberries were finished and Mrs Bignell sipping her Jamaican coffee, both ladies had unfastened mental stays.

"I was dreading it but they were very considerate," said Maureen unbidden. "The coroner offered me the sympathy of the court. He was ever so young. If he'd got the verdict right, I wouldn't have minded. D'you think it'll get sorted out, Mr Pringle? Will there be another inquest when they find out what really happened?" He thought this was most unlikely but didn't want to dash her hopes.

"Can you remember all that was said about the money?" he asked gently.

"Only that it showed up in tests they did. 'Microscopic particles of ash.' They found them in the cab. They asked me a lot of questions about money in the shop. I told them Mr Miller was very strict. We paid the takings into the night safe every evening. There was never more than a five pound float left in the till. Anyway, these were two new notes, they said. Only scraps of them."

"And Roge hadn't withdrawn any extra from the bank?"
"No."

"Perhaps he'd had a win on a horse?" Maureen looked at him in astonishment.

"Roge would never do a thing like that. He disapproved of betting."

The level of noise was much higher now. Windows and doors stood open because of the hot summer night. All round them flushed happy faces shrieked, above the noise of the traffic, across imitation oak tables. Yellow glass in the mock coach lamps cast a pseudo-candle-lit glow. The only thing that was real was the three of them, discussing murder.

"Was anything further said about the money? Did any other evidence suggest where it might have come from?"

"No. The coroner talked to the police about it. I don't think it was that important. It wasn't as if it was a fortune, two five-pound notes. And Roge might have had it left from the money he'd drawn the previous Friday." But why had it been on the floor of the cab?

"It was a terrible holiday when you think about it," said Mavis, pensive now after her second Jamaican coffee. "One girl dead, another one raped—well, nearly raped. Now this. They are all connected, aren't they, dear?"

"Yes." He didn't hesitate. Maureen was stunned.

"They never said anything about that at the inquest." Mavis reached out a comforting hand.

"Mr Pringle's investigating what happened to Elizabeth, you know, and he doesn't believe in coincidences. That's why there has to be a connection."

"Roge heard the verdict about her death on the radio. He said it was wrong." Maureen pushed the fine hair out of her eyes and leaned across, eager to help. "That was the evening before he disappeared. When I asked him, all he said was he'd seen Miss Hurst before the barbecue and that was why he knew."

"Can you remember precisely what he said?" Maureen frowned.

"The radio was on. We were listening to the six o'clock news while we restocked some of the shelves. We both stopped when we realized what they were saying and Roge said 'What a load of nonsense'. I said she didn't look the sort of girl who'd kill herself—because I thought it'd been an accident. All of us did, on the flotilla, when we talked about it. But Roge never joined in those discussions, only Louise and me, he disapproved of gossip. Anyway they said on the radio it was an open verdict, Roge said 'very interesting' or something like that."

"Anything else?"

Maureen sat, going through events of the evening in her mind. "I think when we were going to bed, he said something about being rich hadn't helped her. We'd been talking more about the business, and whether we could raise the capital."

"You do understand, Maureen, what it means if there is a connection between Miss Hurst and Roge?"

"I'd give anything to know Roge didn't kill himself. As it is, for the rest of my life, people will say we quarrelled and that's why he did it."

"But if Roge didn't—then someone else did." Maureen simply shook her head.

"He'd got no enemies. Why would anyone want to kill him? He annoyed one or two people—he was so clever, you see," she explained to Mavis. "He read so much and people misunderstood when he tried to tell them." Mrs Bignell had learned a little about Roge from Mr Pringle. She stayed silent. "It couldn't have been because of money—I mean, we hadn't got any." Maureen finished flatly.

And that, thought Mr Pringle, was the nub of the issue.

TWENTY-SEVEN

"UNCLE—YOU AWAKE?"

Mr Pringle fought back waves of sleep. The last few nights, since dinner with Maureen, had been fitful. The nightmare recurred constantly. Once Maureen had been standing in the sea beside Elizabeth, both women with arms outstretched to catch him as he fell through to blackness. It had taken ages to get back to sleep after that.

The trouble was he knew now, or was convinced he did, but couldn't prove it yet. Any allegation had to be supported by evidence. The last few days he'd spent on the phone, trying to get it.

"Your phone's either been engaged or you've been out."

"I do apologize, Matthew. I've been busy but I should've let you know."

"Sorry to call so early but I've got to leave for work in a tick. I've only just heard about Mother's latest visit—did she annoy you very much?"

"Enid does that every time she opens her mouth."

"Stupid cow!" said her son cheerfully. "Listen, apart from insults, did she tell you anything? Did you know we're all being re-interviewed about Liz's death for instance?"

"No, but I was expecting it. It's probably routine with an open verdict."

"The point is, it was my turn a couple of days ago, and while we were chatting, the officer let slip something about Gill."

"Oh, yes?" Mr Pringle was wide awake now.

"After Charlotte managed to get away from him, Gill claims he heard someone else in the olive grove. He still swears it wasn't Liz. According to the detective, Gill thinks it could've been another man. How about that?''

Mr Pringle put his specs on, to help him think. ''Had he any idea who?''

''No. The detective and I went through the possibilities. We ended up with the same two again: Roge Harper or Clarke.''

''Ye-es,'' said his uncle doubtfully.

''Could we meet to discuss it? I've got some other news, rather special. I don't want to tell you over the phone.''

''How very mysterious. Please, come to dinner tonight. Mrs Bignell and I will be delighted. And can you bring Charlotte?''

''She's visiting her godmother. But it's her I want to talk about.''

''Seven-thirty then?''

''Fine.''

Mr Pringle flung back the bedclothes. There was still a great deal to do.

The secretary at the pathology department recognized his voice even if she didn't think of him as a friend. ''Oh, it's you. No, he's not back yet. Believe me, If I knew where he was, I'd tell you. It's nine days now, you know. If you think you've got a problem, you should see what it's like here.'' Her voice rose in bitterness. Mr Pringle had a ghastly vision of bodies piling up, ready for dissection, overflowing those specially refrigerated drawers. And the warm spell was set to continue! He begged her to let Dr Morgan know of his calls as soon as he returned. His own situation was becoming critical.

''Oh, yes?'' The bitter one was now sarcastic, ''Would you like him to phone you before or after he attends to a complaint from the Director of Public Prosecutions?'' Mr Pringle took the question seriously.

''Before, I fear.''

And because there was no reason for delaying any longer, he set off once again to Hounslow on another voyage of discovery. He'd discussed this particular problem with Mavis. He hadn't told her of his theory about Elizabeth's death, nor his suspicions concerning Roge Harper. He would tell Mavis nothing he couldn't yet prove. But he sought her advice on matters of clothing.

"Who on the flotilla would be the most likely to remember details? I don't want to ask Emma or Charlotte because they weren't at the barbecue the whole time. And neither Matthew nor I are particularly observant. Perhaps, Mrs Hanson?"

"Or one of her daughters?" suggested Mavis, "Didn't you say those two families had teenage children?"

"Yes. There was a girl. With stripey hair."

"She'll be the sort who remembers, dear. Girls that age don't think about anything except sex and clothes."

Mr Pringle rang Mrs Hanson and asked if he might visit her daughter. "Donna's been taken on as an apprentice hairdresser," Shirley Hanson told him. "She's only in her third week. I don't think she could ask for time off just to talk to someone."

"With your permission, I'd like to call and see her between clients. Providing her employer doesn't object either."

"Well, I don't mind. You can tell them I said so."

The salon was on the main road and up a flight of stairs. The walls were covered in green felt and hung with enormous photographs which pouted at every turn. Through plate glass doors at the top, Mr Pringle could see more vivid shiny green. Emerald carpet was reflected in the silver ceiling. Down the centre of the room, gleaming high-tech scaffolding supported the line of basins. Women sat in a row, heads tilted back as though about to be sacrificed, legs splayed, each wearing green and black striped gowns.

"Yes? We're not unisex." The receptionist by contrast, was clad in dark peony red.

"I would like to speak to Miss Donna Hanson when she's free, a few minutes only. I have her mother's permission." She let him wait so that one by one, the assistants could come to peep and giggle. Only when a male person glided down the spiral staircase did the atmosphere change. Mr Pringle opened his mouth to speak but the receptionist got in first. "He wants to see Donna, Mr Christopher."

"Have you told her?"

"I was waiting to ask you first, Mr Christopher."

"What's it about? Can't it wait? She gets half an hour for lunch." But time was short for Mr Pringle.

"It's a police matter," he said blandly. My word! He'd never used that tactic before. Its effect on Mr Christopher was immediate. He strode behind the reception desk and pushed at a section of the green padded wall. It swung open to reveal a cubbyhole beyond.

"In here. It's quite private. And you—get Donna." Mr Pringle pleaded with the proprietor across crates of bleach and mousse. "Please stay. It won't take long." He didn't want to be shut in here with jailbait. He lowered his gaze from Mr Christopher's green eyelids and found he was staring at hands which sported black nail varnish.

Today Donna's stripes were orange and pink, presumably in revenge for the decor. "Yeah?" Mr Pringle had an awful qualm the girl might not remember him at all.

"The flotilla holiday, Donna, in Greece. I was on *Capricorn* with Matthew and Elizabeth."

"Yeah?"

"Can you remember that first night at Parga, what each of the ladies were wearing?"

"That lot!"

"It's not your opinion that interests me, Donna, but what their garments actually were. Blouses, skirts and so forth. Can you remember?" He produced notebook and pencil.

"If we could go through boat by boat. There were only seven boats," he added in a quick aside to Mr Christopher.

Donna started to rattle off names beginning with Kate on *Zodiac*. Holding his notebook close, Mr Pringle pretended to scribble, only writing in detail those descriptions which interested him. He didn't prompt nor draw attention to anyone. When she'd finished he asked, "You are quite certain?"

"Oh, yes." Donna was huffy. "They were a rotten lot of dressers except Charlotte."

"Your memory is excellent." He handed over a folded bank note. "For your time and trouble." She didn't even thank him. When she'd gone, Mr Pringle repeated his thanks to Mr Christopher.

"Is that it?" He'd expected Miami Vice, not Crossroads.

"I'm afraid so. It has been most useful." Mr Pringle went out through the plate glass door. Once outside in the busy street with jumbos bearing down overhead, he knew he had his answer. He still couldn't prove it but there was nothing he could do now except continue to the end.

On his way home, Mr Pringle parked in a side street near his local shops, and argued silently with himself. Apart from buying wine for this evening, as he'd arranged with Mrs Bignell, he was proposing to do something so melodramatic, it embarrassed him.

It was a time of day when children erupted from school, filling the shops, squabbling in the newsagents loudly to distract the assistants while those light-fingered enough, pinched sweets. Mr Pringle selected a note-pad plus two sizes of envelope and stood in line to pay for them.

Back in the car he still felt foolish. He was proposing to write an account of what he believed to be the truth about Elizabeth. To address one envelope containing the account to his bank manager (whom he'd never met) and another to Mrs Bignell with a covering letter asking her to keep the enclosure in a safe place, to tell no one and take it unopened to the bank in the event of his death. He was almost tempted to suggest she give it to the second cashier from the left. She was a nice motherly woman, he'd gone to her for years, she might care if he was dead. Telling himself this was no time to be maudlin, Mr Pringle began his account. He kept it simple. He could only offer one piece of evidence but he knew where the rest might be found, in time. His letter to the bank manager was brief, that to Mavis almost curt. Anything that might be read out in open court mustn't embarrass his friend. Then Mr Pringle opened his wallet and stopped being heroic: he'd run out of stamps.

The queue in the post office was long enough for his whole life to pass before his eyes, let alone his future. By the time he'd arrived at the mesh, he'd decided on second class. He needed to explain to Mrs Bignell before she received it. He didn't want her laughing at him.

He hesitated in front of the post box. Surely he could pick an appropriate moment and simply hand it over to Mavis? Then he remembered what had happened to Roge. And the police were re-interviewing everyone. Time was short. Better be safe than sorry. He posted it.

It was late when he drove round the corner of his street and saw Matthew's familiar Mini outside his door. Mavis greeted him bright-eyed. "Oh, good. Everything's nearly ready. Guess what, Matthew's brought us some champagne. He says we're celebrating tonight."

As HE WALKED INTO the dining-room, Mr Pringle was brought up short by a feeling of déjà vu. Mavis had found an old tablecloth Renée had bought years ago on holiday. Through the drawn-thread work, the battered dining table looked almost gracious. The lights were off because there were candles and these shone on polished glass and his best china. There were flowers in the centre of the table. He was very touched. He never had flowers, not nowadays. But the scene, with Matthew in the easy chair and Mavis standing expectantly, was one he and Renée used to conjure up when they were young, of a time when there would be a son, who'd be a credit to them and how, as his wife, she would be eager to hear the sound of his key in the lock.

But even if they'd had a child, he'd never have been as good looking as Matthew. Mr Pringle moved forward, breaking the spell. "How are you? I'm sorry if I've kept you waiting."

"Not at all," Matthew smiled, "Mavis and I have been demolishing the gin." In the soft light, he looked far more relaxed. "Let me get you a drink. Mavis has been working on a fantastic pud—pure decadence. I've been dribbling down my tie ever since I saw it—ice and lemon?" He swept them along on his buoyant mood. Mr Pringle waited until they were halfway through the melon.

"How did you get on with the police the other day? Were there any other revelations?"

"Apart from Gill, no. We had quite a long session. They took me step by step through that whole afternoon and evening. After all these weeks, it was like remembering an old film. I don't think there was a minute unaccounted for by the time we'd finished."

"Yes," Mr Pringle pondered, "although at the time, it all crowds in, after a while, I think one can see the perspective more clearly. One question I keep meaning to ask . . . ?"

"Fire away."

"When I left to go for a swim, then came back to find first Clarke, then Roge hanging about, what was the precise sequence of action for you and Elizabeth?"

"Well . . ." Matthew finished chewing. "Immediately after you left, I made Liz a sandwich. She was feeling hungry by then and I thought she should eat something before we set off for Parga. In the end, we decided to collect firewood first for the barbecue, which was a bit of a mistake."

"Elizabeth went with you?"

"In the dinghy, that was the trouble. The water was still quite rough outside the harbour and she felt queasy. I wanted to go round to the headland, where Patrick had told us we'd find plenty of driftwood."

"By headland, do you mean by those rocks where Elizabeth eventually . . . ?"

"Yes," Matthew's voice was steady. "Yes, I do as a matter of fact. It was a bit tricky but there was plenty of wood. But before I went round there, I put Liz ashore to recover. She said she was going to have a shower at that place on the beach.

"I went back, collected the wood, took it back to the beach and lugged it up to the site. I was pretty filthy myself by then so I went and had a shower, too."

"Did you meet Liz?"

"Not until later at the restaurant. She left a note on the boat telling me to meet her there."

"So was that when Roge saw her? While she was leaving you that note?"

"It must've been. And she'd left by the time Clarke turned up. At least, that's what I assume. She didn't tell me about either of them." Mr Pringle was about to ask another question but Matthew put down his spoon. "Mavis, that melon was delicious." There was a hiatus while plates were removed and Mrs Bignell came back with what Mr Pringle referred to as her drunken chicken. Vin took precedence over coq in Mavis's version.

"So you met Elizabeth in the beach restaurant," Mr Pringle resumed. "It must have been late afternoon by then."

"Yes, it was. We had a couple of drinks and decided to take a look at Parga before coming back for the party."

"Another potato, Matthew?"

"I shouldn't but I will. This gravy's making my eyes water."

"You would be well advised to consume plenty of coffee before attempting to drive," said his uncle solemnly. "Did you and Elizabeth see anyone from the flotilla in Parga?"

"We may have done," Matthew shrugged, "but I can't honestly remember. The place was full of day trippers making their way back to the ferries by then."

"Yes, of course. What about on your way back to the harbour?"

"Again it's possible but I'm not sure. Why d'you ask?"

"I wondered if anyone from the flotilla managed to speak to Elizabeth, apart from Roge or Clarke."

"Oh, I see. I don't think so. We were together all the time. We took the caique back from Parga to the harbour—I suppose we may have passed you in the beach restaurant. When we got back to *Capricorn*, that's when Liz decided to put on the dress you bought her."

"And wrote her second note? To me?"

"Yes," Matthew's voice was husky. "It really suited her, didn't it?"

Mavis asked suddenly, "Was that the dress she had on when—when it happened?"

"Yes."

There was silence for a few moments.

"I wonder..." Mr Pringle was apparently oblivious, "how Clarke missed seeing you when you walked along the jetty." Mavis frowned at him but he misunderstood. "It was narrow," he explained, "and we had to pass their boat every time we went to our own."

"They weren't there," Matthew answered, putting his handky away. "They'd already gone up to the site, it was dark by then. It was my fault Liz and I were late getting there but after humping all that wood, I felt I'd done my share. And I didn't want her messing about with food. She still wasn't fit enough."

"That was very thoughtful of you," said Mavis firmly and frowned at Mr Pringle again. "You know, Matthew's been through this with the police. Can't we leave it for this evening?''

"I'm so very sorry," Mr Pringle was contrite, "I wanted to be clear in my own mind. After talking to Maureen Harper, you know." They ate in silence.

"Had Roge told her something we didn't know about?" asked Matthew.

"I don't think so... Goodness, Mavis, you have been lavish with the wine in this sauce. I doubt whether I shall make it into the living-room tonight."

"Oh, you'll manage the stairs later, I know you. It's amazing how you recover round about bedtime."

"How is Maureen?"

Mavis sighed heavily. "She's taking it very hard, poor love. Such a nice girl. I hope she'll find another chap eventually, when she's got over it. She's the sort who needs looking after."

"It must be terrible for the one who's left when the other partner commits suicide," said Matthew quietly, "I saw the result of the inquest in some paper or other. Roge must've been desperate for cash to do a thing like that. It was kind of you both to visit Maureen." Mavis waited for Mr Pringle to tell of his suspicions about the verdict. To her surprise, he forgot. "Will you be going to see Maureen again?" Matthew asked.

"I doubt it. There's nothing more I can do." And as Mavis opened her mouth to speak, he said, "Another glass of wine?"

"What about Matthew? Wouldn't he like some more?"

"No, thanks. I want to leave some capacity for champagne."

"Ah, yes. The mysterious news we're to celebrate." And although Mr Pringle could've guessed from Enid's remark what this might be, he gave no sign. "Shall we have our pudding first? Is it your famous Coronary Special, my love?"

"Oh, really!" Mavis rose. "You know, Matthew, this uncle of yours can be very rude. He gives my special treats these shocking names. There's nothing but chestnut purée, sherry and thick cream in this recipe but each time I make it he swears I'm trying to finish him off." And she sailed into the kitchen in mock dudgeon.

"I don't suppose you'll suffer any lasting damage," Mr Pringle observed mildly, "but she serves such liberal portions you'll probably have indigestion for the rest of the night."

Mavis had reached the mellow stage when Mr Pringle suggested brandy with the coffee. She moved with alacrity before he could change his mind. As they passed each other in the kitchen, she with the bottle, he with the tray of cups, Mr Pringle murmured that Matthew was far less cheerful. It was his fault, Mr Pringle acknowledged, for insisting on talking about Elizabeth but perhaps Mrs Bignell could remedy the situation?

It was the sort of challenge Mavis enjoyed. It was why she was so highly regarded at The Bricklayers, more than the younger barmaids. She, Mavis Bignell, wasn't flattering herself when she declared she could bring a smile to anyone's lips.

She began by telling Matthew outrageous anecdotes about her late spouse. By the time she'd described his funeral, when she'd filled the pews with all Herbert's lady loves because she couldn't stand his family, Matthew and Mr Pringle were wiping their eyes. They were in the living-room, sprawling contentedly.

"Oh Lord, what a pity Charlotte isn't here. You're just the tonic she needed, Mavis."

"Did you say she was visiting someone?" Mr Pringle was rosy with brandy.

"Her Godmother. Her father sent her off for a couple of days. I'm afraid the session with the police yesterday didn't go too well."

"Oh, why not?"

"It's probably a storm in a teacup, but Char's terribly upset. The police interviewed Patrick and John again. Afterwards, they told Char there was a discrepancy in her statement."

"What sort of discrepancy?"

"In her estimate between leaving Gill in the olive grove and rejoining the rest of us at the site. Char said it was about ten minutes or so. The police reckon it was nearer forty."

Behind his spectacles, Mr Pringle was pensive. "What about you and Emma? What do you think?" Matthew shrugged.

"That it was probably more than ten—but what does it matter? Nobody was looking at a watch that night. Unfortunately Charlotte was rattled."

"Poor thing," Mavis was momentarily sympathetic. "But what about this champagne, Matthew? When are we going to open it and what are you celebrating?"

"I hope you won't think too badly of me, either of you," Matthew answered a trifle shame-facedly, "especially after all our chat about Liz tonight. But she was such a practical person, she wouldn't have wanted me to brood?" And he glanced at Mr Pringle as if half expecting a contradiction.

"Of course she wouldn't, dear," replied Mavis stoutly. "It won't bring her back. I'm sure she'd want you to put it all behind you and get on with your life—your uncle and I do."

"Bless you!" Watching her, Mr Pringle wished women flowered for him the way they did when his nephew smiled at them. "And Mr and Mrs Fairchild have given their blessing," Matthew went on, "So I hope you'll wish us joy, too. We're getting married."

AFTERWARDS, when Matthew had gone and Mavis finished telling Mr Pringle you could've knocked her down with a feather, they did the washing up in a post prandial lethargy.

Mr Pringle was deep in thought. Mavis declared she was still thirsty and he offered to bring her tea in bed. She waited, propped up against the pillows. As he handed her a cup she commented, "You weren't surprised tonight, were you, dear?"

"No. Enid dropped a heavy hint during her last visit."

"It is a bit sudden though, when you come to think about it. I think they should've waited a little longer. I mean, why do it by Special Licence?" Mr Pringle sipped reflectively.

"Perhaps to avoid the attentions of the Press, although I doubt if that's possible. Perhaps because as you said, the younger generation see things differently?"

"I don't know that it was the younger generation this time, was it?" Mavis said slowly. "Not the way Matthew kept going on about 'her father this', and 'her father that'. If you want my opinion, that Mr Fairchild has made most of the decisions lately."

"Matthew must've approved. He's no giddy youth any longer."

"I suppose so," Mavis put aside her cup. "Come over this side and have a cuddle." But her thoughts were elsewhere. "What's he like?"

"Fairchild? A very important man in the City, I've been told." She sniffed.

"It bothers me a bit, the way Matthew's so . . . so—"

"Subservient?" he suggested.

"Oh, come on, dear, he's no crawler," Mavis was surprised. "It just bothers me the way he jumps when Mr Fairchild tells him to. I wonder—if he'd been left to himself—whether Matthew would've preferred to wait."

"I think you're right. It's fair to say, Matthew is greatly influenced by his future father-in-law. Shall I turn off the light?"

But in Mavis, traces of champagne still lingered. "Not yet," she said.

IN THE MORNING, contemplating the turn of events from the lavatory seat, Mr Pringle's gloom intensified. It didn't ameliorate matters when he remembered the envelope he'd posted yesterday. He went downstairs to tell Mrs Bignell. He'd wondered what her reaction would be. Perhaps, he thought shyly, admiration for his courage. Maybe sympathy for his possible fate. He was mistaken. Mavis was absolutely furious. She waved a cereal box she'd been about to put on the table.

"You bloody fool—don't think you can get away with that!" she shouted. "Risking your neck like some silly schoolboy—how dare you do anything so stupid!" He staggered back from the blast.

"What d'you expect me to do?"

"Do! You can go and sort it out right this minute, before it gets even more serious. You tell me you know how it was done—"

"I *think* I know—"

"Think?!"

"I need proof—"

"Well go and find some. Now."

"I can't go like this!" He was still in his pyjamas, he hadn't shaved, his moustache felt like a worn out nailbrush, "These things take time."

"Well you haven't got time now, have you? I was a fool, giving in over that sister of yours and coming back here. I felt sorry for you, d'you realize? Now you've gone soft and done a stupid thing like this. What's the use of writing a letter for me to post after you're dead? Go and get dressed, stop waffling on about needing evidence—find some. Now, do you want oat crunchies or puffed wheat?"

TWENTY-EIGHT

ON HIS RETURN from Ulster, Dr Morgan made a late visit to the pathology department. It was after the staff had gone home but he had his own reasons for preferring to arrive when the offices were empty. He also had an equally valid reason for not wanting to hurry home. His secretary had left a note stapled to his desk with an amputation knife and, judging by the condition of the wood, she'd done this every night since he'd been away.

Charles,

PRINGLE

Before you start on the various ultra-urgent matters in your In-tray—including what I think is a letter sacking you marked 'Confidential', Home Office, see third item in tray—this boring old fart has been on the phone FIVE TIMES PER DAY. He keeps saying it's about Elizabeth Hurst (the autopsy referral from Greece—see folder on filing cabinet). He also says it's more urgent than the DPP.

Your wife rang, too. She wanted to know if you were still with me—OR HAD YOU MOVED IN WITH SAMANTHA?

WHO THE FUCK IS SAMANTHA, Charles????

I've had the locks changed so if you want to come and explain, ring first. I've also put in for a transfer to Haematology and don't you dare not give me a recommendation.

Trish.

PS. Pringle's phone number is on the Hurst folder.

It wasn't perhaps surprising that Dr Morgan decided to stay where he was instead of returning to whatever bosom, and catch up on his correspondence. Early the following morning, he telephoned Mr Pringle.

THEY FACED EACH OTHER across the desk. "I understand you have information concerning the death of Elizabeth Hurst?" The phone rang. "Excuse me a moment. Yes...?" Mr Pringle tried not to listen. The histopathologist began to doodle something remarkably unpleasant on a pad of Home Office forms. "For the last time, I wasn't with either of them, I was in Belfast!" He slammed down the receiver, recovered and asked, "Yes?"

Mr Pringle explained. The folder with Elizabeth's surname was on the desk but the doctor didn't open it. Instead he sat thinking, and added a few gobbets of blood to his doodle. "That all sounds a bit far fetched," he said. "What's the reasoning behind it?" Again, Mr Pringle explained. "Look, that's way outside my province. That's something you ought to discuss with the police."

"But without your assurance that such an assumption is valid, I would be wasting their time. If the sequence of events I have described is correct, surely the condition of the corpse would provide the only proof?"

"Sorry. There's no way I can even begin to discuss that. Rules are rules—I'm not sure I should even be talking to you. Go and see the police and please, stop pestering my secretary."

Mr Pringle made one last try. "From your knowledge, would you say what I have described was—possible?" The doctor silently added details of the major blood vessels to his drawing of a severed head.

"It wouldn't be impossible," he admitted. Mr Pringle rose. "But you've forgotten one problem. You still haven't said *how* you think it was done. There were no marks indicating violence."

"I've always assumed," Mr Pringle sighed, "that it was done with a plastic bag. There are several stout ones on boats. They're used to protect safety equipment from the elements. Anybody could have got hold of one. As to violence, why would Elizabeth think she needed to defend herself?"

He emerged into a chilly breeze. The warm spell had broken. If this weather continued, it might rain at the wedding. The wedding! So few days left, and before going to the police, he had to see a solicitor.

THE SECRETARY IN Warlingham wasn't very hopeful. "I haven't seen either of them this morning. What was the nature of your enquiry?" Mr Pringle told her. "Oh, that'll be Mr Ridgway. He deals with all the matrimonial work. The trouble is—I don't know whether he'll be in at all."

"If I made an appointment?"

"You could try." She didn't want to disappoint him.

"How about two-thirty this afternoon?"

"Make it three o'clock. It'd be safer," she advised.

"I HAVE SPOKEN to Mr Ridgway," she paused. Mr Pringle nodded encouragingly. It was obviously an achievement. "But he won't be coming in, not today. He suggested you try our senior partner. *He's* in there all right." Both of them looked at Reggie's door, firmly shut against intruders. "The trouble is, he's not all that keen to get involved with matrimonial work."

"It is merely a query, nothing personal," Mr Pringle assured her. They were speaking in whispers, he didn't quite know why. "I could have gone to any solicitor to ask it but this was the only firm I knew, and time is pressing. I need to have the answer by Saturday."

The secretary looked at the calendar. She sucked in her breath, "I hope it's nothing involved?"

"Not at all."

"There is another thing. *He* said…" she inclined her head toward the door, "you were always coming here for free advice. And if I *had* to fit you in this morning, it was to be strictly on a cash basis."

"What are the rates?" asked Mr Pringle grimly. She told him. "Half an hour," he said firmly. "It shouldn't in fact take more than a few minutes but I appreciate I am not speaking to an expert." He was using his normal tones now and she glanced nervously at the door.

"I think he'll need a bit longer than that," she murmured. He stuck at forty-five, he'd be damned if he'd give Reggie an hour. He wondered how many biscuits he could eat in the time, should he be offered them.

REGGIE ROSE FROM behind the desk with what purported to be a smile. "We meet again, Pringle."

"I'll come straight to the point, I know your time is valuable." Reggie didn't even flinch. Mr Pringle asked his question. Reggie leaned back in his chair and gazed happily at the window box.

"Oh, well now… that's a matter which calls for careful consideration. I would have to check the law on the subject."

"It is simply a question of whether what is sauce for the goose is sauce for the gander also," Mr Pringle replied sharply. "And would, I feel sure, be answered by reference to a single work." This time Reggie smiled from ear to ear.

"Come, come Pringle. The law doesn't work like that as I'm sure you are aware." Mr Pringle fought back hard from his corner.

"At present I am aware of only one fact. If this marriage I have referred to goes ahead, it is for the reason I have explained. And if the answer to my question is yes, then it must be stopped. That it is taking place at all is because it concerns Elizabeth Hurst's murder."

"Murder!" Reggie's eyebrows reached the place where his hairline used to be. They didn't want business like that in Warlingham.

"I believe Miss Hurst's death was murder," Mr Pringle temporized but Reggie was shaking his head violently.

"No, no, no. Oh dear me, no!" He was fending off properly and Phyllis would've been proud of him.

"Just give me an answer, off the cuff as it were, yes or no?" pleaded Mr Pringle, but this time Reggie had him on the hip.

"We never give off the cuff answers, Pringle. Far, far too dangerous. But if you want my advice..." Mr Pringle was on his feet: he couldn't afford any more. "Where are you going?"

"To see the police."

"Do remember, under certain circumstances, one is entitled to legal aid." Reggie had won.

IT WASN'T THAT the journey home was more difficult, it was that having reached Warlingham, British Rail saw no reason why anyone should wish to leave it; and, moreover, why that person would want to return whence Mr Pringle had come. He had plenty of time, therefore, to consider his situation.

Until today he had accepted that his theory was the right one, terrible though it was. But he was not naive enough to believe that truth was all that mattered, not as far as English law was concerned. Truth was a bagatelle compared to proof, and proof was what Mr Pringle had not got. The evidence of an apprentice hairdresser when offered up to a tough defence counsel would not be sufficient. Would any middle class jury want to believe a sixteen-year-old with stripey hair? Nor would Donna, with her belligerent attitude, be likely to convince them.

It was possible the pathologist would re-examine his notes but Mr Pringle did not believe the doctor could prove Elizabeth had suffocated inside a plastic bag. She'd inhaled her own vomit but the air passage wasn't completely blocked—there was no apparent reason why oxygen had not continued to reach her lungs. And the bag, if it had been that, had not left any traces. In any medical cross examination, the word 'if' was likely to feature prominently, and that wouldn't convince a jury either.

Then there was the reason for Elizabeth's death. Mr Pringle thought he now understood what it was, but it was so tenuous, most if not all had overlooked it. Were he to draw it to their attention, would he be believed? It was more likely he'd be scoffed at.

There was also one enormous doubt: he could be wrong. He hadn't been able to share this with anyone, there was no one to whom he could turn for advice, or so he told himself. Since his discussion with Donna Hanson he was convinced he was right but there was the possibility he'd misinterpreted basic facts. And Donna wasn't infallible, no one was.

He entered his empty house and made a cup of tea. Then he sat with his notes and wrote in as much detail as he could, the same list of events he'd posted to the bank manager via Mavis. When it was done, he read it through. Not much better than the previous version, in fact it almost read as though he were trying to convince himself. Putting this thought aside, he reached for the card the CID man had given him. It was late, everyone had gone but the desk sergeant pencilled in his name for the following day.

Finally, after he'd rung off, Mr Pringle sat wondering why he wanted to continue. Who would benefit if he did prove Elizabeth's death to be murder? Absolutely no one. Unless he believed her spirit was still crying out for vengeance? His nightmare might be considered evidence of that but it would disappear in time, or so he hoped. Those charities who'd anticipated receiving money from her Trust wouldn't be any better off, nor would the cousin.

He remembered all those interdependent lives that would be ruined if he proved what he believed to be true. Was there one living soul who would thank him? One, perhaps, but that was all. It was time to go to bed.

TWENTY-NINE

THE DETECTIVE INSPECTOR was out. A Detective Sergeant would see him. Eventually. Something much more exciting had happened during the night, to do with drugs. It was so important, television news cameras were expected. Mr Pringle alone among all those in the building didn't share the excitement. He hoped he wouldn't have to wait too long, his nerve was failing by the minute.

When he'd woken today, it seemed a far, far better thing to leave things as they were, to ignore painful truth rather than continue. Then a memory of the awful boat trip at Easter surfaced, and the way Elizabeth had smiled at him then. She hadn't despised him, fool though he was. Wasn't it his fault this farce had continued as long as it had? He owed her something in recompense.

The Detective Sergeant came to reception to fetch him. There was less formality, less intimidating atmosphere but there was also far more haste. "I don't know whether you've heard…a bit of a breakthrough… A swoop nationwide at four a.m. 'Operation catapult'…. Should be on the lunchtime news with any luck." They settled in an interview room with cups of tea and a constable to take notes. "Well now, sir. What can we do for you today?"

"I wish to withdraw my statement concerning events which led up to the death of Elizabeth Hurst."

There was no sudden intake of breath, instead there was a weary, "Here we go again", "Trust this stupid bugger to get things wrong", "Why can't people think before they open their mouths"—but nothing was actually said. Then there was a brief pause because the Detective Sergeant found his biro wasn't working and the other man had to fetch a spare.

"Now sir, if I could have your full name and address?"

An hour and a half later, after it had been written, re-written, read out, altered, typed and signed, he waited for some cross-checking to be done and was told he could go. There was no word of thanks, of belief, of surprise. They would be in touch, he was told. Mr Pringle felt like any actor would when he knows he has just failed an audition.

HE ENTERED HIS HOUSE quickly because the phone was ringing.

"Have you thought about a present?" Mavis asked. "D'you know if they've got a list? Some couples do it through a particular shop."

"I've no idea."

"Would you like me to get something for you? And what about Moss Bros.? It's bound to be formal with that family, even if it is a bit of a rush."

"Mavis, I am not getting dressed up."

"Well, do me a favour and hold your grey trousers up to the light. They probably need a sponge and press. And get your hair cut, dear. It's ever so wispy round the back."

He couldn't bear to talk, not after what he'd just done. He made arrangements to meet at The Bricklayers later in the week and rang off as soon as he decently could.

The house stifled him. He went to his study, to take comfort from his pictures. Two of them, small miracles of perfection, had never failed before but today all he could see were the shapes behind the paint, not the essence of the artist's talent. Nothing in the room could assuage his mood.

He felt a sudden urge to be outside, to walk aimlessly, trying to distance himself from what he'd done, but the very act of being alone among strangers brought back everything with greater clarity.

All he'd done was describe what he believed was the correct version of the facts. He hadn't drawn any conclusions, placed any emphasis nor accused anyone. It was for the authorities to do all those things. Relief broke through his gloom. He'd done what was necessary, that was all. It was silly to pretend he could've carried the burden by himself any longer. The right people knew, now it was up to them to decide the course of action. He must banish the whole business from his mind because it wasn't his concern.

Relief made him light-hearted. He stopped in front of a reliable gents' outfitters and considered whether or not to buy a new hat. The one in the window was identical to the one he had on but it looked fresher. How long had he had this one? Ten, twelve years maybe? He wouldn't judge it to be worn out but he allowed himself the pleasure of going inside to be tempted. This shop pleased him because all the assistants whether young or old felt the same age as himself.

In front of a triangle of mirrors, views of himself he never normally saw disturbed him. His back looked like an old man's, it was so stooped. He straightened his shoulders. From the two profiles, it was obvious the hem of his mac needed a stitch. What good would a new hat do on a dilapidated looking fellow like that? Besides, Mavis would be round, demanding money for the wedding present. He couldn't afford that and a new hat. He settled for two pairs of socks.

The assistant remained equable. He knew Mr Pringle would be back. Men of that generation rarely shopped anywhere else.

As Mr Pringle approached his house again there was something familiar about the car parked on the opposite side of the road. He unlocked the front door and the driver got out of the passenger seat and walked towards him: Charlotte! The setting sun burnished her hair and skin making him strangely uneasy, she'd looked so like an avenging angel. Why had she come? Why now? He was confused.

"May I come in?"

"Yes, of course. How nice to see you." He'd been staring at her. Now he stood aside awkwardly. When he'd closed the door he still didn't know quite what to say. "Would you care for some tea?"

"If you're having some, yes please." He led the way through to the kitchen.

They made desultory conversation; Charlotte asked him about the house, how long had he lived here, how long since Renée died. Mr Pringle answered mechanically. There was no reason why Charlotte shouldn't visit, was there?

"Best let the tea brew for a while." He pulled up a chair and she smiled at him. It felt as though the room had been made luminous. Then he saw behind the smile, how close she was to tears.

"Matthew's told you about the police?"

"He said they'd discovered a discrepancy in your statement."

"I've never lied to them," she burst out, "it's just that I can't remember everything after I got away from Gill. I was too upset!" Blue eyes pleaded that he should believe her. "I don't know how long it was before I went back, it felt like ten minutes."

He poured the tea to allow her time to recover. "There's a difference between ten and forty minutes nevertheless." He'd made her sulky.

"You're the same as they are, that's all they kept saying."

"Milk or lemon?"

Charlotte leaned back, her head resting against the dark fabric of the chair, eyes closed now. The heavy gold hair enmeshed with the cloth made a halo. She was so pale. He remembered how she'd danced that time at Levkas—would she ever sparkle like that again? She looked exhausted. "Try not to worry too much," he said instinctively. She looked at him gravely,

"I'm not. Not any more. Telling the truth is what matters after all." She leaned forward, "Tell me something, do you believe Matthew is being truthful?" Mr Pringle felt himself go red.

"What makes you ask?" She waited a little longer, then gave another smile, mirthless this time.

"You haven't answered my question," Charlotte said softly, "but it doesn't matter because he's convinced everyone, hasn't he? And that's what really counts. Pa believes him. He told me to ask you how your enquiries were progressing?"

Mr Pringle forced himself not to look at her. He didn't want to know how much the answer to this particular question mattered. A fly crawled dozily across the table. He made no move to swat it. An important man, Mr Fairchild, very big in the City, accustomed to getting his way. How far was such a man prepared to go, to ensure his daughter's happiness? Mr Pringle pushed the thought from his mind.

"Would you like to try and tell me what happened during those missing forty minutes?" he asked her instead. Charlotte grasped the arms of the chair.

"I've been through it so often," she said wearily. "Now I've got to the stage when I wonder if any of it was real. I was feeling wild with myself, Gill pawing at me like that, tearing my dress. I was angry for letting it happen," she pushed the heavy hair back from her face, "I should've realized...it's what they always want." Without the hair to soften it, her tired face looked hard.

"No one came to your aid!"

"Do they ever?" she asked bitterly. He blushed for his sex.

"What happened after that?"

"I can't be certain. I wandered about. I was a bit drunk. I went up the hill where it was darker—I didn't want to be seen particularly, not then. There may have been other people around but I wasn't looking for them. You do understand, don't you? The police made such a fuss about that. In the end I went back to the others, sure. Because there was nowhere else to go.''

"According to what Patrick and John remembered," Mr Pringle trod gingerly, "you were still hysterical when you got back. Were they wrong?"

"No," Charlotte said. "Seeing them brought all the horror back. I began to cry. I was still very upset."

"Yes, of course."

But the last obstacle to her happiness had been removed, hadn't it? Pouring himself more tea Mr Pringle asked casually, "Nothing else springs to mind, about what happened before you rejoined the others?" He could feel the large blue eyes staring at him.

"I just—wandered around," said Charlotte. The fly had reached the edge of the table and tumbled on to the floor, its legs waving feebly. Mr Pringle couldn't bring himself to kill it: there had been too much killing. "That's all I can remember," she added.

"Did you sleep on board your boat that night?"

"Yes, of course." She was surprised, "Why d'you ask that?"

"I mean in a cabin as opposed to on deck."

"Oh, I see. Yes, I was in the forepeak. Em and I were supposed to be in there together but she slept in the cockpit instead. She and John had a thing going, it was easier to nip over to *Zodiac* from there."

"I understand." Charlotte stood and he rose automatically.

"I must get back, there's still masses to do." She was a young girl again, fussing about a wedding.

"I can imagine. My own wedding was a very quiet affair but this one must be..." and Mr Pringle used his hands extravagantly, then he remembered it could never take place and felt sick. Charlotte chattered away.

"Tonight was a welcome break for me. This house is so old-fashioned and peaceful." He was too ill to acknowledge the compliment. "Pa's employed a firm of experts to organize everything. All we have to do is say 'yes' or 'no'. They're paid to have the headaches—and make Saturday perfect of course. The house is absolutely chaotic, full of strangers. Your invitation will arrive tomorrow, they're going by special messenger because of the short notice." She paused in the doorway, "You will come, won't you?"

Now was the time to tell her it couldn't go ahead, now! But it wasn't up to him any more, was it? It was up to the authorities. Before he could speak, she said in a rush, "And you never told me—Pa particularly wanted to know—how far you'd got with your enquiries?"

The fly still struggled to live but Roge Harper had died in a burnt out pick-up. How safe was Donna? Without meaning to, Mr Pringle glanced at the sideboard where the manilla folder containing his notes was beside the fruit bowl. "I've passed on what information I had to the police," he said dully, "you can tell your father that. As for this wedding—" but she shook her head to stop him saying anything further, eyes full of tears.

"It's all right, I'm over it now. I'll let Pa know what you said." They went into the hall. He watched her cross the road and get into the car. Had she been an instrument, possibly an innocent one, sent to warn him?—he shivered, holding the door for support—not simply courtesy. What a close-knit family the Fairchilds had turned out to be.

Before he went to bed, he had to carry out one essential task. He found enough dry twigs in the garden to line the bottom of the incinerator. Now that they were a smokeless zone, he had to be discreet, but this was the only sure way

n the stillness, the column of smoke rose straight up, then
piralled off the top into the night. Donna Hanson was safe.
What his own position was now, was another question al-
ogether.

THIRTY

ENID RANG BEFORE he was up. "Matthew spoke to Char
lotte before he left their place last night. She said she'd jus
got back from visiting you. Matthew says you're still pok
ing about, interfering. George wants you to stop."

"I've handed all my information to the police."

"Hmm! I'm sure they can manage perfectly well withou
it. But what we wanted to say is, don't start anything new
It doesn't matter about that open verdict now, does it—"

"Enid—"

"Don't argue. Your trouble is you were never content t
let well alone, even when we were children—"

"Enid, what I've said means it is now up to the police t
decide what action they take."

"I hope they'll do nothing at all!" She was indignant
"We don't want them upsetting the wedding—it's costing
thousands!"

Why was it his sister always managed to nauseate him
"Enid, if there's nothing else?" But she hadn't finished.

"Do you intend coming on your own?"

"I beg your pardon?"

"All the invitations say 'Admit Two'. Are you bringing
that woman?" He was so angry this time, he clenched hi
fists so that the nails dug into his palms.

"I've no intention of subjecting any friend of mine to th
humiliation of meeting my family—" but Enid had got wha
she wanted.

"That's fine," she cut in, "that's all I wanted to know
Don't change your mind, will you? The Fairchilds have in
vited some very important people—and let's not kid our

selves—your friend wouldn't mix very well with them, would she?" He couldn't retaliate: Enid had rung off.

When he'd recovered, a thought began to nag him. His sister obviously believed the wedding was going ahead. Invitations were being sent out despite his visit to the police. Why hadn't they acted? Visited the Fairchilds, or the Registrar, he wasn't altogether sure of the procedure—but why hadn't they done something to prevent the wedding taking place? Mr Pringle had explained the consequences if they didn't. Surely they weren't leaving it till the last minute?

It wasn't his concern any more: he must keep telling himself that, he'd said it often enough to everyone else. And if he kept on repeating it, it might act as a deterrent and stop him doing anything foolish. The police would make a move—wouldn't they? But when the white and silver card with his name on it arrived, he reached for the phone.

"Donna's left for work—hang on a minute. Jason! Have you got your dinner money!" Shirley Hanson dropped the receiver and he could hear the distant domestic fracas. When she picked it up again, she was breathless, "Sorry about that. I'm not allowed to phone her, not while she's an apprentice. I don't *think* the police have been to see her. Why, is it important?" Mr Pringle began to answer but there was a crash as Jason knocked over the bike that stood in the hall. When Mrs Hanson came back on the line this time, he kept it brief.

"Perhaps you could ask Donna to telephone me when she gets home. It is important."

"The trouble is, Mr Pringle, I don't know when that might be," sighed Shirley, "or—if. Have you got children, I forget whether you told me? No? Well, maybe you don't know what it's like. What's today—Thursday? Last week, she never came back at all, Thursday night. When I saw her, Friday, I daren't ask her where she'd been." Mr Pringle's heart sank.

"Do you think it likely she'll be back tonight?"

"I'm afraid I don't. It's pay day, see. Donna and the others go up the West End the minute they leave work Spend the lot, that's all they think about. It's no good say ing don't worry, because I do. You read such terrible things don't you?" Mr Pringle agreed that you do, repeated his request and rang off.

He was reluctant to phone the police. The Detective Ser geant had told him twice, the second time emphatically, to leave everything to them. Mr Pringle had one other source of information. He rang the pathologist.

The secretary who answered this time was an older, confident woman. Yes, she knew where Dr Morgan could be found but she had no intention of disturbing him. Members of the general public must understand that histopathologists were busy men. Were there yet more corpses piling up, thought Mr Pringle wildly, surely the killing had to stop sometime? The new secretary agreed, very reluctantly, to take a message but could not guarantee that it would be passed on today. As soon as Dr Morgan finished work, he went straight home to his family. Mr Pringle didn't fully understand why the doctor could not linger in the office for a few minutes, but perhaps this was just as well. He begged to know if there were any message from the doctor for *him* about the late Miss Elizabeth Hurst but the woman told him triumphantly, there was none.

Dispirited, very worried indeed, Mr Pringle hung up for a second time. Glittering lettering on the invitation card told him the wedding was to be on Saturday at 11.30 a.m. followed by luncheon at the Savoy. Transport would be provided for those who needed it. RSVP to the telephone number overleaf. Enclosed was a map showing the most convenient route to St Helena's church. It was all too much Mr Pringle put aside his qualms and rang the Detective Sergeant. But the man was out! Here he was, worrying himself silly, and the one person who could set the entire machine into reverse was fully occupied on 'Operation Catapult'

'Have you any idea when—" he began but at the other end, the officer replied, "How long's a piece of string? It'll be a few more days yet, sir, I'm afraid. It's a very big operation. Would you like me to tell him you called?"

A few more days? There was only Friday left. "No, no message, thank you." He would go and see Mavis. He had to tell someone.

HE KNOCKED. Although he had a key, he felt diffident about using it when he wasn't expected. The neighbour called from the back door, "She's having her hair done." Of course she was. Mavis went every Thursday, it was part of her routine.

"Yes, thank you." He found the key and let himself in. The other woman watched from behind her curtains. It wasn't decent, him coming round so soon after lunch, not at his age, even if he had retired early.

Mr Pringle settled himself to wait. He picked up Mavis's newspaper but he couldn't see the words. A terrifying thought made the rest of the world go out of focus: if the police could not bring themselves to act, then he must! Mr Pringle nearly swooned. Going to the police station to make the new statement had been bad enough; it had felt like betrayal. But this was far worse. Would he have the strength to carry it out? Would terror make his heart stop beating before he managed it? He had to occupy himself, he would go mad otherwise. He might as well make himself useful in the garden.

From behind the curtains, the neighbour and her particular friend from across the way stood and watched. They agreed it was disgraceful, especially with the children on their way home from school, who might think to ask adult questions. It could give the street the wrong sort of reputation.

"My word, you have been busy." Mavis was delighted, "Thank you for sorting out the lupins." She came further into the room, reached out to embrace him and saw his face clearly for the first time, "Good God, what's the matter!" Tears streamed down far less easily than they had for Charlotte, he was unused to them.

"Mavis, I need your help."

IT WAS A LONG TIME before she believed him. She made him go through it over and over again, completely incredulous at first. Finally, when no questions remained unanswered, Mavis gave in and accepted it. "Oh, my God!" she whispered again.

"I'm so sorry. I didn't mean to burden you but what else could I do? I had to tell someone, I felt half demented."

"Of course you did. I don't know how you've managed as long as you have. All this time, knowing . . ."

"I've only been completely certain since meeting Donna Hanson."

"What about the other business, with Roge? You knew about that when we met poor Maureen, didn't you?"

"I'm still not certain about that," he warned but Mavis brushed this aside.

"It's the only thing that makes sense. When Maureen said Roge wasn't the type to kill himself—she wasn't trying to kid herself, or us, she knew he wasn't. Can't they check where those bank notes came from?"

"There were only scraps. If there were no markings to identify them, I doubt if it's possible to discover where they were dispensed."

Mavis began remembering other events. "What about that evening when Matthew came round?"

"I'm glad he did. I wanted to know exactly what he'd said to the police, to see if it tallied."

"You were taking a bit of a risk, weren't you? Suppose I'd started telling him about the chat with Maureen?" Mr Pringle looked embarrassed.

"Forgive me, Mavis. I poured a little too liberally but I have noticed, at a certain stage when we are enjoying ourselves, your conversation veers towards your late husband's peccadillos. Not that your manner of telling them isn't highly amusing...'' he assured her, ''but that night, I admit I took advantage.''

''You mean when I get tight, I go on about Herbert,'' Mavis sighed. ''It's true, my dear. I'm sorry about it. I still haven't got the bastard out of my system. But when you went to the police that day, and told them all that you've just told me—surely they understood! It changes everything—and what about the wedding?''

''That is what bothers me most of all.'' He explained the reason why. Afterwards, Mavis was silent. Then she asked what he intended to do.

''There's only one day left. I shall spend it trying to discover if the police intend taking any action.''

''But surely they can't just leave it,'' Mavis insisted. ''Not something as serious as this?''

''Perhaps they don't take *me* seriously,'' he said in despair. ''Perhaps that is the problem. They think I'm a silly old fool bumbling away about matters I don't understand. Look at me. I'm not exactly impressive, am I?'' Mavis raised a hand to interrupt.

''Listen dear, you are certain in your own mind?''

''Of course I am. I've checked as far as I can till I'm blue in the face. The only facts I can't be sure about are the medical ones. The pathologist was unable to confirm because of regulations. Nevertheless, he didn't contradict my assumption.''

''It is a pity he couldn't be positive,'' Mavis said doubtfully.

''But then again, there is Donna Hanson,'' Mr Pringle replied with a tiny flourish. She pursed her lips and appeared to be considering. There were no two ways about it, he wasn't impressive when you first met him. He was tidy but he wasn't exactly smart, and he looked as mild as milk until he began to talk. When he was sure of his facts, he didn't give an inch.

"What about this Donna?" she asked. "Would you say she was a reliable sort of girl?"

"She has stripey hair and is obviously at a fairly difficult age. But without my prompting, she answered my question exactly as I'd expected." Mavis sighed. One punk and one dear chap who wouldn't hurt a fly. It wasn't an impressive line-up.

"Do you think the same person killed Roge as well?"

"There were two, I think." This was the one answer he'd avoided putting into words, "At least that's the way it looks. They probably used the same method but of course, Roge would be on his guard."

"Who were they?" When he told her, Mavis said sorrowfully,

"Oh, my dear! How dreadful..."

They sat while the room grew dark but neither switched on the lights. They were like newly bereaved who hope against hope that the clock could be put back. Once she said, "I wish I'd never encouraged you to go."

"But I did. And the least I can do is be true to Elizabeth. After all, I'm partly responsible for obscuring the facts. I admit, if it hadn't been me, it would've been some other gullible fool. There are plenty of us around."

"Please dear, don't let it make you bitter." When they eventually went to bed, it was a long time before either of them slept. "If you can't sort it out tomorrow, what will you do? About the wedding?"

"I shall have to act as I see fit." Mavis felt too emotional to speak. She took several deep breaths to calm herself.

"Would you like me to come with you, on Saturday?"

"No, thank you." God might turn a blind eye to what he intended to do but not if he allowed a second confrontation between Mavis and Enid. In a church.

THIRTY-ONE

THERE WERE PLENTY of Press despite the short notice. There'd even been a couple of headlines in the morning tabloids: "Happiness at last!" Mr Pringle felt sick. Most of Friday, his stomach hadn't given him any peace, he'd had a second sleepless night and this morning he'd quarrelled with Mrs Bignell.

"You keep complaining they won't take you seriously because you don't impress them," she wailed. "Why won't you get your hair cut?" In the end, they compromised. She borrowed his spectacles and went very carefully indeed round the back of his neck.

The light touch of steel made him flinch. Would he survive? He'd been asking himself that question since before dawn. And supposing he was mistaken after all? If it weren't true, he answered himself stoutly, why, then the wedding would continue. But either way, he knew, Enid would make sure he was hung, drawn and quartered.

"There we are . . . that looks better."

He went to his study for a few moments' meditation, not that it helped. But he also wanted to delay departure to the last possible second in the hope of a reprieve. Surely the police would let him know if they intended to act? The house stayed silent. He looked at Renée's photograph. She smiled back palely but he still felt very ill.

"The taxi's here!" Mavis waited in the hall. She hugged him very tightly. "You're the bravest man on earth!" she whispered. "Good luck!" All that kept him moving, out of the house and into the cab, was the memory of Elizabeth calling to him through the spray, "Isn't this marvellous!"

He was ushered into a pew and knelt to ask forgiveness for what he was about to do. "Is there an alternative?" he prayed silently. There was no reply.

He'd been given a seat to the rear of the church so had plenty of opportunity to watch those whom Enid had described, the rich and powerful, assemble in front of him. When the church was nearly full, the principal actors began to arrive: Matthew accompanied by Alan as his best man, Enid leaning on George's arm.

Mr Pringle was surrounded by strangers. On his right, a tall woman held herself aloof, on the side nearer the aisle a man was explaining in whispers to his wife how it was absolutely essential the Volvo be exchanged for a BMW, and high above, in the loft, the organist began a second unsuccessful attempt at Toccata and Fugue. Mr Pringle closed his eyes, to concentrate on Elizabeth, on Roge's charred corpse, but the music changed. Oh, not already! On every side, the congregation struggled to its feet.

He was too far back to catch more than a glimpse as they passed: the susurration of skirts, the floating silvery white veil, that was all, and the set of Mr Fairchild's jaw. The groom was a distant figure at the chancel steps.

"... Therefore if any man can shew any just cause why they may not lawfully be joined together, let him now speak or else hereafter for ever hold his peace."

Mr Pringle turned to the owner of the Volvo: "Excuse me, may I pass?"

The altar was a hundred miles away. His feet grew heavy, he couldn't lift them, couldn't get there—he must keep going! His heart was thumping the way it'd done when he ran back along the beach on that dreadful morning in Parga.

On either side he could feel the shock, the stares and the tide of whispers following him, building into a mighty wave. The Minister was impervious to it but this was only his second wedding; he still hadn't mastered the words. His head was bent over the prayer book. Mr Pringle quickened his pace. He daren't let the next question begin.

"Excuse me," he said again.

He could see the whites of the other man's eyes. The Minister opened and shut his mouth but no sound came out. If it had, Mr Pringle wouldn't have heard it, the blood was pounding so furiously in his ears. His throat had seized up: he gave a nervous little cough to clear it.

"I fear this marriage cannot take place." He heard his words echoing from column to roof and back again, mingling with gasps from the congregation. The Minister said something but Mr Pringle was too confused to understand. He felt dizzy, was terrified he'd fall. He stared directly ahead, ignoring both bride and groom, telling himself Elizabeth had been sacrificed for these two. And Roge. Blackmail, pathetic though it was, wouldn't have cost them much. They could've paid for that wretched little shop.

"Why not!" The Minister's question reached him now and brought him back to the present.

"Because it was murder," said Mr Pringle.

He hadn't been very sure what would happen next. He'd talked about it, in bed with Mrs Bignell. "I remember reading in a book once, when someone did that," she said, "interrupted a wedding."

"So do I. We read the same book. *Jane Eyre.*"

"What happened?"

"The wedding didn't take place for another forty chapters or so, not until his wife had jumped over the battlements and Mr Rochester was half-blind—"

"No! What happened to the man who stopped the wedding?"

"Oh, he got away with his life, I think. There were less than half a dozen people in the church." But Mr Pringle had had an uncomfortable memory of a knife and some staunching of blood. Now the bride's father was shaking him as if he'd break him in pieces and the Minister was imploring everyone to remember they were still in God's house.

Mr Fairchild was shouting incoherently. Behind her father, the bridesmaid stared, as pale as Renée's photograph. Seeing that gave Mr Pringle the last piece of information he needed, but first he had to explain himself. He managed to break free of Fairchild. As he opened his mouth to speak, guests shushed each other, eager to catch every word.

"The reason this marriage cannot go ahead is that in law, a wife cannot be forced to give evidence against her husband nor a man against his wife, and this couple must not be allowed to protect each other like that. Both are guilty."

Beside him Matthew began to whisper, "I didn't kill her, I didn't kill her!" It filled the church and people repeated the word in horror—"Kill?"

"No, I don't believe you did." Mr Pringle turned from his nephew to the bride, "You did that on your own, didn't you? But it must've taken both of you to swim with the body to the foot of those cliffs—"

"No!" He'd listened to that voice all through his childhood but he'd never before heard it so full of pain and grief, "No, Matthew—tell them it isn't true!" Enid pushed past the stunned bridesmaid. "You had nothing to do with it!" In the silence that followed her cry, Matthew began to shake his head but before he could speak, his bride hissed, "Say nothing!" It was the crack of a whip.

Mr Pringle had come so far, he had to make one last try, then it would be over. He moved between, so that Matthew could no longer look to Emma for guidance: "You alone must've been *responsible* for Roge Harper's death? You and I were the only ones he told."

It was tension that changed seconds into minutes so that his mind recorded every detail in slow motion. He knew he'd stripped away any pretence that Matthew might be clinging to. His nephew had been swept along by a much stronger spirit, but now Mr Pringle had told him to his face what he'd done and the congregation had witnessed it. Slowly the face in front of Mr Pringle tightened to a mask, the arm pulled back and, with all the force of despair behind it, Matthew's fist slammed into him, to silence him for ever. Mr Pringle fell into a blackness where no arms stretched out to save him.

THEY DRAGGED HIM into the vestry, splashed water on his face and locked the door so that Enid couldn't get at him. Mr Pringle resurfaced on a semi-plateau where reality was harsh, but the blackness he'd returned from frightened him. He'd heard the crunch of his cheekbone, his face was swollen, now agony filled his mind. Outside was noisy with voices and shouting but Mr Pringle concentrated on staying alive.

Out of one eye he could see dirty, threadbare carpet with an ever increasing stain where the jug of water had fallen over. He could read the label on the jug, "Altar flower ladies *only*" but the letters were blurred because his glasses had been smashed.

When they carried him to the ambulance, the whole world was out of focus. Cameras flashed, the rich and powerful stared and pointed but he couldn't see them. All he was thinking was that no one would thank him for what he'd done; from now on he was a pariah, he was Judas.

His noise had swollen so much he could only pant. He'd betrayed them for Elizabeth's sake, that's what telling the truth had been—betrayal. Before this holiday, he and his family, although indifferent to each other, had lived in peace. The more he thought of this, the more he shivered. They wrapped him in a foil blanket, like a Christmas turkey. Voices said importantly that he was "in shock" but Mr Pringle knew better.

An authoritative female ordered, "Let yourself go limp. This won't hurt," and plunged the needle in. Compared to his cheek, she was right and, anyway, he'd ceased to care. Mr Pringle slid into oblivion.

THIRTY-TWO

HE WOKE TO PAIN but it was separated from his body by a thick blanket. Only when he moved did it seep through to knife his mind; that, and the knowledge of what he'd done. There were lights and distant cries from other anguished mortals but his bed was in a corner among shadows. Then two shapes approached, and one leaned over to speak.

"I understand you don't find talking all that easy yet, sir. Keep the answers as brief as you can. This won't take long." The Detective Inspector and his sergeant pulled up chairs; the sergeant accidentally bumping the bed. Mr Pringle tried to bite his lip but dressings kept his face rigid.

"I have your second statement here, if you'd like to verify the signature?" Something white fluttered above Mr Pringle's eyes. "I see from this you withdrew your first statement because you now believe you did not see Miss Elizabeth Hurst at Parga—correct?"

The wedding, all the torment, might never have taken place. This man was beginning again from the moment he had gone back to the police station for the second time. With a top lip as tight as a drum, Mr Pringle could only lisp, "'es."

"Who was it you think you saw at Parga, sir?"

"Emma Fairchild, wearing the dress I'd 'ought for Elizabeth."

"I see. And when do you think you last saw Miss Hurst?"

"In Levkas. Leaving the restaurant."

"Again, according to this second statement, you say Miss Hurst was helped out of that restaurant by Mrs Clarke and Miss Emma Fairchild. You give it as your opinion Miss

Hurst was not only drunk but her behaviour was affected by some sort of pill?''

'''es. Stolen from Louise.'' He knew he'd been given one of them in that last helping of whisky in the bottle. Had he mentioned that? If only his mind would stop wandering!

"There was a slight trace of a bromide," the CID man admitted, "in the contents of the deceased stomach, but very little."

"Eliza'eth was 'loody sick at the restaurant," Mr Pringle's whisper was as insistent as he could make it. "Given too much 'ine."

"Quite so. Now this Mrs Clarke—ah, thank you, nurse. That's very kind." Two cups of tea, fragrant, brown, warm exquisite nectar, were put on his locker top. The Detective handed one across to the sergeant. It passed within an inch of Mr Pringle's parched throat. For the first time, he realized he hadn't lost his sense of smell. "I can't tell you how welcome this is, sir. We've been on the go for the last forty-eight hours—'Operation Catapult'. A drugs ring. With a bit of luck it should be tied up by the end of next week. Now, when Mrs Clarke and Miss Fairchild took the deceased back to your boat, Mrs Clarke left, assuming Miss Fairchild would assist Miss Hurst into her bunk?"

'''es.''

"But that's when you believe Emma Fairchild suffocated Miss Hurst, using a plastic bag?"

'''es.''

"And again, according to your statement, that attack at Spartahouri was Miss Fairchild's way of camouflaging herself, against possible damage inflicted by Miss Hurst? Sounds a cold-blooded scheme for a young woman . . . ?"

"So's 'urder," said Mr Pringle curtly.

"And when Matthew Shaw returned to the boat, you say he and Emma Fairchild hid the body in the locker stowage under the bunks in the forepeak cabin? Assuming this was so, why did the Greek police find no traces?"

"''lenty of room in the stowage," Mr Pringle insisted faintly, "'ig. Wrapped 'ody large-'lastic 'ag. Delay rigor 'ortis. 'lastic 'ag, easy to dis'ose of." The sergeant was drinking in gulps. Out of his good eye Mr Pringle watched the muscles of his throat bulge as he swallowed.

"I must point out that you said in your first statement, which I also have here, sir, you *heard* Miss Hurst being ill several times during that night when you were moored at Levkas?"

"*Heard*, yes. Heard Emma. Never saw who it was. Door closed."

"But what about during the following day, when you sailed to Parga?"

"Forepeak door stayed closed. Only the two of us. I stayed on deck, on the tiller, all day. Matthew always went 'elow, to the ca'in. I was on deck...not a good sailor." Couldn't the man read? All this was fully explained in his second statement that he'd been through time and again with the sergeant. Something of Mr Pringle's mood communicated itself.

"Bear with me, sir, we're nearly finished. So once you'd arrived and tied up in Parga harbour, you left the boat, assuming Matthew Shaw would continue to attend to Miss Hurst, who he said was recovering?"

"''es."

"But to play his part in that evening's social event, he also had to go and collect firewood. And I take your point, that he also had to recce the shoreline, to decide where to dispose of the body that night as he was a stranger there himself. But during his absence from the boat, that was when you believe Mr Roger Harper came on board and discovered the body?"

"Most people wouldn't poke about on 'oats...respect each other's privacy...Roge not like that...wouldn't see anything wrong... And next day he told 'oth of us he'd *seen* Eliza'eth."

"You think he revealed that discovery with the sole intention of blackmailing Matthew Shaw?"

"'es."

"Assuming you're right," said the Inspector, allowing himself a comment, "Mr Harper must've been the one fly in the ointment so to speak, because up till then, it had been going very smoothly for Miss Fairchild and Mr Shaw." Very well indeed, thought Mr Pringle ironically, and such a carefully designed plan had a tenacious mind behind it, one that Matthew didn't possess. That same mind had suggested the Easter cruise to establish how bad a sailor *he* was and most important of all, how short-sighted.

"Mr Harper needed to raise money, of course."

They all needed money: Roge, Gill and Matthew. Gill had opted for fraud, Roge blackmail and Matthew had agreed to murder because he wanted to marry Emma. She knew her father wouldn't accept a son-in-law without money. He couldn't withhold permission, that was a thing of the past, but he could refuse to bless their marriage with cash—he was that sort of man. And money, Matthew lacked. Emma and Charlotte had been brought up to it, Emma in particular understood its necessity. Mr Pringle's mind was beginning to wander again—Emma had been so clever. Elizabeth had to be killed before she inherited her fortune, that would've subjected Matthew to too much scrutiny. Emma knew that. She must've decided Matthew had to settle for less: for the house with fine pictures and a dinghy in the boathouse, the expensive car—all commodities which could be turned into cash, to provide Matthew with a large enough sum. Afterwards, it would be easy. She could push Matthew upwards once he was established in her father's firm. Mr Pringle needn't think he was Judas; Matthew was the one who'd been bought.

"All this speculation is dependent on the results of a further autopsy," the Inspector reminded him, "and we are in touch with Dr Morgan. However, I think that's as far as we can usefully go this evening—careful, Sergeant!'' The man had jiggled the lifeline attached to the plastic bottle, ''Nurse! We've cut off this man's blood supply!''

''YOU DON'T THINK an iron tonic would do you more good?'' Mrs Bignell was examining the elaborate framework now protecting the blood pack, ''I mean you do hear about terrible germs in these things nowadays. There isn't very much left in this one either, is there?''

''I wouldn't touch it if I were you. It could set off the alarm.'' He could speak intelligibly now but at what a cost. Mavis examined him sadly.

''They've made a real mess of your moustache. Did they have to shave it off in bits?''

''They didn't shave it off. They pulled it out by the roots when they removed the sticking plaster.'' Sister had been extremely cross. His scream had terrified the thrombosis in the bed nearest the door.

''Will it grow again, d'you think?''

''I've no idea. I've never been in this situation before.'' At least he'd gained a private room. The pain had been so awful that he'd threatened mayhem if they didn't grant him privacy. Was it his imagination or were the staff treating him with a little more respect as a result?

''You know why you're in here, don't you?'' said Mavis. ''Enid's been threatening to kill you. It was in the papers. They've even changed the name in the slot outside this door.''

''What are they calling me?''

''Mr Smith.'' Mavis sighed. All the romance had gone while he looked like that. ''D'you think she will try?''

He'd managed to blank out all thought of Enid from his mind until now. He had to face it, he'd destroyed part of her life: why should she not want his in return? ''What's been happening? They won't allow me to have a newspaper.'' Nor a mirror, come to that, to examine the ravages. But vanity could wait.

"Well," said Mavis, considering, "after the wedding the papers were full of it. There was a photo of you on the stretcher, covered in blood, only a little one though. There was a much bigger one of Emma, taken as she was entering the church. She looked really happy, you know the way brides do?"

"Yes."

"It said what had happened in the church. And one of the choirboys was interviewed on television—he'd seen everything. He said your face was smashed to pulp. I was really thankful when I found out it was only pushed in down one side. Then it said the police declined to comment at this stage but investigations were continuing." And with that he had to be content for another 24 hours.

"JUST ONE OR TWO points I'd like clarified, sir. It won't take long. You are feeling up to it, I hope?" Mr Pringle had been allowed to visit the bathroom for the first time and, in consequence, had looked in a mirror. Since returning to his room, he hadn't said a word. "Nice to see you up and about," the CID man said encouragingly. Blimey, he thought, I hope he lasts. We'll need his evidence to make it stick.

"What is it you want to know?" At least he could still talk. The man flipped through his notes. He'd have a word with the Sister before he left, explain how important it was, get her to give the bloke one of these new wonder drugs.

"About Roger Harper..." He'd raised his voice because of the effect this wraith had on him, staring out of his one remaining eye.

"I can still hear perfectly well."

"Yes, of course. Sorry about that. Referring to Harper, you told me the other day he'd spoken to you and Matthew

Shaw when you were together. Can you remember when that was and what Harper's words were?''

''It was the day Elizabeth's body was found and we had returned from seeing the Parga police. Roge was waiting beside *Capricorn*. As far as I remember he said, 'I managed to see her yesterday', meaning Elizabeth. I sent him off with a flea in his ear because I thought he was implying she'd promised him money and he still expected to get it. Why, is there a problem?''

''Yes.'' The detective looked at him. ''Matthew Shaw denies the conversation took place, denies even seeing Roger Harper on that occasion. In view of the fact that the man's now dead . . .''

''Well, Matthew can't have it both ways,'' said Mr Pringle, sounding tart but feeling shaken inside. ''He and Emma must've chosen me because they wanted a totally reliable if stupid witness, but one who would swear to seeing Elizabeth at the barbecue and be believed. If I've turned out to be more reliable than they bargained for, that's their problem.''

The Inspector tapped his teeth with his pen. He was thankful they'd poured enough blood back into the old veins. Perhaps if he ordered one of those oxygen cylinders to be stood by in court, as a precaution . . . ? ''The Fairchilds are bringing big guns to bear.''

''Naturally. One would expect them to. Matthew is the weaker vessel however and, knowing the Fairchilds even slightly, I would guess they may well jettison him in the hope of saving Emma.'' If he was helping to tie the noose tighter around Matthew's throat, that couldn't be helped either.

''Emma Fairchild has denied everything, too, of course. We can scarcely get at her at all,'' the Inspector grumbled. ''What with solicitors and doctors—''

''What about Charlotte?''

"What about her?" The CID man was curious. "We're not bringing up any of that stuff about Gill because it isn't relevant."

"No, but she was in love with Matthew. May still be, in fact. She certainly wanted to marry him. It must've been shattering after Elizabeth's death to find Emma had whisked him off from under her nose. At one time, I wondered if Charlotte herself was involved in all this, but after seeing her reaction in church, I'm sure she wasn't."

"That's interesting though. In love, was she?" The Inspector tapped his teeth again as he pondered. "I wonder if that'll make her any less loyal? Not that Emma hasn't already thought of that one, I've no doubt. A very clever young woman that, not easy to trip up."

Especially with a selection of the best legal brains to help her, thought Mr Pringle. "Have you spoken to Maureen Harper? She told me she remembered Roge mentioning he'd seen Elizabeth."

"Yes sir, we have. But there again, she's a nice, gentle sort of person." Not up to much in court was what he was thinking.

"She cared for her husband," Mr Pringle said quietly. "And although I agree with you, I think you'll find she's tough as steel when it comes to proving it wasn't suicide."

"Let's hope you're right. Counsel usually try and demolish the nice ones first, to stop 'em giving a good impression."

"You've seen Donna Hanson?"

"Yes, sir." The voice had slipped into neutral, "I hope it won't be necessary to call her."

"She remembers very clearly what everyone wore," said Mr Pringle warmly, "including the fact that Emma had on a Greek dress but later reappeared in jeans. Donna couldn't be sure about the colour because firelight made it impossible to judge."

"I don't suppose you know much about Pot, sir. Marihuana? It's got a very distinctive smell. I've been living, breathing, eating that smell for the past two weeks. Donna Hanson reeks of it. She won't last five minutes in court, even if she is telling the truth. And it does matter about the colour because several ladies bought themselves dresses and skirts in Levkas, it turns out. And some of them were wearing them at that barbecue."

"Oh, Lord..." He hadn't noticed. "Does Emma Fairchild have one?"

"I'm sure she has by now," replied the other cynically, "aren't you?"

"What about the autopsy?"

"No worries except that it isn't possible to prove suffocation was with a plastic bag, because there aren't any traces. And with Roger Harper, there wasn't enough left to prove suffocation. We have had one bit of luck, though..." He became more guarded, "It may be possible to trace the notes. They're working on it."

"As I said, Matthew is the less capable one," observed Mr Pringle shrewdly. "He may have made errors. Roge Harper's death was forced on them."

"The day following the inquest, Mr Shaw took sick leave, but he didn't spend the whole time in bed apparently."

"I bet he didn't!" For once Mr Pringle was inelegant. "Tell me, how does he explain his behaviour in church?"

"Very easily. Claims he was overcome when he thought you were trying to destroy his future happiness. Whether a jury will think that was what it was...? Fortunately there were plenty of pics taken, of you on the stretcher. It made me sick as a pig just looking at them."

"I wasn't feeling very well, either."

"The trouble is...he's also a very personable young man. Never mind." The detective got to his feet, "We'll be in touch. Keep taking the tablets, as they say. No more sleeping ones of course!" If it was a joke, Mr Pringle didn't laugh. "Look after yourself." And that, Mr Pringle knew, was vital.

"D'YOU THINK you'll need plastic surgery," Mavis asked, "to make both sides of your face match again?" His dressings had been removed for the first time.

"Nothing has been said so far."

"Perhaps when the swelling's gone down it won't look so odd. Are you managing to see any better?"

"Only out of this eye, using a lens of course. I'm told the other will recover eventually but I have to keep the patch on for several days yet."

"Have you managed to read any papers? Did you know they're reopening the inquest on Elizabeth?"

"Yes."

"I wonder if they'll do the same for Roge Harper? I hope so, for Maureen's sake."

"WE HAVEN'T GOT anywhere with Charlotte Fairchild. To be frank, I didn't think we would. She's not going to get the young man back, is she? All that matters to that clan now is sticking together. I don't know whether Matthew Shaw realizes that yet? I think he will after he's been to court. Nice to see you back home again, by the way. Feeling quite fit again, are we?"

Fit enough to withstand questions from the Fairchilds' barrister was what the officer meant. "Yes, thank you."

"Just one point: you remember the remark you made in church about swimming with the body to the foot of those cliffs, it's not going to be easy to prove. All the marks on the body are consistent with a fall, allowing for the fact the deceased was already dead when she hit the water. There's no medical evidence to prove it wasn't exactly like that, even if it was unlikely. And another thing, according to the Greek report, rigor mortis was still present, even if it wasn't surprising."

"But obviously Matthew and Emma needed to prolong rigor as long as possible. Apart from concealing the body, keeping it in a plastic bag in the stowage, where the surrounding temperature was warm, helped. They knew they had to make it appear death was much later."

"Yes, sir," replied the Inspector patiently. "But none of it proves anything one way or the other. It certainly doesn't prove those two swam across in the dark towing the body between them and left it at the foot of those rocks."

"After first smashing the skull and scarring the limbs," Mr Pringle reminded him, "presumably to conceal any pressure marks in the area of the neck."

"Ye-es. Wonder which of them did that?"

"Emma, I should think. But I'm sure she made Matthew help her. It certainly needed both of them to tow the body. The current was strong under the cliffs."

"It was damn risky altogether."

"But don't you see, plans for the route and location of the barbecue were changed because of the indifferent sailors on the flotilla. Whatever Emma hoped to do originally, she had to fit in with that change of plan—that's why it had to be at Parga." The Detective Inspector shuffled his papers together.

"We'll have to pin our hopes on Maureen Harper and Donna Hanson when it goes to trial, which is a pity." He hadn't pinned his hopes on this visit either but anything was worth a try. The way things looked for the prosecution, this one could end up a no-no.

"That large plastic bag," said Mr Pringle slowly, "the one they used for the body so that it didn't leave any traces in the stowage?"

"What about it? They must've cut it to shreds and dumped them at the bottom of the Mediterranean."

"That's the point. It would be missing. And there weren't many that size on board those boats. In fact there was only one, which held the lifejackets. It was thick transparent plastic in the left-hand side forepeak stowage. It was the only bag large enough to hold a body."

A telex from Patrick on *Zodiac* confirmed that the one on *Capricorn* was still in place but the bag on *Aries* was missing. When he was told they knew this, Matthew Shaw began to talk. "A nice tidy finish by tomorrow if we're lucky. You won't be needed any more, sir. I'd stay at home if I were you. There's bound to be a commotion when the jury bring in a verdict."

"But it's all gone wrong! Utterly and completely wrong!" Disbelief stunned Mr Pringle. Yesterday he'd even tried to protest at what was happening: today during the summing up, he couldn't believe his ears. On his side of the dock, Matthew slumped lethargically, appearing not to see or hear what was going on around him. Beside him, but as far apart as if she were on another planet, Emma Fairchild was as exquisite and calm as a flaxen, blue eyed piece of Dresden.

The Detective Inspector had anticipated this moment. He hustled Mr Pringle into one of the many embrasures in the corridor outside the court. "I did warn you at the beginning about the Fairchilds. We knew they'd got a good Brief."

"But what their Counsel claimed—and the judge *emphasized* it in his summing up—was that Matthew and not Emma was responsible!"

"I'm afraid you may well be right. Mr Shaw did himself no good at all yesterday, going to pieces and making wild accusations like that—"

"But none of what her Counsel said was true!" Mr Pringle's cry echoed down that corridor where so many have protested fruitlessly against injustice, "No wonder Matthew was desperate—we know it didn't happen like that. He simply wasn't capable!" The CID man slipped into his neutral gear.

"Strictly speaking, sir, that's not true either, is it? Now listen to me, please." Mr Pringle's outraged look made him slightly uncomfortable. "We don't actually know what happened, do we? Either of us? Neither you, me nor anyone on that flotilla was there *when* it happened, right? Apart from the deceased, who can say for certain whether it was Emma Fairchild or Matthew Shaw who did it? And it's not up to us to decide anyway, it's up to that jury." Shock threatened to paralyse Mr Pringle altogether.

"You agreed with me! When we discussed the evidence, and my statement—"

"I neither agreed nor disagreed sir, that is not my job."

Opinions like that were expressed in the privacy of the CID room where, since her first appearance in court, Emma Fairchild had been relished in comments ranging from lewd to obscene: her face, her figure, her ability between the sheets, no single aspect had been ignored. And when she began to give evidence, her confidence, her smartness, her class, these added even greater lustre.

As for Matthew Shaw, he was too good looking for his own good, jumped up little clerk. No stamina, either. All that crying got on the jury's nerves. Nobody wants to watch a man feel sorry for himself, it's embarrassing. If, as he claimed, everything he did was because she suggested it, well more fool him. "Please, sir, it wasn't me..." Not that anyone would believe a man, blaming a pretty little thing like that. It was much more likely, wasn't it, the way she told it, that he'd been plain greedy? Wanted to have his cake and eat it. Wanted the heiress's money and this one in bed? Well, serve him right!

Who could really believe that a dainty girl like Emma Fairchild would injure herself on purpose at Spartahouri? That was a bit of rough stuff by that 'Wet' Shaw, that got out of hand. She'd covered up out of loyalty and because she hadn't wanted to upset her parents, plucky little thing. What did it matter if she'd accused someone else, she'd apologized immediately, said she was mistaken. And who could blame her for taking up with that bloke John. Pity for her she didn't stay with him instead of going back to Matthew Shaw.

Charlotte Fairchild had backed her sister up, even if she kept crying. If she said she couldn't remember Matthew being on the road beside her that night, it was because he wasn't there, he was being rough with Emma. Not a very convincing witness, though, in the Inspector's view and far too thin. Strange how unfair it was in families, Emma with all that beauty and brains, Charlotte trailing behind in her shadow. She might've been a good looker once with that thick gold hair but, in the Inspector's view, whoever got Emma had won the jackpot. He turned his attention back to the old chap beside him. "We're grateful for your assistance with our enquiries, sir. But there comes a time in Law when the experts have to take over. You've done what you can. Take my advice: go home and stay there. I know he's your nephew and I'm sorry about that. Perhaps you should consider whether him being a relative hasn't affected the way you look at the facts?" Mr Pringle quivered with anger. The Inspector frowned. "As far as you and I are concerned," he said emphatically, "it's all over, believe me."

He watched him wander off down the corridor. He'd get over it. Thank God they hadn't needed the doped punk or the widow. It was in the bag long before then. He wouldn't be surprised if Emma Fairchild got off with a community service order as she hadn't been responsible. Blimey! He could think of a couple of useful bits of community work she could perform! He looked at his watch and decided he'd got time for a quick one. As he dodged the traffic across the Strand, he thanked his lucky stars they hadn't had to go into that Roger Harper business. That would stay on file, of course, but it wasn't worth bothering about. They hadn't been able to come up with definite evidence about the bank notes; in all probability he had topped himself. Anyway, it would've been a waste of tax-payers' money to spend another day on some very "iffy" evidence.

'I SHALL HAVE TO visit Enid when it's over. I've put it off long enough.''

"What will the sentence be?'' asked Mrs Bignell.

"God knows.'' There was tacit agreement between them that Matthew would be found guilty. ''It's all so wrong, so unfair!''

"Can't he appeal?''

"I suppose he can, once he's been sentenced. Whether it will achieve anything is another matter.''

Mavis put down the iron and looked at him seriously. ''Can't you leave seeing Enid for a bit?'' She was worried about his safety. ''You probably won't remember dear, you were unconscious in hospital at the time, but the day of the wedding she was very vitriolic. The newspapers were full of it. I don't suppose she'll be feeling any more friendly now. Give her time. Leave it a little bit longer.'' But Mr Pringle shook his head.

THIRTY-THREE

HE DIDN'T TELEPHONE. Alan opened the door. "What do you want?"

"Is your mother in?"

"In the kitchen." Alan followed him down the passage, there was no escape. Mr Pringle entered the room. He already knew Enid's hair had gone white. He'd had that shock on the first day in court but it still made him catch his breath. He could remember when she'd worn plaits.

She knew he was there but she didn't look up. "I'll leave you two to get on with it." Alan slammed the door behind him.

"Enid, I am most terribly sorry."

"You made them pin it on him. Because of you the police believed Matthew was guilty. It's your doing, you're responsible—why did you do it!" She accused him out of her old woman's eyes. "Why did you keep on and on? Liz Hurst was nothing to you—"

"There was Roge Harper as well—"

"A nobody! And she probably killed him, not Matthew."

"It's more likely two people were involved in Roge's death—" But Enid didn't want to hear the facts.

"*She* led him on. *She* made him do it. Without her Matthew would never have got involved."

And that, thought Mr Pringle sadly, was undoubtedly the truth. "Will Matthew appeal? There must be grounds."

"What would be the point?" asked Enid dully. "You know the Fairchilds. If Matthew were found innocent it would mean Emma was guilty. They'd go to any lengths to prevent that happening. They've got money, they can afford the best brains, Matthew wouldn't stand a chance.''

"Emma Fairchild wouldn't be in court to influence matters," said Mr Pringle warmly, "it's worth a try, surely?"

"You don't understand. Matthew's given up. He doesn't want to fight any more. He'll stay in prison and rot . . . And you put him there." The quiet voice was worse than her rage. "If you hadn't interfered, if Matthew and Emma had got married it wouldn't have mattered, would it? Not really?"

It was useless to argue with her. "There'll be another chance for him once he's served his sentence." Mr Pringle's assurance faltered. "I'll help in any way I can, Enid."

"There's only one thing you can do," she was full of hate this time, "get out and don't come back. I never want to see you again."

EPILOGUE

HE AND MAVIS didn't discuss it until one autumn day on an excursion to Skegness which Mrs Bignell insisted they visit because she'd never been there. They sat with their backs to the bleak promenade staring at the raging ocean.

"Is this why they call it bracing?" she shouted.

"I've no idea!"

"I bet it was warmer in Greece?"

"The sea was calmer, too."

She turned to face him, hair whipping her eyes, making them water. "D'you remember what you always said about murder? The reason for it was usually domestic, money or sex? Liz Hurst's was all of those things when you think about it. The trouble was neither Matthew nor Emma expected you to work it out."

"I fear I exceeded my role with disastrous consequences."

"You're not still blaming yourself, are you? What about poor Roge Harper? Two people ended up dead. It's a shame Matthew's ended up paying the price for both, that's all."

Particularly if he didn't commit either crime thought Mr Pringle.

"You never got around to telling me what the sailing was like. Did you take to it any better once you were out there?"

"No."

A wave crashed over the breakwater. They cowered before it in their shelter. Mavis looked at it in disgust. "Fancy being on a boat in this little lot. Come on, dear, let's go back to the station. This was a rotten idea."

"Why don't we find a pub and have a drink first. I need one."

Mavis brightened immediately. "I could do with two."

Inside the Hope and Anchor Mr Pringle said nonchalantly, "Actually, while I was paracending over Parga bay, I think I flew over *Britannia*. And d'you know something extraordinary—there was a female lying on deck, absolutely starkers."

"How can you be sure it was *Britannia*?" she asked scornfully.

"Because when I waved at her—she waved back."

"Well I hope you closed your eyes," said Mavis, "otherwise it was *lèse-majesté*."

B. M. GILL

the Fifth Rapunzel

AN INSPECTOR MAYBRIDGE MYSTERY

First Time in Paperback

THE SUDDEN DEATH OF PROFESSOR PETER BRADSHAW AND HIS WIFE WAS RULED ACCIDENTAL....

But in light of the forensic pathologist's damning testimony in the Rapunzel murder cases—in which five prostitutes were strangled, long hair wrapped around their necks in a noose—Detective Chief Inspector Tom Maybridge decided to gently remind Bradshaw's teenage son that his father *did* have enemies....

Nobody had paid attention to the convicted killer's fervent tirades condemning Bradshaw's false testimony on the "Fifth Rapunzel." Perhaps it was time to listen.

"A cunningly twisted suspense mystery."
—New York Times Book Review

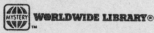

First Time in Paperback

Finders KEEPERS

ELIZABETH TRAVIS

LOSERS WEEPERS

Hoping to acquire publishing rights to the final manuscript of recently deceased literary giant Charles Melton, Ben and Carrie Porter take a working vacation to his Riviera home. They're shocked to find the masterpiece in sections, each one bequeathed to a different heir. Whoever can collect the complete book will own the copyright—and be guaranteed a financially secure future.

Was Charles Melton an evil-minded scamp who set up this devilish scheme in the spirit of revenge? Or did he simply want all his heirs to reveal their true natures? When two of Melton's heirs are murdered, the Porters begin to suspect that a clever author had stuffed his final masterpiece with secrets—deadly secrets—which a killer intends to keep hidden at all costs.

Ben and Carrie are "two likeable, 30-something amateur sleuths."
—*Publishers Weekly*

AN INSPECTOR NICK TREVELLYAN MYSTERY

HOPE
AGAINST
HOPE

SUSAN B. KELLY

First Time in Paperback

DEATH IN THE FAMILY

Aidan Hope is bludgeoned to death in his hotel room in the hamlet of Little Hopford. The prime suspect is Alison Hope, the victim's cousin, a brash, beautiful, wealthy businesswoman who inherits sole ownership of a lucrative software business. Alison maintains she bought Aidan out years ago. So why had Aidan suddenly appeared to claim his rights and his money?

Fighting his growing desire for the red-haired Alison, Detective Inspector Nick Trevellyan undertakes the investigation. Alison has no alibi . . . and every reason to have killed her cousin. But as Aidan's unscrupulous past comes to light, and a second body turns up, Trevellyan begins to hope that Alison is innocent . . . although that may mean she'll be the next to die.

"A pleasant diversion and a promise of good things to come."

—*Library Journal*